Vengeful Assassin

The Boomerang Effect

Vengeful Assassin

The Boomerang Effect

Meagan Collins

Published by: ADVANTAGE BOOKS™
                  Longwood, FL
                  www.advbookstore.com

Library of Congress Catalog Number: 2022930428

Names:	Collins, Meagan, Author
Title:	Vengeful Assassin / Meagan Collins
Description	Longwood: Advantage Books, 2022
Identifiers:	ISBN (print): 9781597556521, (mobi, epub): 9781597556590
Subjects:	Fiction: Mystery, Thriller & Suspense - Suspense
	Fiction: Mystery, Thriller & Suspense - Crime

First Printing: February 2022
22 23 24 25 26 27   10 9 8 7 6 5 4 3 2 1

Acknowledgements:

"In all thy ways acknowledge Him and He shall direct thy path." Proverbs 3:6. I would like to thank God for all His many blessings He has and continues to bestow upon me.

Secondly, to my awesome parents that God has placed so gently in my life. Thank you for believing and trusting in my dream. My mother Jackie Collins, who encourages and remind me daily that, "I can all things through Christ, who strengthens me." CB Collins, such an amazing father. Thank you for exhibiting and demonstrating what a father, husband and Christian man looks like. You have always been my number one fan.

To my godmother Cassie Landrew, thank you for your words of encouragement, your consistent and persistent dedication in assisting me to finish, "Vengeful Assassin." To my godfather, Dr. Paul Landrew, thank you for prayers throughout my journey. When you held me at 2 months, you told my parents that God told you, "Meagan Collins," will one day be a household name.

To my grandmother, Rebecca Johnson, all my aunts and uncles, other family members, friends, and those who in one way or another shared their support either morally or physically, thank you so much!

Special thanks to my former VI teachers, Linda Dunn, Kelly Marks, and Kimberly Finney for assisting and making learning fun. I appreciate your unconditional support and love throughout my adolescent years.

To my mobility specialist, Debbie Fournier – Pursel, thank you for being strict on me, even when I resented you for it. I am so grateful that you continue to encourage and push me. I appreciate your ongoing loyalty and support.

To everyone at Playsmint, thank you for believing in my writing ability and instilling confidence.

To my Publisher Michael Janiczek and Advantage Books for your patience and expertise to get this book published.

Special thanks to Dr. John Adolph for your prayers and for introducing me to

Advantage Books. None of this would have happened without you. God truly created greatness on April 9th.

Lastly, to my grandparents Pa-Pa, (Leon Johnson), and Lightning (CB Collins, Sr), Aunt Yvonne Smith, Ma Mo (Gina Anderson) and Uncle Butch (Sanders Collins), thank you for loving me unconditionally, and I miss each of you very much. I know you would be very proud of me.

1

The Meeting

The doors to the office swung open and a tall, slender man dressed in dark blue walked in with a laptop bag slung over his right shoulder.

"Ah, Andrew, so good to see you." another man said cheerfully, getting up to shake his guest's hand. He was short and fat, with a receding hairline, and he wore black jeans, a hoodie, and sneakers that used to be the same color but were now fading.

"Hello, Pierre, you're looking well." the agent replied, returning the handshake, then letting it go.

"Please, have a seat," Pierre said, offering him a chair.

"Thank you," Andrew Maxwell replied before sitting down and clearing his throat, "what's this about?"

Pierre, the man dressed in black, chuckled and took the seat across from him.

Before answering, Pierre gave his friend a once-over.

Andrew was dressed in a dark blue suit, and he had his honey-brown hair cut short. He crossed his legs at the ankles and waited for his question to be addressed.

"Well, I need some information from you." Pierre said finally, setting his laptop on the table in front of him before opening it.

He eyed Andrew's suit with envy. "About what?" Maxwell asked.

"Who did you say you worked for again?" Pierre said.

"That is none of your business," Maxwell answered firmly.

"Oh, yes, it is," answered Pierre with a satisfied smirk.

"How do you figure?" his guest asked, eyeing his supposed friend.

"Well, you see, before the previous president of your organization died, he asked me to take over," Pierre answered, chuckling again.

"My president?"

"Oui. Did Monsieur Ernest not tell you?" Pierre asked.

Maxwell shook his head, feeling cheated.

"Look, I'm sorry if I've caught you off-guard," he said, but the question was: did the government worker believe him? Not the slightest bit, but he thought it would do his friend's ego some good to humor him.

"Well, let's get down to business, shall we?" Pierre asked, turning the computer on, and Maxwell soon followed with his own.

"Why have you asked me here?" Maxwell wondered, now growing impatient. "Seeing that I am the new president and your boss, I hear that you have entail against America that you would like to share?" Pierre surmised, arrogance both in his voice and on his face.

Maxwell shook his head vigorously. "Why would you say that?" he asked in disbelief.

"That's what Ernest told me and as we both know, Ernest never lied." Pierre protested.

Maxwell looked at him with incredulity.

"Well, he lied to you when he told you that."

"No, he didn't!" Pierre shouted, defending his dead friend and predecessor.

"On that, we will agree, but he did lie to you about this because I do not have entail on them, and whoever told him that shall be dealt with." Maxwell fired back, pounding his fist on the table. The two men glared at each other for what seemed like forever before the man in black pulled something from a bag.

"What's in your hand?" the agent asked.

"A flash drive," Pierre answered, sticking it into the computer's USB port.

"What's on that drive?" asked Maxwell.

"You'll see," Pierre replied as he began to download its contents onto the computer. Moments later, he turned the computer toward his friend and watched with satisfaction as the color drained from his face.

It was the codes that Andrew had stolen from the Russian government, all there, ready to be used at any moment. "You do not call this entail?" Pierre finally asked, stroking the screen as if it were a cat.

"Where did you find those?" Maxwell cried when he could finally speak. He could remember not that long ago when he'd thrown the flash drive into the fireplace at his home and had watched as it had burned.

"Well, Andy, you work for the government and knowing that I assumed that you'd be smart enough to understand that even though the original was burned in a fire, there was still a way to retrieve the file." Pierre laughed. He stared mutely at the screen and read the numbers, all codes that could be used to gain access to the American government's main servers. "With codes like these, it's so easy for anyone to get in there." Pierre mused.

"How did you know they had been burned?" Maxwell finally asked in a quivering voice.

"Just a guess," Pierre answered innocently.

"Burn that flash drive, Pierre," he begged, but the man only deliberated. "Pierre, burn it!" he commanded again before reaching over, grabbing the drive himself, and throwing it into a nearby fire, irritating the man in black.

"Pierre, I have no need for those codes anymore. You should not have shown them to me and if this is all, I shall bid you adieu," he said, getting up to leave.

"You know, you've done well for a traitor!" Pierre called over his shoulder.

"I'm off to do my work, Pierre," he called back as he reached the door, "I'm really glad we had this meeting, but it was a waste of my time. Goodbye!"

2

Missed Information

The cabbie stopped at the curb and waited for his passenger to exit from the stucco-fronted apartment building where he was summoned. The passenger had given him specific directions on how to get to his destination, but that had been all. "What's your name?" the driver had asked at the end of their phone call.

"That's none of your concern." the passenger had said shortly.

"But, sir, how am I supposed to let you know when I get there?" he had asked.

"Just wait," the voice had answered curtly, "I'll be there."

He had hung up after that and now, here he was, waiting for his reward. Ten minutes passed before the passenger arrived at the cab and by now, the driver was dozing off. The passenger knocked on the window twice, rousing him. The driver unlocked the car's back door and after opening it, the passenger slid into the seat, closed the door behind him and thanked the driver.

"Where to?" he asked as both doors automatically locked.

"Bank of London," he replied tersely.

Normally, cab drivers did not ask their customers about their plans, but something about the way he'd said those words made him suspicious. "Why do you want to go there?" he asked.

"Business." the passenger replied before pulling a ringing cell phone from his pocket. "Oh, excuse me, I have to take this." he said, pressing the "talk" button and raising it to his ear. "Hello?" he said.

"So, I've finally reached you." a voice replied.

"Hello, Welsh," Maxwell answered in a hard voice. He recognized Simon Welsh's voice anywhere.

A veteran worker for the government, he was a retired agent for Maxwell's organization. Like his fellow agent, Welsh had worked for the London branch, one step below the American one, though it was only on rare occasions that the Americans ever worked with them.

"Why were you trying to reach me?" he asked after a beat.

"Have you gone back on your word?" Welsh demanded.

"I never agreed to help you with anything," Maxwell said quietly.

"Bullshit. You promised to have my money in 24 hours." Welsh said.

"When did we have this conversation?" Maxwell asked.

"A few months back, on the phone." the voice on the other end answered.

Maxwell thought back to the past few months, but he couldn't remember ever exchanging words with him.

"Welsh, I'm having some trouble remembering. Could you please enlighten me?" he said.

"Back in March, I believe, you called and said that your plans had fallen through, that your boss had died and that you were out of money."

Maxwell gritted his teeth in frustration.

"I gave you $3000000 to help you out. Well, it's August now, and I want my damn money." Welsh said, emphasizing the last five words. Maxwell sighed and frowned. Simon Welsh had a reputation for being questionable, and this was just another example of why people had a hard time trusting him.

"Welsh, whatever money you think I owe you, I don't owe you anything," he said as the driver turned the corner and drove into the bank's parking lot.

"The money's not for me," he said suddenly.

"Excuse me?" Maxwell asked.

"Although I'm asking for the money, I'm not the one who will ultimately decide what is done with it."

"Well, who is?" Maxwell asked, but before he could finish, the line went dead. "We're here." the driver announced and unbuckled his seat belt. He opened his door and walked around to let his passenger out, but Maxwell had already unlocked the door and had gotten out himself. He gave him a $20 bill and thanked him again before walking off.

"Do you need me to come back?" the driver shouted.

"Most likely!" Maxwell called back and walked in.

Once at the window, he waited patiently until a weary-looking teller came to stand in front of him.

"Hello, and welcome to the Bank of London." the woman was saying, but Maxwell stopped her before she could continue.

"Save the formalities, please. I know what I'm looking for," he replied, making her sigh. Unbeknownst to him, he'd just made her job easier.

"Oh, of course, just give me your ID," she said, and he pulled his wallet from his pocket.

He pulled his ID from the inside pocket and gave it to her. She stared at the name on the card for a long moment before collecting her thoughts.

"Is this yours?" she finally asked, showing it to him.

He nodded, and she smiled as he took it and put it back in his pocket.

"What exactly are you looking for?" she asked.

"Money," he replied, not sounding the least bit desperate.

"How much?" she asked.

"$3000000, in cash," he answered without missing a beat.

"All right, do you have a pen to sign this form with?" she asked and watched as he produced one from an unseen pocket.

He signed the form she gave him and patiently waited for the transaction to be made.

"How would you like it?" she asked, shaking her pink hair out of her face.

"In paper bags, please," he said, sitting down at a table as he waited for her to return from the back with the cash. Welsh was going to get his money, but in the back of his mind, he wondered who it was really for and why they wanted it.

Half an hour later, she came back with three paper bags, containing $10000 in total.

After taking the bags, he mumbled a quick thanks and dashed off. As soon as he was outside, he pulled his phone from his pocket and called the cab to come and pick him up, and then it was his turn to wait. A horn sounded a minute later, then the driver stepped out and stood by the back door, ready to open it. Silently, he slipped into the back seat and buckled his seat belt.

After the driver had gotten inside and had buckled his seat belt, he gave the driver directions to his next destination, but this time, he didn't ask why he was going there, which he appreciated. As he drove, a feeling of seriousness washed over him. He drove him to the building on Oxford Street, which is where he signaled the driver to stop before unbuckling his seat belt, grabbing the bags from the floor in front of him, paying the man another $20, then leaving.

Once inside, he walked through the doors and to the front desk, where a brunette receptionist in a tight blue skirt greeted him.

He was going to Welsh's office to hand-deliver the money and to get the answers he needed.

"How may I be of service?" she asked, her diamond earrings sparkling in the dim light of the room. Her eyes were probably twinkling as well, but huge, horn-rimmed glasses obscured them.

"Yes, I'm looking for Simon Welsh. Is he in?" he asked.

"Yes, you can go up now," she answered.

He thanked her and headed up the stairs to Welsh's office, the bags of money growing sweaty from the heat of his hands. He'd been here times before and if he remembered correctly, Welsh's office was the last door at the end of the corridor.

When he arrived at the office, he looked through its tiny window and saw Welsh at his desk with another gentleman. He quietly waited for the men to stop talking before knocking.

"Come in!" Welsh called and softly, Simon's old friend opened up and entered.

"Well, this is certainly a surprise," Welsh remarked.

"I hope I wasn't interrupting anything." his friend began.

"Oh, not at all. I was welcoming my brother here back home from Paris," he answered, patting the older-looking man on the back.

"Well, it's good to see you again, Mario." were his last parting words to the man in the grey suit, who got up and walked to the door.

"Thank you, Simon." Mario grinned, glanced briefly at the unknown man standing in the doorway, then left, closing the door behind him.

"Would you like to sit?" Welsh asked.

Maxwell nodded and walked over to the vacated seat.

"To what do I owe this pleasure?" Welsh questioned. He was tall and heavyset, with grey hair and a handlebar mustache. He wore a grey suit and his hair was short, just like Maxwell's. "I've come to deliver your money," Maxwell announced.

"Oh, you really work fast." Welsh complimented.

His guest grabbed the bags and emptied their contents onto the table.

"Shall I count it?" Welsh asked.

"No need, it's all there, but I do have a question for you." Maxwell began.

"All right, ask away," Welsh answered, staring into Maxwell's eyes.

"Who wants the money?" he asked point-blank.

"Well, before I tell you that, I want to apologize in advance for what I'm about to say," Welsh said.

His guest sat back in the leather chair. "Well, do you remember Ernest's sudden death?" he asked.

Maxwell nodded, confused.

"That was no coincidence." Welsh continued.

"What do you mean?"

"Ernest was murdered. His killers are the ones who want the money," he said gravely.

"Who killed him and why?" he asked after a moment.

"That is for you to figure out," Welsh responded.

"How the hell am I supposed to do that?" demanded Maxwell.

Just then, the door opened, and a sharply dressed man entered the office. "Has he been invited here?" Maxwell asked.

"Yes," Welsh answered and smiled warmly at the man in the blue suit standing in the doorway.

"Who is this?" he asked.

"My name is Riley Peterson." the man introduced himself and extended his hand.

"Nice to meet you," Andrew said warmly, going to shake his hand.

"Peterson works for the Bureau of Assassins. Have you heard of them?" Welsh asked as Peterson stepped aside, letting Welsh's first guest return to his seat.

"Sure, I have. It's based out of New York, right?" Andrew guessed.

"Yes, and fortunately for you, they'd also gotten wind of Ernest's death, and this guy was hot on the assassin's trail until his trail had grown cold. Apparently, he worked for the Russian Mafia when he was in his early twenties, and that's about all I remember about the suspected killer from his file." Welsh turned to Peterson, who straightened in his seat, but neither man had heard him come.

"Why did they send you?" Maxwell asked out of curiosity.

"They sent me because before I worked for the BOA, I worked for the FBI as an investigator." Peterson closed his eyes for a brief second before opening them again and looking around the room.

"Why are you working for the BOA?" Maxwell pressed.

"Just kind of happened," Peterson replied carelessly, flipping his car keys in his pocket.

"What do you do for them?" he asked.

"I just work next to assassins; I don't kill anyone," Peterson stated.

"So, where do I fit in?"

Welsh slapped a folder on the table and leafed through it until he found what he was looking for.

"I have something else on the suspect," he said, sounding businesslike, and the two men turned to listen. "His name is Sebastian Rostanov. He's 46 years old and though he was born in France to Russian parents, he lives in LA now. He's got no wife, but he has a girlfriend that lives with him, he's a well-known assassin and as I've already told you, he worked for the Russian Mafia when he was in his early twenties while living there." Welsh said, speaking quickly and distinctly. "So, you want me to pose as this guy?" his guest asked, trying to put the pieces together.

"You can pass for him," Welsh said, looking him over.

"And my job is?" he inquired, seriousness in his voice.

"Once you're in LA, go to the Chateau Marmont and check in under his name. He usually stays in room 128. He has contacts in both LA and San Francisco that he usually meets up with around this time to discuss business and whatnot. The person that you want to get in contact with is named Eric. Just ask someone around the Los Angeles area. Someone is bound to know who he is, but if they don't, show them this card." Welsh concluded, opening a drawer and pulling out a business card.

"But, Simon, if we already know that this Sebastian character killed Ernest, why do I need to get involved?" Peterson looked at Welsh with the same questioning expression on his face.

"Rostanov's name is just one that's been thrown out there. When Sebastian used to work for the MAFIA, he threatened murder once before as a means to get a rat to shut up about some shady dealings he'd been doing for the government." Welsh detailed.

"Why is he here?" He pointed to Peterson, who now had his car keys in his hand.

"He's going to go with you to make sure that you make it safely to the airport." Welsh smiled.

"What time is my flight?"

"Six o'clock," Welsh replied.

Maxwell looked down at his watch: it was three o'clock now, which gave him three hours to get ready.

"Thanks ever so much, Welsh," he said, walking over to the man to shake his hand once again.

"Don't mention it, but do not blow your cover and be careful."

This was the warning that Welsh, not Pierre, always gave him. But, of course, he expected nothing less from Maxwell, as he expected nothing less from Welsh, but Pierre was another matter altogether.

Pierre Dubois had indeed become president of the Central Intelligence unit for the

English branch of the European government when Ernest Dumont had been killed two years earlier. Still, unlike his predecessor, he did not get his assignments from Pierre. He always drove 45 minutes to Welsh's office, which would have been a problem for him a year ago, but he was used to this communication system by now, as weird and broken as it seemed. Moments later, he was being followed by Peterson to the black sedan parked outside of the two-story building, neither of them speaking.

He had stowed Eric's business card in the pocket of his jacket, still wondering what he and Rostanov talked about when they met up, but before he had too much time to reflect on this, they'd made it to the black sedan. "Before we head out, I have to go back to my home and pack," he said.

"All right," Peterson said as they drove the 30 miles to the agent's stucco-fronted apartment.

An hour later, he emerged from his house carrying two bags, one under each arm. One bag contained two changes of underclothes, two black-and-white suits, and two pairs of tennis shoes; he would buy more clothes in California if he needed more. The other one contained a toothbrush, toothpaste, shaving lotion and other grooming items.

They reached Heathrow Airport in London half an hour later and after helping his passenger out with his bags, Peterson said goodbye and went on his way.

3

Beautiful Vixen

It was five o'clock when the British agent pushed his luggage through the airport to terminal B, where he waited for the "all clear" to board, patiently half-listening to the conversations around him. His mind was on his mission and he hoped that once all of this was over, he would have the answers for which he was looking. When it was safe enough, he looked around the terminal at the people around him, all of them looked harmless enough, but there was one pair of eyes that seemed to follow him wherever he turned.

After nearly forty-five minutes, he was finally given the OK to board. As he did so, he put his bags into the overhead compartment and mentally prepared himself for the long flight. After taking his seat, those watchful eyes he'd felt on his back in the terminal now stared at him from across the aisle for the longest time before the figure got up and walked slowly toward him.

Those eyes had belonged to a short, slender woman with an oval-shaped face and blond hair. The woman wore a teal skirt with high heels, and to top it off, her hair had been neatly styled into a braid at the top of her head. "Mind if I sit?" the woman asked in a low voice.

Maxwell shook his head and she sat.

"Thank you," she said.

"What's your name?" he asked when he'd found his voice again.

"My name is Renee," she replied.

"Do you have a last name?" he asked, making her smile a little.

"It's Anderson," she answered.

"Nice to meet you, Miss Anderson," he said.

"Have you got a name?" she asked. It was her turn now, but he didn't answer.

"Where are you going?"

"California," he answered.

"For work?"

He nodded and sat back in his seat. "What about you?" he said.

"What about me?" she repeated.

"Are you going to California as well?" he asked.

She nodded and looked her seatmate over. She was very beautiful, but he had to be careful not to give too much away to this woman.

"What do you do, Miss Anderson?" he asked.

"Please, call me René.," she whispered as the announcer began to say the directions in both English and French.

"All right, René, what is it that you do?" he asked.

She smiled crookedly, showing all her perfect, white teeth. "I have been sent here to follow someone." she finally answered softly as the plane rolled down the runway.

"Who are you following?" he whispered.

"Someone who was sent on this flight to do business."

"Do you have a name?" she asked again.

"Andrew," he replied, "who are you following?"

"I was told to follow you by Simon," she confessed.

"How did you know what I looked like?" he asked.

She pulled a picture from her pocket and stared at it, and for some reason, he found this amusing.

"Why do you think I kept staring at you?" she asked, putting his picture back in her pocket.

He wanted to say that he'd thought she was a stalker, but he kept his mouth shut.

"You work for him?" he asked instead.

"From a distance. The whole business of the spy trade doesn't appeal to me," she told him.

"Well, why are you following me if this doesn't appeal to you?" he asked.

"Well, I like the danger," she answered.

He didn't want to dash her hopes, but he didn't know how much danger, if any, would be involved in this mission. They sat in silence for a while as the plane took off, but once they were in the air, the woman looked at him again with a comment on her lips.

"You must be well-respected for the work that you do," she whispered, looking around to make sure that the other passengers weren't listening, then she tried to look into his eyes, but he was staring out the window, only to turn back when he heard her voice.

"Hardly," he answered.

"What do you mean by that?"

"I didn't join the government for respect, René. I joined it to protect people," he explained.

"Is that why you're going to Los Angeles?" she asked.

"Yes and no."

"What does that mean?" she asked.

"Somebody murdered my original boss, and I have to find out who did it," he told her.

"Is that the only reason you're going?" she pressed.

"Well, if this bastard's caught, then that's good for everyone because what happened to Ernest won't happen to anyone else in my organization," he explained.

"Why are you going undercover, pretending to be the suspect?" she said.

This girl was smarter than he'd thought, but he wondered how she knew that he to pretended to be the man they were discussing. "I have to meet up with a contact of his named Eric," he said.

"I know who you're talking about." she answered$

"You do?" he said cheerfully.

"Yes, his name is Eric Clay," she informed him.

"What do Eric and his associate usually talk about when they get together?" he asked, feeling bad that he might be getting her too involved with this situation.

"I'm not sure, but I can take you to where he works," she said.

He wanted to hug her, but he thought better of it and stayed in his seat.

"Tell me more about yourself," he said in a conversational tone.

"Not much to tell," she whispered.

"How old are you?" he asked.

"I'll be 30 on my next birthday," she answered.

"When is that?" he asked.

"The 25th of July."

In spite of himself, he smiled in appreciation of this woman. For the duration of the flight, the young woman listened to his stories about his childhood as they sipped chilled wine from small cups, but he didn't say anything about the work he did now.

A few hours later, both were roused by the pilot announcing their descent into LAX. Both of them looked up at the clock at the same time: it was six o'clock in the evening.

"We should get something to eat," René remarked after they got off the plane.

"I'd like to, but I'm exhausted," he said apologetically.

She nodded, indicating that she understood.

After getting their luggage from Baggage Claim, they made their way to a taxi parked on the street. They didn't talk to each other the whole way to the Chateau Marmont, giving her new companion some much-needed time to himself. She rode next to him, staring out the window at the bright light outside.

"Where are you from, little lady?" he heard the driver say.

"I was born in Ohio, but my father was born here, so we'd come here every summer when I was little," she replied.

"What about your friend?" the driver asked, now staring at Maxwell.

"I was born in Russia, but I live here now," he answered, slipping into an American accent and staring out of the car's other window.

"Weird, I haven't seen you here before." the cab driver commented. "What do you two do?"

René shifted in her seat at that question and so did Maxwell.

So what exactly did Rostanov do nowadays?

"I'm only here to meet someone." he lied, hoping that would do the trick.

"What about you?" he asked, staring at her again.

"I'm with him," she said.

"What are your names?" he asked.

Maxwell didn't answer.

"René Anderson," she answered.

This guy's curiosity made him seem nosy, probably more so than he'd intended.

When the driver had stopped his round of questioning, the two people shared a relieved look.

"This is easier than I thought," Maxwell whispered to himself.

When the cab finally arrived at the hotel, the driver helped his customers with their bags and watched them as they walked up to the front to check-in. René's room was on the third floor, and he was only one floor below her.

By eight-thirty, they were both exhausted, and they would need some sleep for the long day they had tomorrow.

"Thank you for coming with me, Miss Anderson," he said, smiling tiredly at her when they'd arrived at her room.

"Whatever, just be ready to meet Eric tomorrow," she replied, unimpressed. He then closed the door to her room and walked away. When he'd finally gone, she pulled her cell phone from her pocket and dialed a number.

"Hello?" the voice on the other end answered.

"Simon, it's René," she replied.

"Oh, did you two make it all right?" Welsh asked.

"Yes, we're at the hotel now," she replied.

"Great," Simon answered.

"Tomorrow, I'm going to take him to see Eric," she informed him.

"Excellent."

They talked for 20 more minutes before she let out a yawn and called it a night. She went over to the window, opened it and looked out at the starry sky. She had read enough sly novels and had seen enough spy films to know that these people were always on their toes and that most of them were smart enough to know when they were lying. She thought about the explanation he'd given her about coming to California, and she hoped that he'd be able to keep that cover long enough to fool the right people.

She trusted that Welsh wouldn't lie to her or put her in danger, but as she'd told Maxwell on the long flight, she liked a little of it.

Before leaving, Welsh had called her into his office and had sat her down. "I have something for you to do." he'd said.

At those words, her ears had perked up, but they had also confused her quite a bit.

"I'm not an agent." she'd objected.

"It's nothing too difficult, Miss Anderson." he'd said.

She'd then agreed to do it.

"Do you know who this man is?" Welsh had asked, pulling a picture from a desk drawer.

She'd studied the picture for a long time, but she had not been able to recognize the person's face. "Can't say that I do." she'd replied after a pause.

"This is Andrew Maxwell, our top worker." he'd told her.

She studied the face again as he talked.

"I want you to go on flight 545 to California. There's a suspected assassin that might have killed a key player in his circle over there." he'd explained.

"Will he be on that flight also?"

He'd nodded before giving her the picture.

"Put this in the pocket of your skirt and whatever you do, don't take your eyes off him and follow him as far as you can without getting hurt or exposing yourself," he'd said and had sent her on her way.

She'd followed him all this way, getting a few bits and pieces of information from her would-be partner himself, and the more she'd heard, the more fascinated she'd become with this story. Finally, when she had grown bored of thinking, she climbed into bed, got under the covers and was soon asleep.

4

Toxic Contacts

"Ready to go?" René asked when she spotted Maxwell waiting for her in the lobby.

After a moment, he nodded and put whatever he was looking at away in his pocket and reached for her arm.

"What were you looking at?" she said as they walked out of the sliding doors.

"I was trying to find out more about Rostanov," he explained.

"Anything of interest?" she wondered.

"I know what he does now."

This comment put a look of surprise on her face.

"Oh? And what is that?"

"He's a hitman," he explained.

"So, he's being hired to kill." she realized.

He nodded and frowned.

"What are you going to do now?" she asked.

"I still have to go meet with Eric," he replied.

They continued walking in silence until they came to a small Mercedes that was parked out front.

Without saying a word, they both climbed into the car's front seats and buckled up.

As René drove, Maxwell silently read his phone's screen, being careful not to say anything that would frighten her. Sebastian Rostanov wasn't a French name by any means. However, he had still made a name for himself as a powerful assassin in the country. While he was still with the Mafia, he'd killed over 70 people, including a French hostage who'd begged for his life. He couldn't go on, but he forced himself to continue reading.

Before his death, the Frenchman had pleaded with him to spare his life for his family. But Rostanov had grabbed the pistol and, with one shot to his head, had killed him. That had been over a decade ago, but the article didn't say anything about what he did now.

"Dammit," he whispered, making René turn her head in his direction.

"Find anything else?" she asked when they came to a red light.

He nodded and let her see the article for herself.

"Christ," she whispered.

"René, this is no place for a girl like you," he said earnestly.

She stared at him, half-knowing and half-surprised.

"This is not for someone like you." he went on.

She knew that he was right, but she had already gone too far to turn back now.

For fifteen minutes, they drove in silence as the building that was Clay's office came into view. Seconds later, the girl tapped her passenger's shoulder, stopped the engine, and got out. He followed her out immediately and waited as she walked up some steps to a gate. She pressed a button and a voice said, "Yes?" seconds later.

"Eric Clay, please," she said into the intercom.

The sound of a door opening was heard and a burly man came out, an expectant expression on his face. His head had been shaved on the sides, leaving the top and back covered in blond hair with a tinge of grey, and he was dressed in a short-sleeved t-shirt, shorts and black-and-white tennis shoes. "Oh, René, it's good to see you again." the burly man greeted the young woman, jogging over to hug her. After their embrace, Clay walked over to Maxwell and looked him over. Silently, they both hoped that this guy was dumb enough to believe that he was his contact. "Hello, my %fr." he greeted, shaking his hand and grinning.

"It's been a long time, Eric," Maxwell replied.

After their quick greeting, he led them into a building and showed them to two seats facing a table. before sitting, their host went to a small refrigerator and grabbed a bottle of Budweiser from the second shelf. "Did you two need anything?" he asked.

René shook her head and so did her partner.

After closing the door, he went to the table and sat across from them, saying nothing. Though Sebastian was an independent assassin now, the article had claimed that he still had links to the Mafia, and he wondered if Clay was one of them. After taking a sip of beer, Eric turned to face his visitors. The building they were in was a small room cluttered with junk, books, many bottles, and computers. In a corner, a small television was playing the news, but it was only background noise.

"Eric, tell me something," Maxwell said, trying to keep this moving.

Eric sighed.

"What?" he asked.

"Do you still work for the Mafia?"

Eric looked down at the table for a moment before answering. "Not since the early 2000s," he said, taking another sip of beer.

"It's a little early for liquor." René cautioned.

"Helps me think," he replied.

"What do you do now?" Maxwell asked.

"I work for the cartel." he finally said.

"You work for the gang?" Maxwell asked in surprise.

Eric shook his head.

"Drug dealers?" he guessed again.

He nodded.

"What do you deal, Cocaine?" he asked.

"Cocaine, crack, ecstasy, you name it," he announced proudly, finishing off his beer in two more gulps.

He was going somewhere with Eric, but it was in the wrong direction. "How much money do you make dealing drugs?" he asked.

"Depends," Eric answered, getting up to put his bottle into the recycling bin.

So far, Eric Clay was no help at all.

"Eric?" René called.

"Yeah?" he called back.

"May we use one of your computers?" she asked, going over to a PC and turning it on.

He said yes, and Maxwell was by her side in seconds. Once they were connected to the internet, he went to Google. He typed the one question he needed answered most right now into the search engine: who killed Ernest Dumont?

He knew that he was taking a risk by doing this and that if word got back to Ernest's killers about what he was doing, they'd be coming after him and whoever they suspected was with him, but he was running out of patience. He waited for the results to pop up on the screen, but there was nothing.

"Anything?" René asked from beside him.

He shook his head in frustration.

He turned his head to the corner, and then he soon turned back when he heard his phone ring in his pocket.

"Hello?" he answered.

"Andrew, I've got some information for you." It was Welsh on the other end.

He might have been questionable, but so far, he was more trustworthy than Pierre.

René leaned forward to listen, so he put it on "speaker" and turned the volume low to make sure that Eric wouldn't hear.

"What's up?" he asked.

"Well, I've had some help, and I've figured out who killed Ernest," Welsh answered quietly.

René leaned in to hear, just as intrigued.

"Who?" Maxwell asked.

"It was Pierre."

René tried to read Maxwell's face, but he was turned away from her. "Anything else?" he asked, his tone alert.

"He was not alone, but whoever he was working with is nowhere to be found," Welsh whispered.

"Speak up, Simon. Clay isn't listening," Maxwell said, turning to confirm his last statement.

As both listened to Welsh's developments, Maxwell thought back to the two men's first meeting.

Even then, he'd had questions about the Frenchman and his motives, but he had just thought that he was overreacting.

As Welsh finished, Eric came back into the room.

Oh, no, René thought, panicked now.

"What?" he whispered, seeing the expression on her face.

She pointed to the figure in the doorway, still panicked.

He acted quickly, taking Welsh off "speaker" and putting the phone to his ear. "Do you know anything about his partner or partners?" he asked.

"As a young man in the late 1990s, he'd been involved in a gang called the Greenridge Killers," Welsh said.

"Where were they based?" asked Maxwell.

"Primarily in France," Welsh answered.

Maxwell stared over at his René, who was staring at the TV screen. "Any motives?" he asked.

"They operated just like the mob, killing whoever they thought knew too much." the voice on the other end answered.

In his mind, he could see the face of the man he now called his boss when he'd announced his new position he now knew had been stolen from him. He'd looked as if the secret he was keeping was one that he was going to take to the grave, and that made him question further if Ernest had known something that could have gotten him in trouble with them. "How did you find this out?" he asked after a brief pause.

"I asked one of my partners in the FBI to do some research on Dubois and to get back to me when they had something." Welsh's voice was cold as he relayed this to him. "They had him on file?" he asked, not at all surprised. He couldn't see, but he guessed that Simon had nodded.

"So, where do we go from here?" he asked.

The other end was silent for a few seconds as Simon considered this. "Stay in Los Angeles and wait for me to contact you.

We're trying to find their whereabouts now." the voice on the other end was sharp yet comforting.

"Thank you," Maxwell said.

"Stay safe," Welsh said and hung up.

"What did he say?" René asked.

He repeated the conversation to her and she listened attentively.

"Did he say how long it was going to be?" she asked.

"No," he answered, and she could see that he was just as worried and anxious as she was.

At that moment, Eric walked further into the room, frowning. "Everything okay?" he asked.

Both of them nodded at the same time, though the future was uncertain.

There was still an assassin out there, and maybe the Greenridge Killers were still out there as well, probably planning to put an end to him and his organization. He asked himself what aspect of the danger the young woman next to him liked: the constant feeling of uncertainty about the future, the daily twists and turns, or the constant feeling that you had to be alert at all times, but that question would have to wait. Eric Clay was back in the room and for his sake, they had to pretend that everything was all right. They turned back to the TV screen and stared at the reporters that were before them, neither of them saying anything for a long time before Maxwell turned back to face Eric.

"Eric, did you hear anything?" he asked, his voice calm and steady.

"No, but I saw you on your phone.

Who were you talking to?" he asked, trying to make conversation.

"My uncle in France," Maxwell replied.

Eric was about to say something else when his phone rang again. "You'll have to excuse me," Maxwell said, stepping outside and onto the porch.

"I should go with him." René apologized before leaving.

"Simon?" Maxwell asked.

"We've located them, but I'm afraid most of them are close," Welsh stated.

"Where are the majority of them?" Maxwell asked.

"Most of them are in New York."

Both stood, tensed at his words. Welsh suddenly told him to take him off "speaker," but he would not explain why.

"What happens now?" Maxwell asked.

"What happens now is that both of you pack up and leave this evening. Your flight arrangements have already been made. Once you arrive and after you've retrieved your bags, a taxi will be waiting at JFK Airport, Terminal C, to take you to the Mariott." Welsh instructed.

"What's my job?" he asked.

"You're his friends. He has contacts there, too, but watch out for Miss Anderson. I want those monsters dealt with and knowing what they've done to you, I thought you'd be the perfect one for this assignment but make one wrong move, and both of you are as good as dead." Welsh told him.

"What about Pierre?" he asked.

He assured him that Dubois would be dealt with when the time came.

After hanging up, René walked up to him as he pocketed his phone.

"Well?" she asked softly.

"When we get back to the hotel, pack your things," he answered.

"Why?" she asked.

"Because," he answered, patting the pocket that held his revolver, "the real work begins tomorrow."

Four hours later, they stepped off the plane at JFK Airport, both of them on high alert. During the ride back to JFK, he had filled in the gaps for René, who'd looked understandably stressed but had said nothing until he'd finished.

"Dear God." she'd whispered.

Now, as they walked along in the airport, listening to the voices around them, his mind worked in overdrive to put the pieces together.

Welsh had sent him a group photo of every member of the Greenridge Killers, and though they were a little older, they still looked like killing machines. He had shown the picture to René, who'd studied it carefully. "How many in total?" she'd whispered.

"Fourteen," Maxwell answered. "I don't see Pierre." she'd told him. "He's in Paris, but he'll be dealt with eventually." he'd said.

Moments later, they stepped outside of terminal C, and it was just as Welsh had said. A taxi waited for them on the curb, and as soon as their driver, a tall, thin man dressed in a wife-beater and shorts, saw them, he hopped out and helped them put their bags in the back. "Thank you," Maxwell said politely and climbed in beside René, who was already seated by the window. They were speeding down the busy streets of New York seconds later, as this driver had already been given specific directions on where to take them by Welsh.

"Have you been briefed on all of the specifics?" Maxwell asked softly after a few beats of silence.

René nodded and said a silent prayer for their success. The driver was silent until they'd reached the halfway mark, but the agent wasn't listening to his speech. He wanted to know why this gang wanted the money and why they made Welsh lie for them. He then asked himself where this Rostanov's contact or contacts stayed and if they could be trusted to help them.

He'd packed his Smith and Wesson Revolver, several .500 magnum cartridges, two bullet-proof vests, and two sets of clothes he'd bought earlier that day, along with his shaving things, his toothbrush, and his toothpaste into the grey suitcase that was now in the back of the cab beside his feet. He was prepared to take down anyone who took the first shot. Before he knew it, they'd reached their destination. The driver got their bags from the car and watched them go inside.

"Miss Anderson and Mr. Maxwell, I presume?" the person at the front desk asked.

"Yes," René said.

After checking in, they were given their room keys and taken to the elevator. Just like in the Chateau Marmont, their rooms were one floor apart and also, just like the previous evening, he walked her to her room. "Welsh says we must be up at eight-thirty tomorrow morning. Do you want me to call you?" he asked.

She shook her head, walked in and closed the door.

Back in his room, after unpacking and making sure his weapon was hidden in the lining of his suitcase, he crawled into bed and looked up at the ceiling.

He asked himself why Pierre would kill his predecessor and how long he'd kept that secret to himself. He thought back to their meeting just a few days earlier, and a different question came to his mind: How the hell had he gotten the stolen codes? Then, an image popped into his mind, though it was blurry. Weeks after finding out that his partners had been murdered in France, he'd gone to Pierre's office. His laptop had been sitting on his desk, and he'd opened his browser to a government agency's website. Pierre had not been there at that particular moment and because he'd been in such a hurry, he hadn't thought to observe the contents of the page.

Maxwell got out of bed and went to a small table where a little notebook, like the one in Eric's tiny room of an office, had sat. After it had warmed up, he had logged in and went to the same website he had gone to in Pierre's office. For five minutes, he scanned the site until he came to what he was looking for. The codes were all there, staring him in the face.

Staring at those numbers brought back the days when he'd worked for Russia. It had only been a few years since that time, but now the memories were as clear to him as they'd been then. Then, he'd worked for a woman named Olga as a foreign agent.

The Americans had been planning something, she'd said. She'd needed the government's codes to stop them before they had time to put their plan into action, but had he been the one who'd gotten them?

No, he could remember that he'd had two partners, maybe more, but he couldn't remember their names. He concentrated harder, and one of the men's' names came back to him. Peter Neovich. The other one had been his boss's assistant, but he'd never worked closely with either of them. They'd gotten the codes from the government, and he'd downloaded them onto a flash drive, which he'd then handed over to the Russian government, but at the last minute, their golden worker had had a change of heart and had stolen the codes back from them. Eventually, they found out about it, and someone had sent over an assassin named Nikoolai to kill him. Before he could get there, however, he'd been murdered as revenge for a spy's death in France.

That's when he'd burned the drive, and it was only after that when he'd found out about the deaths of his partners. Both men had also been murdered in France by an unknown enemy of theirs, leaving two empty seats in Russia's branch of the CIU.

He had stayed for another month until Olga was targeted just a few days before Christmas. Her death had been felt all over Russia, and after her funeral was over, he'd left.

He'd spent a short time on his own, lying low at a friend's flat in London until he'd received a call one night. The call had been from Ernest Dumont, asking about a job offer.

"Who told you about me?" he'd asked warily.

He'd explained that a colleague, only known as X, had referred the English spy to him.

He'd then gone on to tell him that although he wouldn't be paid much, Ernest was interested in him and his services.

"I'll think about it." he'd answered. Two weeks later, after many late-night talks with his friend, he was on a train to the building that housed the new organization that he would now be working for.

Who was this X, who did they know, and for whom did they work?

Those were questions for another time. Right now, he had to focus on his assignment; maybe after he was finished, his boss's death would be avenged, and with that thought in his mind, he drifted off to sleep.

5

The Hardest Part Begins

At half-past eight, Maxwell awoke and stared out the window. The city had already come to life. People were going about their business, street vendors were opening their stands, and all-night partygoers were being driven back home for their early-morning naps.

He knew that René would be up soon, then their car would come for them. So he got up, stretched, and went to the spacious bathroom, still thinking about the previous couple of days.

All of the codes had been on that laptop, and he'd found out that Pierre Dubois had killed his predecessor. All of that had led him here, to busy New York. The easiest part had been meeting the woman he now called his partner for this assignment, but in the back of his mind, he was suspicious of her motives. It was probably the spy in him talking. Yes, she was nice, but could she be trusted?

He took a quick shower, washed his face, brushed his teeth, shaved, and dressed in a buttoned-down shirt, blue jeans, sneaker, and a jacket. Then, he pushed those thoughts from his mind and focused on his current assignment.

How were they going to find these men? He didn't know the answer to that question or any others that came to his mind. But now wasn't the time for such musings. He grabbed the .500 Magnum and stuck it under his shirt, then looked at the clock on the wall. The time was now eight o'clock.

He decided that he'd see what she was doing at nine o'clock if she didn't call. So when she hadn't called by then, he left the room and started for the elevator when an unexpected presence made him stop.

He looked up and grabbed the handle of the gun, then tightened his hold on it.

"Hold your fire." the voice said. René looked at him terrified and bowed her head.

He took his hand away from the gun and flexed his fingers. His hand was sweating, but he smiled down at her.

"Hey." he greeted her.

"Good morning," she said, smiling at him.

It would take him a while to get used to having a partner. "Are you ready to go?" he asked.

She nodded and they walked to the elevator together in silence. Once they were there, René turned toward him.

"Where exactly are these men located?" she asked.

"I'm afraid that's the hard part," he answered wearily.

"Do you think they'll believe our story?" René asked.

He didn't want to frighten her, but he knew that there was only a small chance of that happening. "Let's hope so." was all he said.

They walked the rest of the way to their waiting cab in silence. Maxwell paid the driver $30 for the day. As he gazed out of the back windows at all the scenery, he paid particular attention to the men that crossed the street. They passed over the Brooklyn bridge before going through the Harlem tunnel and all the while, he kept a watchful eye out for anyone who looked suspicious. The men in the picture had been dressed in faded black hoodies and khakis, but there was no chance that they would be in plain sight. "Be on guard at all times," he told her.

From time to time, René glanced at Maxwell, but he kept his gaze hard and serious. He was certain that this day was going to be uneventful and lacking in action. In time, he tore his gaze away from the window and sighed. Then, a few feet from Times Square, the driver suddenly turned to him and cleared his throat.

"Where am I taking you?" he asked.

"Times Square," René said.

The driver stopped, gave them both a look of warning before getting out and opening their doors. They walked along the busy streets crowded with fast-moving people, making Maxwell curious as to where most of them were going.

Cigarette smoke filled the air around every corner. It seemed like every few minutes, a taxi or another car sped down the street. "Are you ready to look for them?" he asked.

René nodded, though she was nervous about the whole idea of facing these monsters. They passed a group of street vendors selling all sorts of things, from sandwiches to umbrellas, even though it wasn't raining. Maxwell took his phone from his pocket and searched until he found the picture Welsh had sent him of the group they were trying to find.

He examined the figures more carefully: they sat in a circle, coldly gazing at the camera. Their faces were covered by their hoods, but there was no concealing their weapons. All but one held semi-automatics, but the last one had a pocket knife with a freshly sharpened blade. Then, after a long and careful examination, he handed the phone over to the person beside him, who gazed down at them with mild interest.

"Memorize what you're seeing," he ordered.

She looked down again and tried to concentrate. After a few moments, the faces were ingrained in her mind and so were their poses. They were all posed as if they were hunting their prey: crouched, with their muscles tensed, ready for the attack.

"Simon wants you to kill them?" she asked, surprised.

He nodded and grabbed the phone from her. In a flash, he was on Google with his back to her. Then, after a few moments, he turned back to her and held the phone out.

On the screen was a picture of Sebastian Rostanov, the man who'd been wrongly accused of the murder of his boss. He was dressed in black, and slung over his shoulder was a military rifle. His eyes were cold like he knew something but was not about to give him away.

René stared, wide-eyed, at the image on the screen, then looked back at Maxwell. "Is this the man you suspected of the crime originally?" she asked.

Maxwell nodded.

"He was wrongly accused of committing the murder," he said before putting the phone back in his pocket. He looked at his watch: it was now almost noon.

Both images were now in René's mind as they continued their walk, and now she was more focused than ever. She had more questions for him, but he had to concentrate and so did she. They ducked into a library and waited as the librarian approached them.

"May I help you?" she asked. The librarian, a short, fat woman, wore a skintight black dress and sandals. Her face was stretched into a tight smile, and her brown hair was piled on top of her head. The Englishman stepped closer to the woman, who flinched.

"Yes, as a matter of fact," he said patiently.

The place wasn't crowded: just a few people that had come for a day of reading.

"What do you need?" she asked patiently.

"You can begin by telling us your name," he replied.

She grabbed her name tag and held it out to him.

Her name was Melody Williams. "Now that you know my name, what else do you want to know?" she asked.

"We're after information," he said, his voice businesslike.

"All right, I'll tell you whatever you want to know, but first, you must tell me who you are and why you're here," she answered, matching his tone.

How to answer this question?

"I am a friend of this man's. Have you heard of him?" he asked, pulling his phone from his pocket and pulling up the second picture René had seen only moments ago.

She studied the image and a spark of recognition lit up her eyes. "Barely, but what does this have to do with this situation, and who are you?" she asked, her patience vanishing.

"Fine. If you must know, we're looking for some people. Have you ever seen these people anywhere?"

She looked at the other picture on his phone and tensed. "No," she whispered, but there was a hint of something in her eyes that said differently.

"Your eyes tell a different story, Miss Williams."

The woman looked at him, both worried and scared.

He slowly drew the gun from its hiding place and aimed it at her head.

"I don't know anything." she whimpered.

He put his finger on the trigger and threatened to shoot her if she didn't stop lying and tell him what she knew. She backed away a few feet, her eyes sparkling with fear.

"Some guys in hoods came here about two weeks ago," she confessed in a weak voice.

"Go on," he said, lowering the gun and digging the butt of it into her stomach.

She squirmed, but he had to remind her several times to stay still. "They were wearing black sweatshirts, blue jeans, and black steel-toed boots," she said, now gone robotic.

"Were they carrying weapons?" he asked, his voice and eyes cold.

She shook her head. "If they had been, they had them hidden somewhere," she whispered.

"Where are they now?" he asked.

"I don't know," she said, and he released her.

She looked over at René, who had grown still beside him.

"One more thing," he added and went over to her, "did they say anything to you?"

She shook her head quickly. "Thank you, Miss Williams." he waved and grabbed René's hand and shook her gently. They ducked out of the door, leaving the librarian shivering.

"Are you all right?" he asked when they were outside.

She managed a nod and a shaky smile. The hardest part was the beginning. They had to find these men who never showed their faces to their victims, not even the ones they let go free. At 5th avenue, they hailed a cab and went back to the hotel for lunch.

They both ate steak, baked potatoes, spinach, and for dessert, a chocolate lava cake. They had little to say.

Maxwell was still thinking about the librarian and her answers.

She had known something, but she had withheld it. Had she been afraid of being murdered by them if she said the wrong thing?

His thoughts were interrupted by a sharp poke in his ribs on his right side.

He looked over and saw a man dressed in grey with a Glock pistol in his hand. The two men glared at each other for a long moment before the one with the gun that had poked him spoke in a deep voice. "I've just come back from the library about a block from here."

Maxwell answered the man in a calm and relaxed voice. "Did you now? And what happened?"

"That girl, Melody, told me that you paid her a visit and that you'd probed her for information."

Maxwell nodded serenely.

The man then turned to face René cleared his throat. "I know who you are and why you're trying to find them. It's a very interesting situation you're in, Mr. Maxwell."

René sat back, desperately wishing for this guy to go away.

"So you've heard of me?" he asked.

The gangster nodded. "You're trying to get revenge for a murder, yes?"

Maxwell smiled tightly.

"Do you know anything else?" he asked, suddenly very interested.

The man reached over to his table just in front of them and grabbed his glass of Merlot, sipped from it once, then put it down.

"The victim was Mr. Ernest Dumont, the boss. You and your parents worked for your organization's London branch. Your younger brother died at birth. Am I missing anything?"

For a moment, he was caught off-guard. How the hell did he know so much?

The French gangster saw the unasked question in his eyes and smiled. "I work for the government myself," he said, though like Pierre, he didn't believe this guy, but he didn't admit this.

Was this was his cover: a worker for the government when he was, in fact, one of the members of the very group they were trying to find?

"Who sent you?" Maxwell asked.

The man produced a card from his pocket and slid it across the table. It said that his boss was X, but the card did not give a first or last name. He'd heard that name before; his original boss had mentioned someone of that same name had recommended Maxwell to him, and he asked himself if this was the same person.

"Why are you here?" he asked.

The French gangster smiled, showing his nicotine-stained teeth. For a moment, Maxwell thought about asking him what brand of cigarettes he smoked, but he pushed that thought out of his mind and told himself to focus.

"I've got a message for you." the gangster said menacingly.

"Well, let's hear it," Maxwell said, turning to stare at the unnamed Frenchman, who was staring at René.

"Both for you," he emphasized and reluctantly, his partner stared into the Frenchman's eyes.

"It's from the very group you're looking for." the stranger said and picked up his wine glass again. Both of them waited as the glass was drained, then set back down.

"What do they want?" René asked, impatient now.

"They want you to terminate your search." He watched as the waiter came by and refilled his glass, then left.

"Why?" Maxwell asked.

The gangster rearranged his facial features but for an instant, Maxwell thought that he had seen rage in his eyes; however, when he next looked, his face was blank.

"They'll kill you if you don't," he said stiffly.

Maxwell shook his head. "I'm not dropping out of this assignment until it is finished," he replied sternly.

The nameless man gave a cold smile and raised his gun to his chest. "Your loyalty to your government is very touching, but which do you value more? Your job or your life?" The man sipped from his glass again.

Maxwell turned toward the hall and looked out at the room that was now filling up with people. "My job," he said simply.

The supposed government worker sighed and fixed René with a hard stare.

"And the girl?" the other man asked.

"What about her?" Maxwell questioned, his voice hard.

"Is she with you?" he asked angrily.

René shook her head.

"Excuse me?" the man asked.

"No," she whispered.

The man lowered his gun and stared at the two figures in front of him. René looked scared, but her friend stayed relaxed.

He picked up his glass for the last time and drank the rest of the wine down. He then set the glass on the table and put his gun away in his pocket before turning toward the door. Then he turned back and stared at them for a long time before saying in a cold voice, "Do what you want, but it's your funeral. Goodbye."

After paying the bill and putting the gun away, he left with ice in his eyes and his hand on the pocket with the gun in it.

René and Andrew stared silently at one another from across the table for a few minutes. The image of the man's face and his words seemed to be haunting both of them, but the look in the Englishman's eyes was one of determination, not fear. Half an hour later, as he went to check on his new partner, Maxwell thought about the nameless man who'd come up behind them. The man had claimed to be a government worker, an employee of X's, but he still didn't know what this mysterious person did, nor did he know what the man's real intent had been.

Five minutes later, as he waited to be let into René's room, his mind began to spin again. He wanted to get his hands on those men, to let them know that this man's death was going to be avenged whether they were prepared or not. His next impulse was to call the airport and send René back to Paris or London, but he'd promised Simon that he would watch over her; this was a dangerous situation she was getting into. He hoped that she was prepared for it. However, it was going to end.

Seconds later, René opened the door, still in her red dress and sandals with a weary look in his eyes.

"May I come in?" Maxwell asked. She nodded and led him through the door to a chair by the window. He stared out at the crowded streets for what seemed like forever before he turned to her. "René, tell me something," he said, and at the sound of his voice, she flinched.

"All right." she finally said.

He sighed and prepared to ask the question he'd waited so long to ask, but she read it in his eyes.

"You're doubting me," she said accusingly.

"No." he objected.

"I can see it in your eyes, Andrew. You doubt my ability to keep up."

"Please, René, you're jumping to conclusions." he tried to explain.

"All right, so what is it, then?" she asked calmly.

"I'm just concerned," he replied in an authoritative voice.

"Why?" she asked.

"You might get hurt," he argued.

"You should be more concerned for your safety." she retorted.

"I am, but since I have you here, I have to worry about one extra person not going missing." he fired back.

"So, I'm a burden?" she asked, tears welling up in her eyes. He reached over and grabbed her hand. "No, René, I'm just trying to figure out why you're here on this mission. What is it about this business that intrigues you?" he asked softly.

"I told you, it's the danger," she said, all the tears gone now.

"What does that mean?" he asked.

She explained that the sense of adventure attracted her to this business, not so much the killing.

"Aren't you afraid they'll kill you?" he asked seriously.

She nodded but told him that she would die with the knowledge that she had helped save her country if it came to that. They sat in silence for a while, just thinking, but it was he who broke it first.

"Enough of that," he said. "We still have to go find Rostanov's contact."

"Do you think he can tell you anything?" she asked.

He said he hoped so and got up. He told her that he would take a nap, and they agreed to meet in the lobby at half-past four. Back in his room, Maxwell stripped down to his underwear, put on a housecoat, and climbed into bed.

He was now left with his thoughts. He wondered what his contact's name was and where they were located. He got up and grabbed his phone from the bedside table and called Welsh, who answered on the second ring.

"Have you found the contact yet?"

"No, I've just called to ask a question," he said.

"Go on," Welsh said.

"Who are we looking for?" he asked.

Welsh gave him the information he asked for and more.

The other contact's name was Alexander Ritzkov, and he lived somewhere in Brooklyn, but he kept in touch with people in Moscow. He'd worked for the very group they were looking for, but they'd lost contact when he left in 2001. Welsh said that this guy was the one to ask because, in his own words, he "knew things," but what those things were, he wouldn't say. Finally, after spending some time in jail for the murders he committed, which had not been as many as his companion, he vowed to change. So he did, though he still prefers his nickname: The Poisoner, the one he used back then.

"Has he kept in contact with anyone else from his GK days?" he asked.

"I don't think so," Welsh said.

"Why is he called The Poisoner?" Maxwell asked.

"He used to poison his victims as a means of torturing them for answers, but if their answers weren't to his satisfaction, he would kill them."

He then went on to explain what he did now. After Olga's death, he'd moved to Washington and had worked for the FBI."

"Is he still an assassin?" Maxwell asked.

"No," Welsh replied.

If necessary, he was the one who recruited the killers to do the dirty work for him. Who had hired Nikolai's killer?

Though he knew that it had been an act of vengeance for another spy's death, what exactly had led Nikolai to kill the Frenchman? He then asked himself who had hired Nikolai to murder him. He wanted to ask these questions, but he thought he knew the answer to all of them: Olga.

Simon was saying something on the other end, but Maxwell was preoccupied with his thoughts.

He soon found himself thinking about Ritzkov. What was supposed to be done about him? How much information was he supposed to get? His thoughts were suddenly interrupted by the sound of a throat being cleared.

"Is something wrong?" Welsh asked, immediately snapping him out of his thoughts.

"No," Maxwell replied quickly.

"Have you got enough information from me?" Welsh asked.

He said he did, thanked him and hung up.

At four twenty-five, he got up and put his clothes back on. Before leaving, he grabbed the two guns and hid them under his shirt and jacket and grabbed his key. He then opened the door and headed toward the elevator, hearing nothing but the sound of his footsteps in the silence. At four-thirty, he arrived in the lobby and waited for René, his mind still wandering. If all of Welsh's information was accurate, how much did Alexander Ritzkov know, and how much was he willing to tell them? He texted Simon and asked him where he worked.

Half an hour later, they were in a car, heading to Ritzkov's office building for the answers they needed. Before they had left, Welsh had cautioned them not to waste Alexander's time. He'd said that he was a very busy person with a full schedule and little time for talking. Two hours later, they had gained access to the building and were waiting for someone to speak to them.

"What?" the receptionist asked coldly.

"We're here to see Alexander," René said, and they were immediately led to an elevator.

On the 8th floor, the man showed them to a door in the corner and knocked.

"Yes?" a voice called.

"Visitors are here to see you!"

Within seconds, the door opened and they were ushered into the office. Then the door was closed behind them.

"What do you want?" a voice sneered in a thick Russian accent.

"I'm guessing you're Alexander Ritzkov?" Maxwell asked.

"You'd be correct." the person agreed and fixed them with a cold stare. He sat behind an oak desk with a leather-bound book in front of him, but he was not looking at it.

"What do you want?" he asked after a moment of silence.

"I have some questions for you," Maxwell said.

6

Rapid-fire

Alexander turned his head toward his guest, and he could see that the years of torturing people had gotten to him. Circles were under his eyes and lines were around his mouth, but his eyes were still as hard as the man's in the picture had been.

"Ask your damn questions." he snapped.

"Do you remember a lady named Olga?"

Alexander smiled sadly and sighed. "Vaguely," he replied, clearly not in the mood to answer any more questions. But they had come for answers to their questions.

"Do you remember her death?" Maxwell asked.

Alexander got to his feet and went over to a cabinet. René could see the veins in the back of his hands when he showed them. He opened it, got a glass from a shelf, then reached for a bottle of vodka.

"I remember the day quite clearly, yes," he answered, filling a glass to the rim before replacing the bottle on the shelf.

He finished half the glass, wiped his lips on the back of his right hand, then set the rest on the counter in front of him.

"What happened?"

"An employee knocked on my office door and told me that Olga had been targeted by a pissed-off man," said Alexander, looking around the room.

"Who hired the killer?" Maxwell asked.

Alexander's cold eyes finally settled on Maxwell and held his gaze.

"Their identity was never revealed to me." he finally said, his voice emotionless.

He stared at what was left in his glass for a long time, then turned back to face his guests with annoyance. "I've heard of you," exclaimed Alexander, staring at his guest with intensity.

"Have you?" Maxwell asked.

Their host nodded and gave a cold smile. "You used to work for Olga as a foreign agent, and the last thing you did before your partners and dear, sweet Olga were assassinated had something to do with America. I'm glad to see that you were able to get another job after all," he sneered.

René opened her mouth to speak but closed it when she saw her partner's hard eyes look her way.

"Go on, you must have more." Maxwell encouraged.

Alexander downed some more vodka, then turned back to face him.

"You were stupid to take those codes away from the Russians," Alexander whispered menacingly.

"Why?" asked Maxwell.

"The American government was plotting against us.

They wanted to destroy our government, but we wanted to get them before they got us." Alexander explained and took another sip of vodka.

"What are you talking about, Alex?" Maxwell asked, annoyed now.

"We used to be allies, we used to be on the same side, but things have changed since then. There have been recent reports that the Americans were going to switch codes with us in an effort to screw us over, so we were going to shut their government down. We were so close to reaching our goal, but before we could, guess what happened? You stole the drive. You did what you were told for the first part, but why did you have to take the codes away?" Alexander was shouting now, so loudly that his guest flinched.

"There was an investigation into it, Alex. The Americans did nothing wrong."

"Oh, no? It was an American that targeted Olga, but he was never caught, never prosecuted." Alexander turned back to the liquid in his glass.

"How do you know that it was an American that did it?" Maxwell asked skeptically.

"I have my sources," Alexander said.

The room lapsed into silence, with only the sound of the clock ticking loudly on the wall to fill it. Maxwell gritted his teeth in frustration. He was beginning to realize that Alexander, or The Poisoner, or whatever he called himself, was just as useless as Eric had been.

"Who hired Nikolai?" he asked.

"Who?" Alexander asked, clearly caught off-guard.

"Nikolai, the person who was sent to kill me." he clarified.

"Olga hired him after your so-called change of heart." Alexander continued.

"How does the French spy tie into all this?"

"The French spy had been responsible for the death of one of his closest friends. He'd killed him after learning that he was having sex with the woman he'd been hired to take down. No one knows her real name, but she goes by the code name M13, I believe. The enemy had tricked the poor fool."

Alexander paused to refill his glass and sipped from it again.

"What happened after that?" Maxwell asked.

"Once word had spread about his death, Nikolai had been sent to find the Frenchman. It didn't take him long, but his death had left everyone divided. Some had thought that it was right to kill him. Others didn't. On the day that Nikolai was supposed to kill you, one of the people who'd disagreed with his choice confronted him and shot him point-blank." Alexander explained.

The room was silent again after that as his words sank in. Maxwell looked at the clock: it was now five forty-five in the evening and though he'd gotten some of the information he needed, he still hadn't found out what he'd come for.

"Alexander?" he called sharply.

The former assassin turned away from his glass and frowned. "What?" he snapped.

"Have you ever heard of the Greenridge Killers?"

Alexander snorted.

"Sure." he finally answered.

"Do you know where they are?"

Alexander nodded, his attention on his glass again.

"Can you take us to them?" asked Maxwell.

Alexander snorted again, then asked what they wanted with them.

Maxwell told the whole story as Alexander listened. They watched for any sign of emotion in their host's cold eyes. But as always, they were lifeless. He reached inside his desk and handed him a sheet of paper with an address on it.

He said that they were temporarily stationed somewhere in Harlem and were planning some kind of attack.

"Thank you," Maxwell said.

Alexander gave a short, brittle laugh before hurrying them out the door.

"What now?" René asked as they walked to the elevator.

Maxwell didn't answer. He was still surprised that Alexander had been willing to help them. He held the sheet up to his face and stared, transfixed, at the list of numbers.

He read the numbers carefully until he memorized them, then put the paper in his pocket.

René had asked the right question: what were they going to do now? It was too early to confront them, and acting like they were old friends would be too risky.

They were now on the main floor, both in their own worlds but worrying about the same thing: the mission. They only had a limited amount of time to find and "take care" of the group responsible for his boss's death, then Maxwell would have to get on the plane back to London.

They always had a little talk before he and Welsh parted and he went home.

He was again pulled from his thoughts by the sound of a honking horn, but he had not even noticed that they'd gone through the outside doors. He looked up and saw their car in the distance. His eyes wandered to René, who was waiting by the car's door with her back to him.

He slowly walked over to her, his eyes hard and distant. He watched as she opened their doors, then climbed into the front seat. The drive back to the hotel was long, and they barely spoke to each other.

From time to time, René tore her gaze from the road to stare at the man Maxwell. She wondered if there was a story to the face that now peered out the window and was void of emotion.

The question that she had asked seemed to have no answer. If they went through with their plan, millions of lives would be lost. The thought suddenly occurred to Maxwell that these people's lives were in his hands. The drive seemed to take forever until the building loomed in the distance.

Once inside, they approached the front desk. Their faces still looked empty and full of exhaustion.

"Any messages?" Maxwell asked the receptionist at the desk.

She asked his name and he told her. She looked down at the pad in front of her, then turned back to him. "No."

He thanked her and they walked to the elevator. He watched as she got off on her floor, then the doors closed again, and the numbers flashed until his came up.

After the elevator's doors opened, he walked silently to his room and opened his door. Once he'd closed it, he looked around and saw that nothing had been broken and nothing had been misplaced, but as he walked farther in, he sensed a presence behind him. He spun around and confronted a burly man dressed in a brown striped pantsuit, his eyes sparkling with mild anticipation. The man was hiding in the shadows, but it was clear who he wanted.

He was staring intently at Maxwell, but he had not come out of the shadows yet. Maxwell walked to the closet to put his things away, but the hidden man suddenly lunged at him, and Maxwell lurched forward and put his hand on the gun's trigger.

Both his eyes had been blackened and his hair reached his shoulders. He was short and stocky. The man cleared his throat and grabbed at the back of Maxwell's jacket.

"Not so fast, buddy." the man said in a gravelly voice.

They stared at each other for a long moment before his guest gave a smile full of pain and resentment. "We have something to discuss."

7

Message From An Assassin

"Who are you?" Maxwell asked in a calm, hard voice.

"The question you should be asking is, why am I here?" the voice answered, asking the question for him.

That question seemed to be the better of the two when he weighed them in his mind. Maxwell's finger was still on the trigger, and he could sense that he was probably going to be needing the gun soon.

"All right. Why are you here, then?" he repeated.

The man smiled that painful smile again. "You are very good at staying hidden, Mr. Maxwell," he explained softly.

His guest spoke with a strong accent, but Maxwell couldn't place what it was. The man pointed at his conquest but didn't wait for a reply. "You see, we've been playing hide-and-seek with you for weeks now, but you have been such a good hider that it was hard to seek you out." he continued.

"We?" Maxwell asked, confused.

"Yes, we," his guest answered, "you've been working for an enemy of ours."

Maxwell turned and faced his company, ripping the hand off his jacket in the process. "Let me guess. You work for the government," he predicted.

"No, I work for M13," he replied.

"I've heard of her," Maxwell said.

"Her?" the man laughed.

Maxwell nodded, making the man laugh harder.

"M13 isn't a person." the man finally answered, pulling from his pocket a card and handing it to the one he called an enemy.

M13 turned out to be another group of assassins, but unlike the ones they were searching for, they took victims in America. This card provided more information, but he wondered why this man was looking for him.

"What have I done that was so terrible?" Maxwell asked after studying the card.

"The European government has always sought to divide us, and you have been a part of that effort. Would you like to know how?" his guest asked.

Maxwell nodded.

"When Ernest hired you, he was hiring the most divisive man out there." He was whispering now.

Maxwell was staring intently at his unwelcomed guest, latching on to his every word, just as he had with Alexander.

"I also work closely with the Greenridge Killers, and I realize that you want to avenge Dumont's death, but you'll be angering a lot of people if you killed them." the man cautioned.

"Why?" Maxwell asked.

"If you kill them, I assure you this will not be the last time we meet." the man threatened.

"If I kill them, you're going to kill me?" Maxwell said incredulously.

"Think of it as an eye-for-an-eye kind of thing." The man smiled again.

The two men looked at each other again, neither of them speaking for a long time. He wanted to know if Alexander had lied to him about the circumstances surrounding the French spy's death. "I have a question for you," he stated.

"Of course, but make it good." the nameless man snapped.

"Since you work so closely with them, I'm assuming you know Aleander Ritzkov?" he asked.

The M13 associate turned toward the window and stared out at the clouds that darkened the sky before he answered. "Yes, why?"

"He told me something very interesting. An agent who worked in Paris was killed for having sex with a girl whose code name was M13. Is that true?" the agent asked.

The man smiled that painful smile for a third time. "It is true that the agent you're referring to had sex with a villain with a code name, but her code name had been Rattlesnake," he explained.

"What happened to her?" Maxwell asked.

"She's... around," he said, that menacing edge back in his voice.

The man turned and walked to the door, then turned back to face the man he had come to see. "It was nice meeting with you, sir, but remember my promise!" and with those words, he was gone.

Maxwell watched as the assassin rounded the corner, and when he was sure that he had gone, he sighed and released his hold on the gun's trigger. He walked past the closet door and into the bathroom and examined his surroundings, taking the time to make sure that nothing had been stolen or tampered with, and he was pleased to see that everything was as it should be, but upon leaving, he noticed something on the sink's mirror. He went back into the room to his suitcase and grabbed a magnifying glass.

He stared at the mirror again, and it took him a few minutes to realize that the object was a message written in the assassin's blood. It didn't look fresh, making him wonder when the killer had gotten there and how long he'd stayed. He stared at the spots until they formed two sentences: "Let them go through with their plan.

If their plan is thwarted, someone will come for you and whoever is associated with you.

It took him only half a second to realize that this was a threat and he was conflicted. He was an agent whose job always came before anything else, but would he be able to make the ultimate sacrifice if necessary? He stared at the sentences for a long time until beads of sweat formed on the back of his neck and a feeling of anger washed over him, almost enough to make him sink to the ground.

He tried not to think of the looming question that weighed heavily on his shoulders, but it was impossible. The bloody message on the mirror spoke louder to him than if someone had said it out loud.

He told himself to stay calm, but the more he stared at the mirror, the more he asked himself if killing these assassins was the right thing to do after all. Ernest Dumont was in the ground, never to be seen again, unable to give him an answer. It was up to him to decide what to do, but as he looked from the door to the mirror, then back to the door again, he felt trapped by indecision. Welsh had given him the assignment because of what they'd put him through, but his mind was now frozen in time. When he had finally come out of the trance, he grabbed a wipe from the bottle on the sink and scrubbed away every last bit of blood, then threw it into the trash can, leaving it and the words behind him, but the question was still in the back of his mind. He slowly walked over to his bed, took off his shoes, and climbed in without taking off his clothes.

The message on the mirror haunted his dream that night. The killers had gotten the girl and a car chase had ensued. They were chasing each other all over New York: he was in a Mercedes, and she was in a car with tinted windows, being tormented by the man that sat next to her.

The two cars eventually found each other, and her captives were in front of him, ready to fight to the death. Both cars had pulled up to an abandoned building, and as soon as they were inside, a fight had erupted and blood was soon splattered all over the walls and the floor.

It was a gunshot that woke him hours later. He looked at the clock: it was only two o'clock in the morning. The whole thing had been like a scene from a movie.

René had been in danger, and it had been up to him to save her from the people who'd wanted her dead, but this did little to solve the conflict that he was now facing. The message on the mirror had been clear: do anything to stop their plans, and someone was going to come after him and his associates.

On the one hand, death seemed so peaceful, so comforting, but on the other, some things needed to be done to keep millions of people safe. He stared out the window at the darkened night sky, though he knew that down below, there were still parties being held and people going to them. He would have to get up soon, and their search would begin again.

His thoughts then turned to Peter Neovich, his dead partner. He wanted to know what he'd done before working for Lyoma and Olga. He'd heard something about a wife and child that had lived in Japan with him. Last he'd heard, they still lived there, and the little girl, whose name was Tiffany, was now almost two.

Soon, his mind was spinning with thoughts of a past that could never be changed and a future that was still uncertain. For hours, he lay awake, trying desperately to ease his mind, but his thoughts were too tangled. The dream soon came back to him and he then realized that he'd have to be the hero, but what about that damn message that had been written on the mirror?

He decided to get up and busy himself with the task of getting ready, even though it was still too early. Later in the morning, as he and René discussed their plans, he told her about the message on the mirror and the visitor.

"What does all this mean?" she asked.

"If we do anything, he'll come after me and anyone who's with me, meaning you," he said.

"What about the mission?" she asked, defeated.

He didn't answer for a long moment. Instead, he looked at the faces around them. They were seated in a little room on the first floor at a table by the back windows. The girl had a mug of untouched coffee in front of her, and Maxwell had the sheet of paper with the address on it still folded in front of him.

The little room was crowded with hungry patrons having their own conversations, and to their relief, no one could hear them with all the noise.

"Aren't you worried about Simon?" René whispered.

"Of course I am," he said, resting his eyes again on the first couple of numbers on the sheet.

René looked at the mug of steaming coffee in front of her and sipped from it once.

"If you're going to terminate this assignment, are you prepared to tell him your decision if that's what you choose?" she finally asked, her eyes not meeting his.

Is that what he wanted? Did he want to give these killers the satisfaction of staying? He pondered this for a long time, but that question always made him stop short.

He studied the faces around him again; most of them wore smiles, and some wore serious expressions like him.

Alexander had given them the address for a reason, but did that even matter now? "I don't know." he finally answered honestly.

They stared at each other from across the table, both dreading the imminent decision that needed to be made. It was unusual for someone in his line of duty to be this emotional. They were the ones who got the killers, the ones who protected the world from these bad people, like the police, but unlike police officers, their real identities had to be kept secret from the world.

"What are you thinking?" René asked, but Maxwell just pointed to the sheet and her eyes scanned it.

He lifted his head and reached into his pocket.

"What is it?" René asked.

"I've got to call someone," he answered, dialing a number. "Welsh," he said, his tone clipped.

A moment of silence followed as Welsh spoke on the other end.

"I'm all right, and so is René," Maxwell responded. More silence as he listened to Welsh's words.

"The message has been wiped away," he replied.

He stayed silent as Welsh spoke again, and René stared in anticipation, trying to read his face for any information, but his face remained empty as Simon continued speaking.

Eventually, he removed the phone from his ear and sighed.

"Well?" René asked cautiously.

"He told me that it was my decision, but if I chose not to take care of them, he was going to choose someone else," he said.

René stared forward blankly and sighed. She felt bad for Maxwell, having to choose between his country and his job. If he chose wrong, both their lives would be in danger, and if she looked at it the other way around, all of their loved ones would die. Could they win in the end?

She turned toward him and watched as he studied the address for the millionth time. She wondered what he was thinking, but she kept her mouth closed.

He eventually straightened up and looked her way and saw her eyes on him.

"What?" he asked with mild urgency.

"Whatever you decide, I'll support you."

He stared at the clock on his phone: it was ten-thirty, then he looked around at the now half-empty room, then turned to her and gave her a small smile. Most of the tables were empty, including the one next to theirs.

They'd been sitting at the same table for almost two hours, and many more questions still needed to be answered, including the toughest one. René pushed the mug of coffee away and rose, leaving her partner a few feet away, still staring at the numbers on the sheet.

He was lost in thought, but he looked up at the clock every now and then. He stayed there for another hour until the place got crowded again, then he left.

He walked along the first floor until he came to an empty room. The door was unlocked, so he walked in and closed it behind him. He looked around for a place to sit and found a couch in the corner.

He grabbed his phone from his pocket and went to Google, unsure of what he was looking for.

He went to a news site and scrolled through the stories but found nothing useful. So he looked around until he found a TV with the remote on top of it.

It was a flat-screen, the kind that was on the wall. He walked over, turned it on, and watched the news wearily, but he could tell that it was going to be a slow news day. As always, the politics lead was first, but his ears perked up when the reporter said the name of the group they wanted.

"In other news, the notorious group of assassins, the Greenridge Killers, are back after a long hiatus." the lady's voice announced.

He turned the volume up and began to listen.

"The Greenridge Killers have announced today that they will be holding a rally in downtown New York. The rally is a cry for all supporters of theirs to come and help them prepare their plan, which, by now, is still in the early stages of development. However, they have said they will not stop until they get what they want." the lady concluded before switching to a story out of Russia.

That story sparked mild interest within him. The Greenridge Killers were back in the news again, and he questioned if what they wanted was a victim and who their victims were going to be. He needed more information, but the internet was clean, and he was sure that the news anchors wouldn't be talking about it again for some time, which frustrated him. He sat back and turned toward the windows, not staring at anything.

Informing Welsh and René about this was going to be easy, but what he worried about the most was where they were located and what they were going to do with them when they were found. He went to Google again and searched for further information about the rally, but information was scarce. The rally was going to be held in front of the Rockefeller center, and every supporter was instructed to be armed with small weapons, like pocket knives, just in case it came to that.

The sound of his phone ringing suddenly broke through the silence, and the sound was so loud that he was sure it could be heard outside.

"Hello?" he said, trying to sound casual, but there was no answer. He looked down and saw that it was just a news alert, which he opened and read. It informed him that the rally would be taking place in just a few weeks, on a Tuesday, but there was no date on the bulletin. After looking at it for what seemed like hours, he closed it wearily and sighed, bracing himself for what he was going to do.

He opened up Google and typed M13's name into the search engine and tried to shut off his mind as he waited. There were many results matching that group. On one page, there was a picture of the members in their assassin's outfits: they were dressed in all black, and their faces were covered by black hoods, just like the other group, but the only difference was the weapons.

Most of the other group members held semi-automatic weapons, but, like the last one he'd seen, some of the members in this group held pocket knives. Did they think those were better for the kill? He was curious to know why their faces stayed concealed from their victims and how many people had fallen victim to their killing method, as ordinary as it was?

He exited the page and went to the search engine. Unlike the last time, though, he knew what he was looking for.

He tried gaining access to the group's Wikipedia page, but an error message popped up on the screen. Just great, he thought, realizing that he would have to locate a room with a computer. He closed the pages and put the phone in his pocket, then got up to turn off the television before replacing the remote on it and leaving the room.

After half an hour, he found himself in another room that looked like a library. He was still on the main floor and the door, like the last one, was not locked. This room was also empty, and there were three computers, one on each of the three tables, and behind them were shelves of books arranging from autobiographies to romance and spy novels. He chose a computer at the center table, powered it up, and took a minute to scan the shelves behind him. Both biographies and autobiographies of musicians alone took up one shelf and encyclopedias took up three-and-a-half, but there was no time for leisurely reading right now.

The computer had booted up and was now showing the "home" screen. He worked quickly, getting to the page within seconds, then waiting as it loaded. He looked through the windows at the sun that was now high in the sky, indicating that it was early afternoon.

When he turned back to the screen, the page had finally come up. He scrolled through it, glancing down at the screen from time to time, getting only the key information he needed. He found out what he wanted to know about this group within only a few minutes: unlike the Greenridge Killers, M13 did not hide their faces from the ones they killed, and only 50 people had fallen victim to them. With a sigh, he logged out of the site and closed the browser. He turned around and read the titles on the shelves, left with nothing else to do.

Cookbooks also filled the shelves, but he hadn't noticed them until now. So he skimmed right past them and pored over the many books about musicians.

The assignment and all its problems were momentarily forgotten as his mind began to wander, and his eyes stayed glued to the middle three as his thoughts swirled around in his mind. He shook his head after a moment, trying to clear it. He needed to get back to his assignment.

He knew that René would be waiting for him somewhere, so he turned and headed out the way he came. He heard low voices murmuring as he made his way back to the elevator. Once he was in and the doors were closed, he pushed the button for his floor and watched the numbers flash until it came to his floor, then he headed to his room.

As he stared out the window at the blue sky from his bed, the news report played over and over in his mind. The Greenridge Killers were back in business, and they weren't as far away as they'd predicted. Then, suddenly, a question popped into his mind along with everything else: how many supporters did they have?

Several minutes passed before a morbidly delightful image popped into his mind: the assassins were all dead, and their bodies were spread all over the ground.

Blood and brain matter stained the streets of town, and their supporters were also dead. He closed his eyes and wondered what he was going to do next.

A knock at the door startled him, but he quickly recovered and went to answer it. "Who is it?" he called.

"It's me," René answered, "can I come in? I have news!"

8

New Recruits

"You heard the same thing?" she asked, facing him as they sat on his bed.

"Yes, earlier this afternoon," he replied somberly.

René had brought her computer with her and was now setting it up. "Did they say when it was going to be?" she asked, leaning over the screen.

"No, but I've been looking," Maxwell said.

René's face was blank as she went to the news site and sifted through the stories as he glanced over her shoulder.

"Anything yet?" he asked.

She shushed him and continued scrolling through the items on the site, tapping the side of her head and knitting her eyebrows together. Finally, after a moment of silence, she relaxed and pushed the computer toward him. On the screen, there was an article with the headline:

Greenridge Killers Are Back!

He clicked on it and began to read. The article stated that the rally would be held in two weeks outside of the Rockefeller Center and also according to it, more than 200 people were expected to attend.

He stopped reading abruptly and closed his eyes. They only had two weeks to decide what they would do and how they would gain their trust.

He slowly opened his eyes and looked over to where René sat, unmoving. He quickly went to YouTube and browsed through the results until he found a video of an activist for the Greenridge Killers and clicked on it.

A few seconds later, a female voice came over the tiny speakers, along with a male reporter's voice.

"Will you be going to the rally?" he asked.

"Yes." the woman said in a soft voice.

"Can you tell us why?" he asked.

"These are not assassins, these are heroes," the woman answered.

"How?" he pressed.

"They're doing us a great service," she replied.

He swore under his breath and went back to Google, where he looked up information about this woman. She called herself Angela, and she had aspirations of someday being a part of this group. She'd become infatuated with them some years earlier after reading a tweet from their official Twitter account.

Our time has come!

"Grab a pen and a pad," Maxwell ordered.

René opened her mouth to ask why, but he put his hand up to stop her. She rose from the bed and grabbed the items from the night table and sat them on the bed. For the next hour, she wrote down whatever he read and by one-thirty, they had a little stack of notes on one side of the bed.

Maxwell shut the computer down and after the girl had gone, he reviewed the notes they'd taken. For the rest of the day and into the night, he looked through their notes on the rally, but he kept coming back to the question of how they were going to get in there without being noticed. He finally settled on breaking into a car and driving there.

Every afternoon for the next two weeks, the girl came up to his room to finalize their plans until the day of the rally finally came.

On that day, they left at one o'clock and wandered the streets until they came to the parking lot of a Ruby Tuesday, where a lone car sat in a parking space. René looked around quickly and when she was sure they were clear, she looked through the window at the man that sat in the car with his feet on the dashboard. She knocked on the window and the man stared, confused by his visitors. Half a second later, she grabbed a rock from the ground and broke the window, leaving glass everywhere and the driver startled.

The guy looked up into René's fierce, demanding eyes. He then opened his mouth to speak but snapped it shut when Maxwell pointed his gun at his head.

"Where are your keys?" he asked.

He held them out, but both of them shook their heads.

"You're driving," René told him.

The driver nodded as his new passengers went around to the back, unlocked the doors and scooted inside. "Where to?" he asked weakly.

"Rockefeller Center," René said, her voice calm.

"For what?" the driver questioned.

"None of your damn business." René snapped.

They drove in silence, but the girl kept a sharp eye on the driver as a silent reminder not to make any wrong moves.

After a few minutes, they had reached their destination, but as they looked around, they saw no one with a knife nearby. A stage and mic had been set up, along with chairs in a circle.

"Turn the engine off," Maxwell commanded.

The driver obeyed and stared out the space where the glass had been, awaiting his next command. They sat in silence for what seemed like forever before the first attendees arrived.

"Now?" René whispered.

Maxwell nodded and they rushed out, leaving the driver staring after them. Some of the members were hidden in the bushes beside the stage, watching to see who came.

They kept their distance and watched as more people arrived and took their places.

When most of the chairs had been filled, both parties moved as one to the center of the stage, but René and Maxwell stayed a few feet behind them, out of sight.

After clearing his throat, one of the group members stepped up to the microphone to deafening applause and grinned at the many faces around him. "Thank you!" he called in a clear, strong voice, still smiling.

After the roar of the crowd had died down, the lights were dimmed and everyone became still.

"I have one question for you: why are we all here?" he asked.

An answering silence tore through the air.

"We are here to take back that which was stolen from us," he shouted in his strong French accent.

The other members gave him a thumbs-up and smiled. "This world, our lives, and the lives of our children and grandchildren are under attack, and it is all thanks to one group: lying conspiracy theorists, radical people who want nothing more than to divide us!" he continued, raising his gun to his chest.

Maxwell and René watched from their perch among the bushes with undisguised horror. They asked themselves if they were making a mistake by doing this while the crowd clapped and cheered, showing their approval.

Another member then stepped to the mic and cleared his throat. This one had more gray hair and more wrinkles than the first, but he also wore all black like his partner. "We have worked very hard to rid the world and the country of horrible people and we are moving forward with our plan, but we need your help." the man said.

A moment of silence followed, and the government agent peeked up at them. A

Powerpoint had been set up and was on the first slide. The sound of a remote clicking was heard and muffled speaking soon followed, but the images were clear. The first slide showed a picture of the American flag with happy children standing next to it, smiling but the image soon changed to a school shooting.

The children were now dead and the flag had been burned to the ground.

"Do you see those dead children?" he finally asked sharply.

The crowd cheered.

"Good," he said, "remember those images because in due time, we will be in the spotlight, and you will help us."

Their "guests" listened on, trying to contain their horror and shock as he continued.

"In the near future, we will be back and better than ever, and no one will know what hit them." he declared to cheers. "I know you think that we are French and that we do not hurt our allies. This is true, but we have seen how you operate when left to your own devices and we are assassins, so we do not care what you want," He chuckled once before continuing. He gave the projector's remote to a man in the shadows, then turned to face the dozens of people that had come to see them.

"For almost a decade, we've been trying to come up with the perfect plan to get our names back in the spotlight, and we think we've come up with it!" he shouted to the many faces around him. Murmurs suddenly filled the area. "Blood is what we're after, so our plan is to kill as many people as we can," he said ominously.

"How are we gonna do that?" someone asked.

"Excellent question," the man answered.

Another man pushed the button again and a whole new set of images popped up onscreen.

"Burn down a building or two," he said.

The horde of people looked at the man at the mic as though he were their teacher.

"What if they try to run?" another man asked.

The Frenchman pulled a pair of cuffs out from behind his back and pointed to the watch on his wrist. "Due to the departure of some of the members from our group over the years, I have inherited some... supplies." He winked at the rest of the group, who only stared back blankly. He pointed to the watch again and put his finger on a button. "When I push this button, it opens a compartment and shoots a poison that paralyzes our victim for five minutes, and the handcuffs are to prevent them from moving once their strength has returned." he smiled.

Minutes passed as the rally went on and their guests chanted things, getting more and more excited with each thing that was said. Then, the rally finally ended and the guests filed out until only the group, Maxwell and René were left.

"May we help you?" the speaker asked.

"Are you taking any new members?" Maxwell asked.

The member that had spoken first eyed his guests suspiciously. "Who is asking?" he asked.

"My name is René, and this is my friend," RENTH spoke up, pointing to the man beside her.

"Does your friend have a name?"

"Yes, but that's not important."

He continued to eye them with doubt. "Is this a trick?" he finally asked.

"No," René said stiffly.

"All right," he said, "I'll have to speak with my companions."

The members walked a few feet away, leaving their possible recruits to stare at each other. "Are you sure about this?" they heard him ask.

They were conversing in French now and whispering.

"Maybe we should give them a chance." another one spoke up.

"I agree, let's just see how they do." a third one chimed in.

After a moment, the speaker walked back to his guests with the others flanking him. "All right," he said, speaking in English again, "we've decided to give you a chance, but make one wrong move and you're out on your asses."

Though it was meant to be a threat, Maxwell held back a laugh. As they walked away from the meeting spot, the realization of what had just occurred sank in: they had gained the trust of the assassins. Phase one was complete. Now came phase two, the hardest part.

He looked over at René, who smiled a tiny bit back at him. She was happy about what they had just accomplished, but there would be no premature celebration just yet.

As they walked outside, René turned back in the direction of the building and frowned before turning back to her partner. He was going to call Welsh when they returned to the hotel or wherever they were going with his findings. "Hey," the member called, walking toward them, the doubt in his eyes now replaced with recognition, "where do you think you're going?"

"To our hotel," René replied.

"Great. Grab your stuff and meet us at this address," he said, putting a piece of paper into her outstretched hand.

She thanked him and watched as he walked off.

Hours later, they were headed to the address that had been written on the sheet, both now in need of a rest. Welsh had been pleased to hear about what had happened. "Be careful." he'd warned, and those words rang in Maxwell's ears as they came up to the building.

It was a small office building with a sign out front that said it belonged to a man named Jonathan Westwood.

The building looked old and abandoned, with the paint from the windows gone or smudged with dirt spots in some places and the glass rusting around the windowpanes.

It had already been a long day for the pair, but both had a sense that it was about to get longer as René shut off their car's engine and stared out the driver's-side window.

"Changing your mind?" he asked, staring out his window.

"No," René said in an offhand manner, "I swear, these have been the longest days of my life."

They continued to stare out their windows, grateful for the silence. Although he didn't admit it, he agreed with the person sitting next to him. They had done so much already, but the process to get here had been exhausting, and there was still more that needed to be done. Then, one by one, cars began approaching and turning into the parking lot.

The guests were arriving, most of them the same people from the rally. Maxwell touched the gun that was tucked under his bulletproof vest and the jacket he wore. He hoped that he was equipped enough to handle anything they threw at them. After another minute, they exited the car and followed the last of the guests: a group of four boys across the parking lot to a crumbling walkway that led to a door that was barely on its hinges.

The boys were dressed in faded blue jeans, sweatshirts, and scuffed tennis shoes, and their heads were shaved on the sides. "I don't understand why we're here." one of them said, his tone whiny and bored. They all looked to be about thirteen or fourteen, and all but one looked like they knew what they were doing there and were comfortable to be doing it.

"I told you. This was the address on the invite," another one said.

They had reached a rickety elevator that looked as though it would break down at any minute. "Why the hell would you hold a meeting in such a broken-down office?" the same boy asked, his tone still bored and his voice cutting through the air like a knife.

One of the other boys elbowed him in the ribs, signaling him to be quiet. Soon, the boys, René and Maxwell entered the elevator, the sulking one standing between the tall, graceful one and the short, fat one.

In his hands, he held a spiraled-bound notebook, which stayed closed and by his side. The group stayed silent as the elevator went up one floor, then stopped and opened its doors. They walked out and the group's newest members followed the four boys, careful to stay out of sight of them, to a heavy-looking metal door.

Jonathan Westwood had died in 1990, though his cause of death had never been revealed to the public, but he wasn't theirs, or anyone's, problem anymore.

Someone had opened the door, and they were now standing in a cozy-looking hallway that was dimly lit by candlelight. There was no one behind the desk, but a cup of coffee sat far enough away from the edge that it wouldn't spill with a bagel and cream cheese next to it. Then, suddenly, a door opened from somewhere down the hall, and a woman dressed in black stepped out of a tiny room, her high-heeled shoes click-clacking on the tiled floor. Her lips were painted with pink lipstick, but besides that, no other makeup painted her face.

She carried a cell phone in one hand and looked very bored. They watched as she strode toward them, her eyes still on the phone's screen. She gave the appearance of being late for a meeting, and the new additions to the group wondered if the four boys were somehow involved.

"You're here for the event?" a female voice asked.

Everyone turned to find the woman standing in front of them. After a brief silence, one of the four boys spoke up. "Yeah." It was the fat one who answered. The girl went to the desk and stood in front of the bagel, gazing at it hungrily.

Five minutes later, she led the six of them to a room at the far end of the hall opposite hers and knocked. As they waited for an answer, she studied each of them as they had studied her moments earlier. The sound of shuffling papers could be heard from inside, then the clicking sound as the lock turned and the door opened. "You've made it." the member greeted them heartily.

He then turned to the girl and smiled warmly. "Thank you, Ennette," he said.

"You're welcome," she answered and turned on her heel.

They could tell from her tone that she was used to people coming and going as they pleased.

"Is she from London?" Maxwell asked once Ennette was out of earshot.

"No. Ireland." the man standing in the doorway answered before taking the man's, girls' and the boys' names down on the top sheet of his clipboard and inviting them in.

Thirty others stood in the center of the room with glasses of wine in their hands, but the ones that weren't holding anything turned to see who had come in. Their faces suddenly looked familiar to Maxwell, though it took him a minute to understand why.

He glanced at René and tapped her shoulder. She turned toward him and they shared the same look of immediate recognition. Most everyone from the rally was there, wearing smiles and conversing quietly. Some group members lingered by the door, taking down names of people on a clipboard as they arrived, while other attendees mingled about.

The four boys had gone off somewhere, but René stayed by Maxwell's side as they looked around the room that could have easily fit over one hundred people but as of now, over half of their attendees were missing. She asked herself if they were even coming and if they were, how many people would even bother to show up.

Half an hour passed before anyone addressed the crowd in full. "Welcome!" one of the members called, holding up his hand.

The group's chatter quickly turned into murmurs as everyone got their last words in. "We are very happy to have you here. Please make yourselves at home," he announced before rejoining his group by the door.

As others talked around him, Maxwell gazed around the room once more and noticed, for the first time, the suitcases lying against the far wall.

Those that had come with coats had replaced them with glasses of wine while their coats hung on hooks just a few feet away. Members came around every once in a while to refill wine glasses before going back to their post.

"Are you getting anything of use?" René asked hopefully.

He shook his head and frowned. "Maybe it's coming," he answered and returned to listening and watching the people around him.

A crowd had gathered around the bar, and whatever they were watching had captured their attention. "How much?" someone asked, their speech slurred.

"$20." someone replied to hoots and titters.

"40 dollars." someone else shouted and the crowd looked pleased.

"All right, 40 bucks it is," the voice said, followed by silence as the sound of liquid being poured into a glass was heard.

René moved in closer to see what was going on and suppressed a laugh at the sight of a girl clumsily dancing on her knees. Some cheered while others took photographs and videos on their cell phones. From this vantage point, it looked like her friend had been passed out for a while and had no intention of moving from her spot.

The woman had almost finished her dance when she suddenly fell to the floor and began to vomit. Everyone moved away from the spot glumly, knowing that their fun was over. One of the men turned and looked in the room with a half-amused, half-frustrated expression, then turned back to his colleagues. "Oh, God, it's happened again." they heard him murmur to someone.

When the woman had finished, the space surrounding the bar was covered in vomit and broken glass, though no one had seen her drop anything. Then, out of nowhere, Ennette strode to the door, carrying a mop and a broom. "It's happened again?" she asked. The men nodded stiffly. She quickly walked past them and into the room. "Seriously," she muttered when she saw the mess: one passed-out girl on her back, one flat on her butt and both of them covered in vomit, "one girl drunk on her ass, another drunk on her back."

She led the crowd away before throwing water from a pitcher she had found on the bar onto the passed-out girl, who woke up immediately. "What?" she asked, disoriented and shivering.

"Get up," Ennette demanded sharply.

The girl slowly got to her feet and followed the woman into the hall.

It was only then that she saw the state of her clothes. "Dammit, Marissa!" she muttered angrily.

Ennnette pointed in the direction of a bathroom and told her to go change.

"After that," she continued, "you and your friend go to the downstairs kitchen. I've already put the coffee on."

Once she was gone, the young woman set about tending to Marissa.

"Where's that other girl?" she asked, her speech still slurred.

"She is in the ladies' room. I suggest you go there as well, then you can go to the kitchen and have a cup of coffee with her," she said sternly.

She then walked off, muttering about how she shouldn't have let herself get so drunk.

Finally, Ennnette went back into the room to find the mess where she'd left it and the little group scatted. She reached into the pocket of her apron, pulled out some latex gloves and snapped them on. She then pulled up her pants legs, got down on her knees and began picking out pieces of glass from the mess. Once all the glass had been separated, she went to work on cleaning up the vomit.

More people had shown up in the chaos, but they had been told to wait outside with the men until the girl had gotten everything straight. René and Maxwell stood still and watched with admiration and sympathy. She did this task with an urgency that told them she'd done this before and that this girl hadn't been the first to stain the floor.

Forty-five minutes later, the mess had been cleaned, and their new guests had finally been let in.

"All right, roll call," the man at the mic said, clearly ready to get down to business.

After checking that everyone was accounted for, chairs were brought out for the guests to sit in and stretch their legs, but some chose to stay standing.

"As I've already said, we are very happy to have you here with us," the man said for the second time that night.

Clearly, he didn't have anything else to add, but he remained where he stood.

"I will tell you something now that may shock you," he said, regaining the attention of the people who'd had it elsewhere.

Maxwell silently counted the faces around him, then jotted the number down on a sheet of paper in a notebook he'd gotten off a nearby table. There were now sixty-eight people in the room if you counted the eight members standing around.

"In the early 2000s, our group was branded as terrorists worse than Al-Qaeda," he shouted.

Some people in the room gasped out of sympathy and some simply stared and looked as if they were frozen.

He paused and watched as most of the people in the room composed their expressions while the information sank in.

"The world was ready to run us out of town, but before they could, we went into hiding. During that time, some of us raised families and tried to be normal, productive members of society, but the urge to kill has come again."

These remarks drew some applause.

"Recently," he went on when the applause had died down, "we killed a man for going to the media about us. That murder has only made us more infamous and famous!"

Maxwell's stomach muscles tightened as he fought the urge to grab his gun from its compartment and shoot them all dead right here.

An image of Ernest Dumont's dead body suddenly appeared on a screen and everyone turned toward it. He was lying on his stomach, shirtless and bloody. His back was marred with scars, including one that reached to his rib cage.

His hands were chained to the floor by his sides, showing he'd tried to escape some time before.

René stared at the image for a few minutes more before turning away. She wasn't squeamish, but she had seen enough to make the image stick in her mind. She was going to be up for most of the night and was pretty sure that he would be as well.

His lips were parted as if he had something to say, but the look in his eyes told everyone in the room that he was dead. Maxwell stayed frozen, his eyes glued to the screen. He had been at this long enough to know how to hide his anger from others, but his insides were screaming at him to kill the monsters responsible for his former boss's death. So he went on for a while longer, talking about how the murder had put their names into the same category as Jeffrey Dahmer and Gary Ridgeway, even though one was dead and the other was in prison.

Before everyone was dismissed, they were told where the extra guns were just in case they needed them, then they were taken to where they would be sleeping for the night, but Maxwell was sure they weren't going to be sleeping at all.

Eight-thirty found Maxwell on top of his sheets, staring at the ceiling. Who had taken the picture, and why had they shown it tonight? Who had been with him, and had anyone tried to call for help? Just then, his cell phone rang, a shrill sound in the darkness, but it was a sound he was most grateful for.

"Yeah?" he answered, trying to clear his mind.

"It's me," Welsh said.

"Is anything wrong?" he asked.

"I've just called to check in."

"It's not going so well," he lied.

"You're lying, mate." Welsh laughed. The man on the other end gritted his teeth, trying to fight a smile. "All right, Simon," he confessed, "we are in the early stages of planning."

"Not as bad as I'd thought," Welsh replied, still laughing. "How's René?" he asked.

"She's all right," Maxwell answered, then went on to describe the events of the evening, careful to keep the details about the pic of Ernest's dead body scarce.

"What about Ernest?" he asked, tired of dancing around the subject.

"He was lying on the floor, on his stomach, shirtless and bloody," Maxwell said, as though this were just another bit of everyday news.

"Did he have scars?"

"A few," Maxwell said.

"Were his hands chained?" Welsh asked.

"Yeah," he said.

"Where?"

"On the floor, by his sides."

"Dammit," Simon murmured.

He suddenly regretted telling his friend everything, but he decided that it was better coming from him than from someone on the street.

"Did they have a motive?" Welsh asked.

"They say it was because he was threatening to tell the police and the media where they were hiding."

"And you believed them?" asked Welsh. A sharp knock sounded on the door, making him jump, but he quickly recovered.

"Sorry, I gotta go," he said quickly and hung up without waiting for a reply. "Come in," he called, but no one appeared.

The sound of footsteps crept away from his door and all was quiet afterward. He stayed up until midnight, switching between images of Ernest: one of the last time he'd seen him alive and the other of his scarred, bloodied corpse. As he dozed, he wondered if the people they'd murdered before him had been in worse shape. Then, finally, a blurry image of the man's face as he'd described their motive appeared behind his closed eyes.

The way he'd looked when he'd said those words had seemed suspicious, but he doubted that anyone else had noticed. Though his face had been kept smooth, Maxwell could tell from the secretive look in his eyes that he'd had more to say, like he'd been hiding the truth, or part of it, from the people who seemed to trust him and his group the most. But, then, a knock sounded on the door at a quarter past nine the following day, rousing him.

"Come in," he said sleepily, rubbing his eyes.

René stood in the doorway, tired-looking and holding a cup of coffee in one hand.

"You decent?" she asked.

"Just give me ten minutes," he said, yawning.

Ten minutes later, he came out of the bathroom, dressed in a pair of blue jeans, a blue sweatshirt, and sneakers.

She was now perched on the edge of his bed, the mug of coffee sitting on the table next to her. "Have you slept at all?" he asked, concerned when he saw the circles under her eyes. "No," she sighed, grabbing the mug and taking a sip, "but I can see that you have."

"What time do we have to be out there?" he asked.

"Noon," she said, trying to hold back a yawn.

"What time is it now?" he asked, unenthused about what they were doing.

"Ten," she replied just as flatly.

"I'm sorry about last night," she said suddenly.

"Why? You didn't do anything." He gave a slight smile.

"I just didn't know they were going to do that." she shuddered at the image still behind her eyelids.

He too shuddered slightly at the memory of his boss's bloody, scarred corpse on the ground.

"Have you spoken to Simon?" she asked.

"Yeah, he called last night," he replied.

"And?" she prompted.

"He wanted to know everything," he said with a look that told her that he would share no more details.

They walked out of their respective rooms at eleven-thirty, more haunted by the events of the night before and filled with even more unanswered questions.

Most of the guests were already at the table when they arrived, but none looked at them when they walked in. A plasma screen TV sat in the corner of the big room, but it was only background noise.

Figures with made-up faces moved around on the screen, but no one seemed to be paying them any attention, either.

Finally, René and Maxwell took seats across from a couple of girls who were staring out the back windows. Then, promptly at noon, the eight members from the previous evening filed in one by one and approached the people at the table.

"It's nice to see you all again," the group's leader said, "I hope you all had a good night's rest because what I'm about to show you requires your full attention."

9

First Round

"And now, the news." a shrill voice called.

It had come from the television, but neither Maxwell nor René had noticed that someone had changed the channel and turned up the volume. The female reporter read from a teleprompter, turning from time to time to correspondents to get their take.

The people in the room had grown still, their gazes filled with praise for the young girl in the striped pantsuit.

Five minutes later, the TV was turned off and the oldest member of the group stood at the head of the table. He grabbed his phone from his pocket and pulled up a video of another news report. The video was dated July 1st, 2016 and from the look on the reporter's face, this story was serious.

"Some heartbreaking news to share with you tonight," the reporter said in a somber tone, "known and beloved government worker Ernest Dumont has died."

René took a deep breath while Maxwell only seethed in anger.

"Ernest first made a name for himself as an agent for the United States in the early days of the Cold War, and he was also instrumental in helping get the Berlin wall torn down in 1989," she said and cut to a picture of a young man dressed in black and hugging a young girl to his chest.

"After that, in 1993, he began working in London as an agent recruiter, where he picked up several agents to work for his branch of the government.

His last client had been a veteran government worker by the name of Andrew Maxwell."

The video cut off after that and another one began, showing many photographers standing outside a darkened house, clicking away on cell phones. Some leaned forward to get a clearer picture, while others stayed back, but several minutes passed before anything happened. Whoever had emerged had their face covered by a black veil, like they were in mourning.

"Mrs. Gonzales," one of the photographers called out, "do you think your husband killed Mr. Dumont?"

The woman raised her veiled face in the direction of the camera-wielding paparazzi and lifted the covering with one hand while waving with the other.

"No comment," she said, moving briskly in the direction of a car.

Seconds later, a burly man wearing a wedding ring and dressed in shorts and a t-shirt slowly walked out, carrying a baby in his arms and wearing a diaper bag on his back.

"Mr. Gonzales, did you kill Ernest
Dumont?" another photographer called.

The little girl in his arms turned to look at the camera with a curious expression before giggling.

"No, but you will know all you need in a few minutes," he said and turned away, the giggling girl still in his arms as they walked.

Maxwell found himself wondering who these people were and if their denial was genuine or just for the cameras. The video was still playing when news vehicles began parking out front and reporters raced out, making a beeline for the front lawn, joining the photographers that were already there.

The couple eventually returned to the scene, their daughter, niece, or whatever she was to them, in tow. The man set a briefcase down on the ground and turned toward the cameras. "My department has done an autopsy on Mr. Dumont, and we have discovered that foul play was involved," he announced to the waiting crowd, whose cameras were now silent.

The little girl began to whimper, so the woman gave her a toy to quiet her.

The press conference lasted for five more minutes before the couple scurried away with the baby.

Before he'd left, the officer had said that the body of Ernest had been found on his bedroom floor, covered with bloody stab wounds, including one that ran from his rib cage to his left side, and his hands had been chained to the floor. The knife had been found on the bathroom sink, the blade gleaming from the bleach that had been used to clean it. The officers had performed CPR on him for 20 minutes, but he'd been pronounced dead by midday on July 1st, 2016.

Once that video had ended, the phone's occupant pressed a few more buttons and another video came up.

"This video is perhaps the most important one, so listen and look because this will be you soon," Pascal said before tapping the screen and the video began.

"After three-and-a-half months of investigation, we finally know who has killed

Ernest Dumont. Legendary assassin group, the Greenridge Killers." said the news anchor. She then cut to a picture of the fourteen-member ensemble grinning broadly while holding guns of various sizes, all of which were loaded. A crowd surrounded them, but they kept their gazes focused on something in the distance.

He abruptly closed out of it and put his phone back in his pocket. The others stared in awe, but René and Maxwell kept their eyes lowered. As he spoke, the whole building seemed to be staring at him, taking in his every word. All pairs of eyes in the room were focused on his face. "Do you want what I've just shown you?" he called.

Several people nodded eagerly while several others gave thumbs-ups.

It was two o'clock when they emerged from the room as a group, but they stayed silent as they made their way to the elevator.

"Where're you goin'?" Ennette shouted from the open door of her office.

One of the men turned to stare at her and held up his hand. She seemed to understand because she backed away from the door and closed it.

The second oldest carried an empty backpack. The old elevator creaked as each member and aspiring member filed in, then it was down to the main floor. Once on the main floor, they walked a short distance to a kitchen and were directed to take seats around a table. A cup of coffee was set in front of each of them, making Maxwell and René wondered how long they'd be down here.

In the center of the room, a TV showed a weary-looking woman sitting on a bench with her head down, staring at the novel in her lap. Her black hair was combed into a bun at the back of her head and her glasses were sliding down her narrow nose. She looked to be enjoying herself, but she often cast glances over her shoulder at a phone that was resting on the table next to her. The member with the grey beard stood up from the table, walked over to the stand and grabbed its remote.

He began flipping through channels, and within minutes, Maxwell realized what they were doing. From inside his pants pocket, he grabbed a pen and started taking notes in the notebook he'd gotten off the table the night before. Various houses were shown. Some had people outside, and others stood empty. He stopped at a building that looked similar to theirs, but unlike where they were now, the building was small and one lone person sat at a table over a small pot.

The person wore a pair of gloves and had their shirtsleeves rolled up to their elbows. A thick tangle of curls covered their face and they were dressed in a long-sleeved sweatshirt and blue jeans. On the table beside them was another pot of dirt and another one with sprouts growing in it next to that one. The TV behind the worker was muted, but a radio was softly playing a classical piece. The room was stocked with boxes of rubber gloves and bags of seeds, but the worker didn't seem to be paying it or the radio any attention.

Two-thirty came and went, and the only thing that had changed was that a big pot of coffee now sat on the stove.

The worker on the screen was now standing in the doorway of another room talking quietly to a woman, but to everyones' disappointment, nothing exciting was going on. Most of the members had fallen asleep, but those still awake watched the screen for anything of importance. Then, the worker suddenly jerked away from the door and ran across to a ringing phone. "Hello?" they whispered.

"Have you heard the news?" a male voice down the line asked.

The phone had been put on "speaker," but that didn't seem to matter right now.

"No, what's up?" the worker asked.

"The GK is back," the voice said.

"The what?"

"The French assassins you've been tracking," the voice said.

The people in the room turned sharp, focused eyes on the worker, who was now red-faced and alert.

"When did they come back?" the worker asked.

"A few weeks ago."

As the voice on the line spoke, the worker meticulously took notes in a spiral-bound journal, the pot and the seeds completely forgotten. The person stayed on the phone for fifteen minutes, feverishly taking down information and reading the lines back to the disembodied voice until the first two pages were stained with ink. After hanging up, the journalist grabbed a black jacket off the back of a chair and headed for the exit. They turned back toward the room where the woman sat and gave her a quick explanation before leaving and closing the door behind them.

As they walked, the men stared, wide-eyed, at the slim figure making their way to a car. They exchanged a look that told Maxwell that this person was well-known to this group.

"I think we've shown them enough." one of them whispered.

His neighbor shook his head before replying, "Let's just see what she does."

The woman reached into her purse, grabbed a set of car keys, pushed a button to open the driver-side door, and slid into the seat. After closing the door and starting the ignition, she pulled her cell phone from her pocket and dialed a number.

"Yeah?" a bored voice said.

"It's me." the woman said.

"Anything?" the voice asked, sounding more pleasant and more alert.

"We can stop tracking them now because they're back in the states." the woman said.

The sound of heavy breathing, like someone had just finished a workout, was then heard for a second or two before the person spoke again. "Think there's a story in this?" the voice asked.

"Could be."

"You've got this one, Jessica. Do your homework tonight and have a draft on the boss's desk within a week or two." the voice instructed.

The men and women in the room had not moved an inch, and it was now past three o'clock. The men in the front row, in particular, kept their eyes on Jessica as she pulled out of the parking lot.

The man who'd operated the remote earlier slowly got to his feet and seconds later, the screen went black.

"Who's that?" one of the four boys asked after a moment's pause.

"Jessica Morales.

She's a reporter for the New York Times." the man stated.

"Why were we watching her?" another person asked.

"Jessica was the one who reported our return, and it was because of her that the police were able to find out we killed Ernest." another man said, his tone peppered with underlying rage.

"Was she the one who reported it on TV?" René asked.

The previous remote's operator shook his head and narrowed his eyes. "That girl's name was Andrea."

"Jessica had been tracking us for months, and once someone had had a lead, she'd been the first one to report where we were." the oldest man said.

"So?" Maxwell asked.

"That was the first reporter with whom Ernest had contact." the man explained.

At nine-thirty, everyone was dismissed for the night, but Andrew stayed downstairs alone with his thoughts.

Nothing about this made sense. Why had they shown them the video, and where did the reporter fit in? So many unanswered questions were running through his mind, and the answers he was getting weren't adding up. Finally, he walked over to a computer desk and sat down, weary but determined.

He waited for the computer to boot up before going to Jessica Morales' website.

Sure enough, she had been the one Ernest had confided in, but again, that feeling was telling him that he'd hadn't gotten all the facts. He clicked on a clip of an interview she'd given just a few weeks after his boss's death from her office in New York. "He was a broken man," she said to the camera, "of course he knew the risks of coming to me, but he needed someone to talk to. He was desperate."

"What did he say?" the interviewer asked.

"That he'd gotten entail that the Greenridge Killers were back, and he was scared they'd come after him," she stated, nervously fiddling with the blinds over the windows.

"Did you ever ask yourself if it was a good idea to talk with him?" the interviewer asked.

"I did, but my job comes before anything else." Jessica snapped.

"So, you felt bad for him?" the woman pressed.

"Wouldn't you have tried to help if you had the chance?" Morales shot back.

Stunned, the woman cleared her throat, looking flustered. "I suppose," she answered before the video cut off.

After it had finished, he went back to her website and looked for any more information on why he'd come to her and if she'd seen anything on the day of the murder, but there was nothing of interest on the page. At midnight, he shut the computer down, pushed the chair underneath the desk and walked back upstairs to his room, only to find René waiting up for him in the hall.

"What were you looking for?" she asked.

"Just taking some last-minute notes," he said wearily.

"You look tired," she commented.

"I am," he said.

With that, he closed the door and undressed. He was not a detective, but he was beginning to wonder if that was the route he was meant to take.

Like the previous night, he switched between images of his former boss in his mind until finally, he fell into a troubled sleep. He saw a coffin in his dreams that night, but the body in it looked nothing like Ernest's. There were no scars, no chain marks and every ounce of blood had been cleared away, but perhaps the most frightening part was the fact that those haunted eyes looked into the eyes of the person whenever he stared at the figure in the casket. It was as if they had unfinished business to attend to.

Maxwell woke up in shock an hour later, the image of the ghostly face appearing behind his lids. He stared over at the notebook he'd been writing in lying on the table by the bed with his pen. He then stared up at the clock: it was only half-past four in the morning, but his thoughts were already racing.

After a few minutes, Maxwell grabbed his phone off the table opposite the notebook and opened Google, intending to do some research to take his mind off the nightmare. Once Google had come up, Maxwell went to Jessica's Wikipedia page and silently began to read. She'd grown up in Arizona and moved to New York in her early twenties after college. She married when she was thirty-three to an airline pilot, and they shared two young children together. She'd gotten a bachelor's in journalism from Columbia University and began working for the newspaper at thirty. After closing out the page, he went back to her website and looked for any contact information. He was rewarded with a phone number, but he wasn't sure if the number belonged to her or to someone else.

He opened the notebook to a blank page and jotted the number down, telling himself he'd call it before the day was through. The day dragged by slowly, with most of the house guests scattered. The eight members stayed together for most of the day, conversing in French, only parting ways to eat lunch with the others before reconvening soon after they were done. At three that afternoon, Maxwell retrieved his phone from his room and called the number he'd gotten from the internet.

"Hello?" a voice said after three rings.

"I'm looking for Jessica Morales," he said.

"How can I help you?" the voice asked.

"I'm calling because I have some questions for you," Maxwell told her.

A long, awkward pause followed before she spoke again. "I'm all ears," Jessica said nervously.

"I was hoping we could meet somewhere." he clarified.

"Um, all right. Where?" she asked.

He suggested Planet Hollywood a few minutes from Times Square.

They agreed to meet at noon the next day before hanging up. He spent the rest of the evening replaying the words and images from the previous day in his mind, trying to gather his thoughts. At seven-thirty, he emerged from his room and entered the dining room for dinner. A cartoon was on the television behind them, but only a few people watched as the animated characters moved around on the screen.

He went to bed early that night, the questions he still needed answers to in the back of his mind. He hoped that Jessica would have something to tell him, but there was also the question of what he would do if she had nothing to offer him. He woke at ten o'clock the following day, showered, cleaned his teeth, washed and shaved his face, then dressed in a black suit, tie, and dress shoes, a far cry from the ratty t-shirt and jeans he'd worn the previous day.

"Where are you going?" one of the other guests asked as he passed the kitchen table, where they all sat looking as if they were waiting for something or someone.

"Got a lunch meeting at noon," he answered absentmindedly.

"You're leaving now?

Dude, it's only ten o'clock," one of the men said.

"I know, but the place where we're planning to meet is two hours away," he said and continued walking to the exit. He headed for the elevator without saying anything more and rode down to the main floor.

Once outside, he flagged down a cab and told the driver where he was headed. Half an hour later, he was seated at a table for two in the packed restaurant.

As he waited for Jessica, he grabbed his phone from the inside pocket very his jacket and turned it on, hoping she wouldn't mind going on the record. A waiter dressed in slacks came by and took his drink order before disappearing again.

Thirty seconds passed before a brunette walked toward him, smiling nervously. "Are you the one who called?" she asked, extending her hand to him.

"Yes, how are you?" he asked, shaking her hand.

"Fine," she replied, going to the other end of the table, "why have you asked me here?"

"I have some questions for you," Maxwell repeated.

"Who are you?" she asked, now staring down at the table before a spark of recognition lit up her eyes. "You were Ernest's last client." she declared happily.

"Yes, and I'm assuming you're Jessica?"

She nodded and watched as the waiter returned and set a glass down in front of him.

After giving her drink order, she looked over at the sharply-dressed man sitting across from her. The teal dress she wore reached her knees, and her facial features were accentuated by the little makeup she wore. Her hair fell to her shoulders, and the diamond ring on her left hand sparkled dimly in the sunlight that shone through the window.

Maxwell put his phone on the table in front of him and glanced around the restaurant cautiously before hitting "record" and launching into his questioning.

"What day did Ernest come to see you?" he asked.

"The first of February, 2016." she paused as the waiter came with her strawberry shake and set it down in front of her, then took their meal orders and left.

"Did you two have a conversation?" Maxwell asked once the waiter was out of earshot.

"No, it was all one-sided," she said, putting her straw in the cup and taking a long sip of her shake.

"Whose side did most of the talking?" Maxwell asked, leaning forward and sipping from his water glass.

"He did," she said, twirling the diamond ring around on her finger.

"What did he say to you?" he asked.

"Did he hire you as a detective or something?" she asked, a bit suspicious now.

He quickly shook his head, staring at her skeptical expression.

"Then how did you know where I worked?" she asked, some of the suspicion in her voice now replaced by doubt.

"One of the members of the GK told me," he said.

"So, you're one of them now?" she asked, jabbing a finger in his direction.

He shook his head again, leaning forward to take another sip of water. "I'm sorry if I've given you the wrong impression," he said when he'd swallowed.

Jessica stared down at her cup, asking herself if he was worth believing. Finally, she sat up straight and looked out at the street, internally debating whether or not she should stay. After a moment, she turned back to face him, her expression a bit softer.

"Is this detrimental to what you're doing?" she finally asked.

"Would I have asked you here if it wasn't?" Maxwell asked.

She considered this question for only half a second before agreeing to continue to help him. "OK." she finally said, facing forward again as the main course came.

"What did he say to you?" Maxwell repeated after the waiter had gone in an effort to get back to where they'd left off.

"Your boss had been falsely accused of something, and he was afraid that somebody was going to kill him," she said, taking a bite of her burger.

"Where did you two meet?" he asked, thinking that this was the question he should have started with first.

"My office," she said, shoving a ketchup-covered fry into her mouth, "he'd come down from London a few hours before our appointment. At first, he'd been hesitant to talk to me until I finally convinced him. He agreed to do it but only if we could do it in private."

"Did anyone take notes when you met?" he asked.

"Yes, he eventually let me take them." She took another sip of her shake. "A few minutes after he'd sat down at my desk-"

"What do you mean by, he was hesitant about talking to you?" he interrupted.

"He came to New York seeking help and when he first came to my office, he wasn't sure that talking to a reporter was a good idea," she admitted with a guilty smile.

"How did you finally convince him to talk to you?" he asked after swallowing a mouthful of hamburger.

"By promising that whatever he revealed wasn't going to be shared with any of my colleagues."

"Is that why you were granted the story?" Maxwell guessed, a question she seemed to find offensive.

"I was not granted it. I took it on because I was the only one he trusted." she corrected in a brusque tone.

"Was he mad when you put it in print?"

She had, by now, eaten half her hamburger, but her attention had been diverted from her meal to the handsome man that sat just a few feet away from her. "If he was, he didn't tell me."

The waiter came by for their plates, then scurried away to get the check.

"Are we done here?" she asked, standing up, giving him a better look at her figure and clothing.

She had a blue sweater tied around her tiny waist, and on her narrow feet were black stiletto shoes. She reached into her purse and pulled out a wallet.

"Yes, I think I have everything I need," he said as the check was brought to their table.

She paid the bill and turned to leave, but just as she reached the door, she turned to see his silhouette only a few feet behind her. He'd stowed his phone away in his pocket, but once he caught up to her, he took it out once again. "Have you forgotten something?" she asked, checking her watch.

"Yes," he said, inching his way closer to her, "what can you tell me about the day of the murder?"

"Nothing out of the ordinary. I got a call from my boss, explaining that a man had been found in his room." Jessica said, her eyes still on her watch. It was twelve forty-five and she wanted to get back to the office by one-thirty.

"And?" he prompted.

She groaned inwardly, desperately needing to get back to her desk. Her boss had given her a midnight deadline for a story she was working on about an up-and-coming New York attorney. She'd been in the middle of organizing three weeks' worth of notes when her cell phone had reminded her of the time.

"I did some research on the story and was shocked to learn that he'd been the one they were talking about," she said hurriedly.

She waited as he turned the phone's recorder off and stuck it back in his pocket. "Are we done here?" she asked again, her patience completely gone.

Maxwell nodded, his attention already elsewhere.

Half an hour later, as he sat in the back of a cab, he reviewed the recording from the restaurant, but to his disappointment, it wasn't as much as he'd hoped. He eventually went to the New York Times' website and clicked on the article. Jessica had been right: he'd come to her office and had sat at her desk. The article had a picture of his former boss with his eyes half-closed, a panicked look on his face.

"The Greenridge Killers want revenge on my department." he was saying.

"Why?" Morales had asked.

He hadn't said.

"Have they come after you?" Jessica asked.

He continued to read but soon closed out of it, already tiring of the article.

When he finally returned to the dilapidated office building of Jonathan Westwood fifteen minutes later, he felt like a weight had been placed on his shoulders. Once inside the creaky elevator, he carefully leaned his aching head against the wall as he tried to turn his thoughts away from his boss and back to the mission at hand.

"There you are!" René exclaimed, rushing up to him once he entered the dining room, but her smile disappeared when she saw his tired expression.

"What's wrong?" she asked.

"My lunch with Jessica didn't go as I planned," he said, falling into a chair.

"What lunch?" she asked, frowning.

"I'm sorry, I forgot to tell you that I was having lunch with Jessica Morales," Maxwell apologized.

"Why did you meet with her?" the girl asked.

"To see if she could be of any help," he replied.

"Was she?"

He shrugged, feeling as if he'd failed his former boss. His head began to ache again as he turned to leave before turning back to face her. "Do me a favor," he said, rising to his feet.

"Depends on what it is." She half-smiled.

"Tell the others I'm going to bed early tonight," he said and walked away without waiting for a reply.

10

Disturbance

Maxwell woke up seven hours later to find that the place had gone quiet. He reached for his phone and looked at it, shocked to see five notifications waiting for him. He opened each one and read, both intrigued and annoyed, but the one that seemed most important to him was an e-mail from Welsh with the link to a story that had come out a few days after Ernest's death.

The story was from the BBC, and the headline read:

News of the Death of Famed Government Worker Spreads Like Wildfire Across The Globe.

He opened the attached link and waited as a video loaded.

"A few days ago here on the BBC, we brought you the shocking news of famed government worker Ernest Dumont's death. Well, now, we have more news for you on that front: in the days since it broke, the story has gained a lot of traction across the globe. Watch this." the female reporter said before showing a clip from a network in South Africa.

"Breaking news for you out of London tonight," the male reporter said, "famed and acclaimed government worker Ernest Dumont has been found dead at his home in Hyde Park, investigators say. Police found him in his bedroom, shirtless and bloody with scars on his back, including a long one that ran from his rib cage to his left side."

As the reporter described the extent of Ernest's injuries, the image from a couple of days earlier made its way, bit by bit, into his mind.

"Police say they suspect foul play was involved, but at this point, it's too early to know. We will bring you details on this story as we get them," he said before the BBC reporter's voice was heard again.

"And this morning, it also made its way to France."

"Monsieur Ernest Dumont vient d'étre retrouvé mort chez lui." the reporter began before going on in the same way as the other reporter had.

The last piece of evidence, as if he didn't believe her already, was from the American network Fox. Unlike the last two reporters, this one was female, like the one reporting this story.

"This is a Fox News alert," she said, "police have just found famed veteran government worker Ernest Dumont dead at his home."

Maxwell fast-forwarded through her report, not interested in hearing the same thing again.

Five minutes later, the officer who'd been responsible for the discovery, Nathan Gonzales, joined the BBC reporter in the studio. The guy's face became instantly recognizable to him. The man on Skype with the redhead was the one from the video they'd seen in the kitchen.

"Nathan, you say you found his body in his bedroom. Where?" the reporter asked.

"Hello, Rosemerry," he said, "that is correct. First, we'd got the call that a man was unresponsive in his home and to come quickly. Once my team and I were there, we found him by the window."

"I won't ask you to describe his condition, but were you shocked at what you saw?" she asked.

"Yes," he replied.

"What about his family? Have you told them yet?"

"Last night," he said.

"And how did they take it?" asked Rosemerry.

"As to be expected, his wife was distraught, and as for his five-year-old daughter, all she knows is that her father isn't coming home," he said.

"Last question. If this was indeed murder, do you know of anyone who'd wanted him dead?"

"Not at this point, and we don't think he had any enemies," Gonzales said.

"Nathan Gonzales, thank you." the reporter said.

After it had ended, Maxwell stared up at the ceiling, not bothering to replay the video that waited for him on the screen. Everyone seemed to have the same story: the man was found dead in his home, and the police had suspected foul play was involved, but no one seemed to know his killer's true motive. All he knew was that he had gone to the media, but for what?

"And you believed them?" Welsh had asked when told the explanation he'd been given.

The skepticism in his voice had been palpable during their conversation and since then, it sometimes came back to gnaw at him.

At around ten o'clock, the place became lively. The guests emerged from their rooms and went about their morning routines before once again convening in the dining room. Maxwell scanned the room for René until he found her sitting by the door, looking at something in her hands. He went quietly to her side and looked over her shoulder as the outline of Rosemerry appeared on a tiny screen.

"How'd you get that?" he asked, causing her to pause and look up at him.

"Simon sent me the link," she said.

"Have you found it useful?" he asked.

She shook her head and laid her phone on the table, frowning slightly. "Have you seen it also?" she asked.

"Yes," he said.

The first half of the case had been solved: they had found the GK and knew the first part of why they'd killed him, but Maxwell sensed that they were still hiding something from him. The odds weren't on their side at this point. He hated the thought of letting them go free but if the mission's time ran out, he would have no choice but to do so.

The message on the mirror he'd wiped away nearly two weeks before also found its way into his thoughts from time to time. Though it had only been a few days ago, it still haunted him as if it had happened yesterday. It was clear that the man had been looking for him, but he wanted to know who had hired him and how much he'd been paid to track him down.

Then there was the man who had come up to them in the hotel's main dining area. Although their encounter had been brief, the French gangster with the nicotine-stained teeth and the gun in his pocket had made his point clear.

He, like the other man, had been more interested in their conquest than in anything else. But, despite their warnings, he now faced to face with Dumont's killers, and also, despite their warnings, he was going to take them out. When it all came down to it, he was glad to have a partner, but could she be of use when the time came?

Along with everything else, he still needed to know who X was and if he or she was working for the good guy or if that was a lie.

There was also Nathan Gonzales, the police officer who had been responsible for finding his body. He walked away from the table and out of the room without saying anything to anyone, leaving René to stare after him. His room was only a few doors down from the dining room, where everyone else but the eight group members sat. The door to his room had been left open a crack for this purpose.

He stopped and listened to the silence outside his bedroom door, hoping that René had stayed where she sat. When he didn't hear any footsteps on the carpeted floor, he quietly opened the door, went in, then closed it behind him. He walked over to the bedside table where his phone was charging and sat down on the bed.

He put the phone on his lap, then grabbed his notebook and pen and set them on the bed beside him. He searched through the officer's Wikipedia page, Twitter account, and Facebook account for the next fifteen minutes, but there was no contact information.

"Damn," he muttered before checking one more place.

At the bottom of the Wikipedia page, at the right-hand corner of the screen, was an e-mail address. He grabbed his pen, flipped the notebook to a blank page and jotted the address down.

It was noon when he wrote the e-mail, asking if they could meet for lunch and saying that it was very important. After he pressed "send," he considered the possibility that his questions and e-mail would go unanswered, but he couldn't afford to wait around any more.

It was an hour before he got a reply, and though the message was only two sentences long, he decided that it was better than nothing.

I can meet you for lunch at twelve-thirty on Friday. How about the Ruby Tuesday in Midtown?

That's perfect. Maxwell said.

Today was Wednesday, which only gave him two days to get his questions in order. After sending his response, he emerged from his room and searched for René in the hall leading to the dining room, but when he didn't see her, he walked into the room to find it half-empty. She had not moved from her spot, but she was now talking to a woman with dark-brown hair, looking relaxed. He was about to turn around when the brunette got up, thanked rené for her time and left. It was then that she saw him and beckoned him forward.

"What was that about?" he asked.

"Remember Angela? The girl from the video?" she asked.

Her name rang a dim bell when she spoke it. "Vaguely." he finally answered.

"Her story is fascinating," said René, who then proceeded to regale him with her story, but he was barely paying attention until she got to the part that had led her here.

"Her younger sister had been killed in an accident, but when it was time for a trial, the murder suspect was nowhere to be found. She had gone to the police to find out what had happened, but all anyone would tell her was that she'd been hit, and the suspect had mysteriously vanished," she said and paused to glance over at the brunette who was now sitting beside a guy that could have been her brother.

She was dressed in a pair of faded blue jeans and a grey turtleneck. Her hair was tied back with a rubber band, and around her neck, she wore a cross. She had her legs crossed at the ankles, and a pair of high-heeled sandals were on her feet. She and the boy were exchanging glances at each other and quietly talking.

"Anyway," René went on when she turned her attention back to him, "after months of searching, her family had given up, and she'd felt like a failure until she saw that tweet."

"Is Angela her real name?" he asked when she had finished.

She nodded. "Angela Bradford," she said.

He took the chair opposite her and put his elbows on his knees.

"What's up?" she asked.

"I was able to get in touch with Nathan Gonzales," he informed her.

"Who?" she asked.

"The officer who found Ernest's body," Maxwell said.

"When are you two meeting?"

"That's what I wanted to talk to you about," he said, "I want you to come along."

"Why?"

He wanted to tell her that there was no immediate danger she had to watch out for, but he simply said he wanted her there. She agreed.

"When is the meeting?" she asked.

"Friday at twelve-thirty at Ruby Tuesday in Midtown."

"What are we meeting about?" she asked.

"I want to find out who they brought in for questioning following the murder," he answered.

"Do you think he'll answer your questions?" she asked.

Maxwell tried to keep the uncertainty out of his voice when he answered.

"Once he finds out that he was my boss, he might not," he said.

The investigation had ended nearly three years ago. It had been all over the news when the identities of his killers had been revealed.

On the day of the announcement, time had stood still. The whole world seemed to hold their breath collectively as the moment grew closer.

News reporters had teased a big story, but instead of it being the first item of the morning, noon, or nightly broadcasts, they had "saved the best for last," as they had put it.

"Are you hungry?" René asked, bringing him back to the present.

Food had been the last thing on Maxwell's mind, but as he came back to the present, it was all he wanted.

He nodded eagerly and watched her get up from the table and head to the kitchen. What time was it now? he wondered as his train of thought resumed where it had left off.

The days following the big reveal had been nothing short of difficult for him. His had been one of many pictures they had chosen to show on TV when reminding people of who had worked for and with the acclaimed agent-turned-boss, garnering him unnecessary and unwanted attention.

"You're famous!" a friend had excitedly exclaimed while having dinner at his house not too long after that night.

"What?" Maxwell had asked, looking up from his plate.

"Your picture. It's in the Daily Mail." his friend had said, thrusting a copy of the paper at him.

He'd grabbed it and looked at the front page with annoyance.

Under an article about the identities of his former boss's killers finally being unearthed was a picture of two men standing side-by-side; Maxwell, the one on the left, held a gun in front of him like a shield, while the one on the right had no way to protect himself if someone came at him. The outline of a building was behind them, but only the first word of the sign was visible: WELCOME!

He then threw the newspaper down on the table in exasperation before throwing his friend a pissed-off look.

"Oh, for Christ's sake," he'd said.

"What's the matter?" his friend had asked, staring at the picture calmly.

"My boss has just been murdered. That should not be glorified!" Maxwell had roared.

He opened his eyes and sat up straight when René approached the table carrying two glass plates with forks already on them. "Hope you like spaghetti," she said cheerfully, setting a plate in front of him.

"Thank you," he mumbled, grabbing his fork and digging in.

"Where's everyone else?" he asked after swallowing a mouthful of pasta.

She pointed to a closed-door a few feet behind them and he followed her finger. The sounds of loud voices emanated from the closed door, but the walls muffled their words. They ate in silence for several minutes while the others in the room continued their conversations.

"How long are you expecting this lunch with Nathan to last?" René asked, twisting her fork around in the pasta on her plate.

"Depends on how long it takes him to answer my questions," Maxwell said, hoping Nathan wouldn't be too difficult.

The sounds of muffled chatter from the other room grew louder, and he wondered if someone had gotten in an argument.

"Do you already have your questions in mind?"

Maxwell shook his head, still eyeing the closed door.

They ate the rest of their meal in silence, then she got up and cleared the table. "Why do you keep looking at that door?" she asked when she'd returned.

He shushed her, walked over to the door and leaned against it, listening carefully to the noises that came from inside. He heard the sound of movement before someone finally spoke.

"I'm just having trouble thinking of something." the deep voice said.

"There has to be a reason you wanted all of us here." a second, a more high-pitched voice responded.

"And your attendance will be greatly rewarded, don't doubt that." the first voice promised.

"Pascal, no one is after you. Who's left for us to go after?" a third voice asked.

"The reporters who broke the story."

Maxwell kept his ear to the door, eager for more information and cursing himself for not bringing his notebook and pen.

"The reporters were just doing their jobs." the second voice said.

Pascal, who he assumed was the leader, let out a short, brittle laugh. "They were, but haven't you ever wondered what those reporters know?" he asked, a sinister edge to his voice.

"What the hell are you talking about?" the second voice demanded.

"Of course, they had a responsibility to their loyal fans, but reporters are sneaky in their own right," he explained.

"Meaning?" another female voice asked.

"They tracked us for months, but we didn't know it until right before Ernest's death."

"What about the one who found him? That Nate something-or-other?" the third voice asked.

Pascal considered this for a moment and gave an audible sigh. He then said something too low for Maxwell to hear before asking, "Does that please everyone here?"

A chorus of "yes's" then filled the room and Pascal seemed satisfied.

Maxwell wanted to know how many people had gone into the room and how many had been involved in the discussion.

The sound of a lock turning was heard and Maxwell hurried away from the wooden door.

"What did you hear?" René asked, getting up to follow him as he ran to his room. "They want to kill the two women who reported the story," he said, panting as they reached his door.

"What about Nathan?" she cried.

He shook his head and ran for his notebook and pen.

"Stay outside," he ordered, closing the door behind him.

He walked to a desk and began to put pen to paper. As he wrote, he considered calling Welsh, but the urge to do so quickly vanished.

By the time he'd finished, the page was filled with paragraphs of ink, but he found himself thinking about if "handwriting was legible to anyone else. So he carried the notebook, still opened to the newly-filled page, out to René, who was still standing by the wall.

"I normally don't do this, but I need you to see if you can read this," he said, holding the freshly-inked page out to her.

She took the notebook and looked over it silently, bristling at the words she read.

"It's legible," she said through clenched teeth.

"What's the matter?" he asked as she handed the book over to him.

She only pointed to the words on the page in front of her.

"How much do you think those ladies knew?" she finally asked, but he wasn't listening anymore.

He stared at the page, asking himself if he should warn his lunch guest on Friday or if he should let him figure it out on his own. Finally, he took the notebook back to his room and set it on the table next to the bed, then left and closed the door behind him.

11

Second Round

"Is that him?" René asked for the fourth time as a heavily tattooed man entered the restaurant.

"I don't think so," Maxwell said as the man passed by their table without looking their way.

They had arrived at Ruby Tuesday at noon and had waited outside for fifteen minutes before going in. The sun had been warm on their backs and they had enjoyed it, but they had not come for pleasure and warmth. It was almost one-thirty now, and he was beginning to worry that Nathan had forgotten about their meeting, but just as he was about to take his phone from his pocket to contact him, the doors opened again, and someone else came in.

"Are you the man who e-mailed me?" a voice asked. It belonged to a heavyset man with a long, narrow face with pinched cheeks that, for some reason, reminded Maxwell of people who got Botox. He had brown eyes, and the little hair he had was gray. He looked like he could have been a male model before joining the police force.

"Yes," Maxwell said, standing up to shake the officer's hand.

"Nathan Gonzales," the man said, "nice to meet you." He pulled out the chair next to Maxwell and sat down.

"I hope I didn't pull you away from anything important," Maxwell said.

"No, just paperwork," Nathan replied, his eyes flickering to the girl across the table. "Who's that?"

"She's working with me right now," Maxwell said, grabbing the notebook and pen from his pocket.

He flipped the page to his prepared questions, looked down at them, then looked over at his guest. "Are you up for answering any questions about the day you found Ernest in his home and afterward?" he asked.

"Are you one of those Goddamned detectives?" the officer asked, frowning.

"No, I was Ernest's last worker." Maxwell clarified, suddenly aware that he had not seen his picture on television or in the newspapers or wherever else a copy might have been.

Nathan smiled again and removed his suit jacket, revealing a two-piece denim suit, and put the jacket on the back of his chair.

"That jacket looks expensive," Maxwell commented.

"It cost me a fortune." Nathan laughed.

René smiled as the waitress came and sat their drink orders in front of them.

"Water, please," Nathan told her before she walked away.

"Who called you with the information that Ernest had stopped breathing?" Maxwell began.

"One of his neighbors," said Nathan.

"What time did he call you?" asked Maxwell.

"At two o'clock that evening," Nathan said as his drink arrived.

He grabbed his straw and used it to stir the ice cubes and water around in his glass, making the cubes clink.

"What did this neighbor say?" Maxwell asked.

"That a man was lying on his floor, unresponsive, and police were needed right away," Nathan said, still stirring the ice around in his glass.

"Who did you bring in for questioning following the discovery of his body?" Maxwell asked.

The officer tapped his clean-shaven chin with one finger as he thought back almost three years. "The first person was his oldest sister Mel." he finally said.

Melissa Fitzgerald had been born in California to a Spanish teacher named Emelia and an investment banker, but that was all anyone knew about her; her age, birthday, and birth month were all mysteries to the public.

"What was her story?" asked Maxwell.

"She was angry, as you can imagine. Her brother had just died." Nathan paused to take a drink of water.

"What did she say?" Maxwell asked.

"Her story was that she was at work all day, then she went to go pick up her daughter from preschool," Nathan answered, not looking at Maxwell.

"How long did you keep her there?" Maxwell asked, keeping his expression detached as he looked from Nathan to René.

"An hour," Nathan answered.

"Did she cooperate?"

"She did."

"Who was the second suspect?" Maxwell asked.

"A friend of his, but I don't remember his name."

By now, Maxwell's and René's food had arrived, but only he gave the impression that he was hungry. "What did he say?" Maxwell asked.

"He was in denial.

He just started screaming and crying and asking if I was screwing with him." Gonzales stated.

"Did he answer any questions?"

The officer shook his head.

"Have you heard of a woman named Jessica Morales?"

Nathan gave two quick nods.

"When did you two meet?" Maxwell asked.

"A few days after the murder," Nathan answered, munching on an ice cube.

René grunted in frustration, and both men turned to her, surprised to hear her make a sound after all this time, but she had already turned back toward the windows.

"Where'd you meet?"

"She had come down to the station to interview me about what I saw at the house," Nathan said and looked at his watch.

"I have to go back to the office, and I have an hour-long drive. Is there anything else?"

He needed more information, but instead of asking his questions, he thanked Nathan and let him go.

"By the way," he said, putting on his jacket and turning back to them, "the Greenridge Killers have a flash drive stashed away somewhere with something on it that you might find very useful."

"What's that?" Maxwell called, but the officer had already left.

They waited until they saw him around the corner before saying anything. "What do you suppose is on that drive?" René asked.

"I don't know, but it might be the key to helping us find the truth."

It had grown noticeably cooler when they left the restaurant at a quarter to two, but it was still warm enough not to need a jacket. They didn't talk again until they were safely in a cab and their driver had diverted his attention from his passengers to the road.

"He seemed nice," René whispered.

"Yeah," Maxwell said, still thinking about the unknown flash drive hidden away somewhere.

It was after two o'clock when they returned to find that nothing had changed. The building's occupants were sitting in a circle around the bar, drinking cocktails and talking softly to each other, but no one made a big show when the two missing members of their party suddenly showed up and took the two empty seats at the bar. "Has anyone ever met Jessica?" a woman asked, gulping down her second Mimosa. She was wearing a strapless pink dress, and gold bracelets lined one of her wrists.

One by one, the others shook their heads.

"Does anyone know what she looks like?" the woman in the pink dress asked.

"She gave an interview on 20/20 a year ago," Angela informed the crowd.

"Pull her video up." someone else chimed in.

It only took her a few minutes to find the video, and the room soon filled with the familiar sound of Jessica Morales' voice, but whatever she was saying wasn't clear. René guessed she'd been on there to talk about her meeting with Maxwell's late boss. She looked over his shoulder at the woman speaking into the camera. Jessica's dark-brown hair was styled into a braid at the back of her head. She was dressed in an orange pantsuit, and the only makeup she wore was a light shade of black lipstick.

She tried to turn her thoughts from the dark, twisted path they were taking, but her mind had a mind of its own. Would anyone miss her when she was killed? Who would be the one to speak at her funeral, and what would they say in the eulogy? Her train of thought was interrupted by a tap on her left shoulder, but the sense of relief she felt was greatly exaggerated.

"At midnight, I need you to help me get that flash drive," Maxwell whispered.

"Why?" she asked.

"Whatever is on there may be important," he said.

"Fine." she agreed nervously, but inwardly, she was beaming.

In every spy novel she'd ever read, this was the moment you were supposed to be looking forward to. It was the calm before the highly anticipated storm, the thing that made coming face to face with killers worth it. The woman on the video had stopped talking, and the people around the table were now looking at pictures of Andrea, the one who'd first reported it in her column in the paper.

The picture on the screen was of a thin, smiling woman in her mid-20s with her hair cut close. She was facing the camera with her eyes half-closed, like she was concentrating on something. She was dressed in a pair of yellow overalls and high tops, and her face was made-up like a doll's.

Poor woman, René thought, she doesn't even know she's about to die.

They were still analyzing the picture when Pascal, dressed in an old pair of slacks and a faded sweatshirt, walked in alone. "What are you looking at?" he asked, peering at the screen.

"A picture of Andrea." the woman in the pink dress announced.

"She's very pretty, Pascal," Angela chimed in.

"She is." Pascal agreed, that sinister edge in his voice again.

As she listened to this, René asked herself what they had in store for her. Would her death be slow and painful or quick and easy? Would they take her somewhere, or would they do it at her home?

"Did you know she's pregnant?" the man sitting beside Angela asked suddenly, making everyone, including René and Maxwell, jump.

"How far along?" the lady in the pink dress asked.

"Six months," Angela interjected.

From the corner of his eye, Maxwell saw Pascal frown a tiny bit.

"Show me a picture," he ordered in a steady voice.

Both could hear the exasperation behind the facade, though whether he was angry at himself for thinking of killing a mother and her baby or at her for getting pregnant was unclear. He scowled at the picture of her showing off her baby bump in a pretty dress, then ran off in the direction of the hallway, where the other members waited.

"What?" one of them asked.

"The bitch got knocked up," he said sharply.

"Who's the father?" another voice asked.

He shook his head, indicating that he didn't know. "If she wanted to have a baby, she should have had it years ago." he lamented.

"How far along is she?" the same voice asked.

"Six months," Pascal said angrily.

"Do you think they'll still go through with it?" René asked later that night after they'd gone downstairs.

"I don't know." Maxwell sighed, reaching out to open the door that led to the office Pascal shared with the seven others.

It was past midnight, and they had all retired for the night. The room was cluttered with stacked boxes, but they were able to squeeze their way in.

Aside from one of the walls covered in black spots, the room was colorless, no vases of flowers sat on the table, and the air smelled strongly of stale cigarettes. "Where is the drive?" René asked.

Maxwell threw her a look but otherwise kept searching. René's job, he'd told her, was to stay back and take the flash drive when it had finally been located.

"Why?" she'd asked.

"Better for you to pocket it than for it to be in plain sight." he'd reasoned. After half an hour of searching, the drive had been located in the bottom drawer of one of the file cabinets. Relieved, she took the small disk and pocketed it, then followed the government agent out.

It was half-past one when they returned upstairs and closed the bedroom door behind them. They had gone back into the agent's room and were now sitting on his bed, with Maxwell looking at the screen of René's PC as the drive's contents loaded onto it. When it was finished, he turned the computer in her direction.

The files had already been sorted out and put into three separate folders. The first folder was filled with journal entries from the past few years, each describing their kill in more detail than the last. The second was filled with gruesome images of corpses lined up in a row. Some of the bodies were missing certain limbs, and others had been beheaded. René gasped and covered her mouth with her hands to keep from screaming but continued to look at the frightening images on the screen, reminding herself to be strong for the man beside her.

The last folder contained a long list of names and addresses of potential victims.

"Where do we start first?" René asked when she could finally speak.

"The journals," he said, going back up to that folder and opening it.

The killers' journal entries they were looking at had been dated back to 1997.

"May 1st, 1997," Maxwell read aloud, "I finally know what it's like to be in a group. Three years earlier, I became the newest member of the Greenridge Killers. I was an outsider before June of 1994, but now, I'm getting what I want: revenge. Last week, we murdered a woman and her husband, both had worked for the FBI, and both knew damning things about my friends. They were going to go public with them, so we looked up their address, went to their home armed with guns, shot them in their sleep, then ran away. Weeks later, the news reporter showed pictures of them which showed their blood splattered all over the sheets and blankets and pillows. It was cruel, yes, but they should've never investigated them."

There was no name at the bottom, just the initials Pd.

"Dear God," Maxwell whispered, shocked.

"Jesus Christ," René said, echoing his sentiment.

"Who do you suppose Pd is?"

"Pierre Dubois," Maxwell stated in a flat voice.

"I thought the GK was formed in the late 90s," René said.

Maxwell did a quick search for the Greenridge Killers on Wikipedia and looked over it quietly.

"The Greenridge Killers, also known as the GK, is a group of assassins consisting of fourteen members. They are famous for murdering anyone they consider to be a threat to their way of life. Formed in the late 60s in Paris, it first began advertising itself as a haven for anti-establishment and at-risk youth, but in the first three months of 1970 alone, six people they believed had connections to the FBI had been murdered. Still, the murderers were never caught by police."

He stopped reading and closed the page, then took the drive out of its port and stared down at the object in his hands. "Are you all right?" René asked from beside him.

He didn't answer. She wondered idly if their temporary hosts were going to be waking up soon and whether they'd notice something was missing from their messy office. She turned to read the numbers on her computer's clock: it was nearly two in the morning, but she was committed to staying up with the agent until he got all the information he was seeking.

"René, you should get some sleep," he said without looking up.

"No." she yawned, still looking at the clock.

She took the drive from him and stuck it in her computer's case while he resumed looking at the information they'd stolen from the downstairs office. The second journal entry was dated November 22nd of that same year, and this one described that date's kill as "the bloodiest, most satisfying kill in the past three years."

It was written by someone with the initials PL, and the object of their kill had been a former FBI agent. According to the entry, the person had investigated the shady past of a suspected drug dealer they'd been told was a close friend of theirs.

The entry stated:

We asked him who had been the one to come forward, but the guy said he was sworn to secrecy.

He scrolled down to another entry that had been written by someone named Garrett in June of 1999.

Garrett had written that earlier in the day, and the news had reported the disappearance of the BBC sports reporter Richard Witherspoon. He'd said that the police had been looking for him for weeks. The last person to see him was his wife, but investigators had determined that she was clean after hours of questioning.

"He disappeared a few days after his 42nd birthday," an unnamed friend had said, "it's rather unfortunate, isn't it?"

There was no description of the murder or the body and the blood that must have been all over the room or wherever they had done it. The last entry in the folder was from 2004, but it was only to announce their plans to go into hiding. They were all going their separate ways, detailing how they would live their lives before promising their return. He scrolled back up to the first entry, which had been written sometime in 1967, making him wonder where they'd kept them before computers came into the picture.

He closed that folder and opened the next one, and spent a few minutes looking at the disturbingly familiar images on the screen. He glanced over to see an empty spot on the bed where René had been sitting. He wondered where she had gone, then decided to let it go and returned his attention to the screen. The haunted eyes of many corpses stared back at him, asking the silent question of why.

At two-thirty, he called it a night and set the computer by its case on his bedside table before climbing under the covers. As he drifted, he thought of Andrea and the child she was carrying. He suddenly found himself hoping for the safety of a child he had never met and likely never would meet. As he closed his eyes, thoughts of his boss came back to him, but before he was fully under, he heard the bathroom door open and the sound of footsteps.

His body tensed and he automatically reached for his gun. The figure came closer to him, their breath smelling of mint toothpaste and mouthwash. "I just finished brushing my teeth, so I thought I'd say good night." the voice said.

His eyes flew open then and he saw René standing before him, staring at him, and he saw the same question mirrored in her gaze.

How many had it taken to kill him? That was the question on both their minds but neither René nor Maxwell had an answer. The man had given very little away, but the agent could tell that there was something he had forgotten to mention. All fourteen of them could not have been involved in the crime; after all, he had only been shot and stabbed, and it only took one person to stab you to death and another to shoot you. But then, another thought occurred to the agent: he wondered if the same person who had stabbed him had also chained his hands to the floor, and then there was the big question: Had they only killed him for threatening to go to the police with their whereabouts?

"Are you going to bed now?" he asked.

"Unless you need me for something else," René said.

He shook his head and told her to leave.

"Are you sure?" she asked. "I'll be fine," he promised.

With that, she walked out of the room, leaving him with his thoughts as he fell into a troubled sleep.

12

Confrontation

René stared out the window of her room at the darkened night sky and sighed.

There was no movement tonight, a rarity for New York, but she laughed quietly when she remembered where they were. Jonathan Westwood's office building was located in a secluded part of town, but the longer they stayed here, the more she wondered if this was where he'd spent his final days. She thought about getting up and going back to retrieve her computer, but the thought vanished from her mind as soon as it had come.

She grabbed her phone from the bedside table and typed Jonathan Westwood's name into the search engine. Two Jonathan Westwoods popped up onscreen, and out of mild interest, she clicked on the first one.

The page said that Jonathan had been a famed NYC attorney. He'd graduated from law school in 1974 but got his big break five years later after winning the murder case of a famous celebrity. The case had been all over the news, and the man at the center of everything had earned enough money to be able to part ways with the Ebstein and Company law firm he'd started working for after graduating college at the age of 20. The office building they were now in had been built in 1985 with specific orders from Westwood on how to design it. His death had shaken everyone that had either known him personally or had been represented by him.

According to this, Westwood had been involved with someone named Gabriela Rodriguez at the time of his death. For many years after his death, the building had remained vacant until 2014, when a member of the French-based Greenridge Killers had bought it in an auction for half a million dollars.

Without realizing it, she had gotten to the bottom of the page, to the last bit of information. Her eyelids felt heavy, but she fought against them and won.

Jonathan had died mysteriously at the age of 40 in 1990, and everyone in the lawyer world had been distraught. An autopsy had been performed on his body, and the coroner had concluded that he had died of a rare disease, though what he had had never been given a name. However, in 2011, new evidence had come to light, suggesting that maybe he'd been murdered, but the coroner had not been willing to do another autopsy.

She read over the last line twice before exiting out of the page and replacing the phone on the bedside table before flipping over on her back to stare up at the ceiling.

Her thoughts suddenly turned to the man sleeping in the next room over. She told herself that when this was all over, she had to repay him somehow. It was three o'clock when her eyelids grew heavy, but the information she'd just read fit into a slot, like the missing piece of a puzzle. This would be another question for him, and Welsh would be curious about this new development, no doubt. She began to wonder if the eight figures on the first floor had anything to do with his death. She did not dismiss this as a possibility, but her mind was not sharp enough to form coherent thoughts at this hour. A montage of images suddenly flashed through her mind: the scene at Ruby Tuesdays earlier that day, the picture of pregnant Andrea, the interview with Jessica, the group around the kitchen table.

"The bitch got knocked up," Pascal had said, all the anger he'd hidden from the people at the table in those five words.

The woman's baby bump had been on full display in the form-fitting black dress she'd worn for the picture, but her hopes of having a future with her child would soon be dashed. One floor below her lay eight of the deadliest assassins while the others had stayed behind in France. She wanted to know if they were staying in contact with the six others while also enjoying their stay but not only that, she wondered if they stayed in contact with their wives or girlfriends and children.

At nine-thirty, she dressed quickly and walked to their usual meeting area, surprised to find only one person sitting at the usually full table.

"Have I thanked you for helping me last night?" Maxwell asked, leaning over a cup of coffee.

"Yes," René answered, startled.

She was not used to seeing him before ten o'clock, and she also wasn't used to seeing him drinking a steaming mug of coffee.

"Where are the others?"

It was her turn to ask.

He pointed over his shoulder at a partially closed door where the soft sounds of laughter could be heard from inside the room. She wanted to know what was going on in there, but from the kitchen, she couldn't see their faces. René absentmindedly pulled up a chair across from him and continued to stare at the cracked door he'd pointed to.

She heard someone ask something and another voice reply

"Have they all gone in there?" she asked after a second.

Maxwell turned away from his mug and plate. "They've been in there for quite a while," he said after another brief pause.

"Aren't you hungry?" he asked, digging into his plate of scrambled eggs and bacon.

She was about to shake her head when her stomach growled, making her frown and Maxwell smile as he pointed to the pan on the stove.

"It might be cold now, but there's still some left for you," he said apologetically.

"Thanks," she answered, grabbing a plate from the cabinet and filling it with food.

She walked back to the table, sat the plate down, and stalked back to the kitchen to get a fork and a cup of orange juice.

"I went to Jonathan's Wikipedia this morning," René said, scarfing down the still-warm food.

"Did you find anything?"

Maxwell asked.

She told him everything she'd learned, and he listened intently, trying hard to keep his face blank.

"Do you think they murdered him?" he asked.

She nodded but looked toward the closed door with an unsure expression.

"What did the autopsy state?" he asked, staring down at his plate.

"That he'd died of a rare disease," she said, frowning.

They continued to eat in silence for a moment or two before René spoke again.

"When did you knock off?" she asked, still facing the door.

"Right after you left." Without being prompted, he described everything he'd seen, right down to the clothes the corpses had worn.

"Did it give you nightmares?" she asked, trying to keep her tone light, but panic made her insides ache.

"No, but I wish they'd had," he answered.

That admission surprised and frightened her.

"Why?"

"Strangely, it makes me feel better knowing that someone is more damaged than me," he muttered.

"Why do you put it like that?" she asked.

"I wasn't the one who ruined everything for them," he said, his back to her.

"I've been playing this game for nine years, and I've seen some pretty bad things, but when I saw those photographs, I thought back to every life I had taken, and at that moment, every corpse, past and present, seemed to ask the same question: why?"

At his words, she whipped her head around to face him, dumbfounded by all that he'd said.

"Those people were already going to Hell. You were doing the world a favor," she told him, barely able to speak above a whisper.

"Oh, yeah? In 2014, I tracked down a suspected ISIS member in Syria. He'd been all over the videos, pledging allegiance to Jihad, and in one, he'd held up the severed head of a woman. But when asked if he'd killed her, he'd said no. Anyway, I tracked him down, and you know what I saw?" He paused to shudder before continuing.

"Two children: a three-year-old boy and a six-year-old girl, were in the corner of a tent. They shook with fright when I came near them, but I eventually gained their trust.

In the end, I killed him and got the two children back to their home, where they soon died. I'd gotten there too late." He finished lifelessly.

She turned away from him and buried her face in her hands. She was paying no attention to the people in the room behind them, but their muffled voices still reached her ears. "Are you having second thoughts?" she asked, her voice muffled by her skin.

The two sentences that had been written in blood on the hotel's bathroom mirror came back to him, word by word until it was once again stuck in his memory.

Let them go through with their plan. If their plan is thwarted, someone will come after you and whoever is associated with you.

He thought about what the person next to him had said only seconds ago. Then, in quick succession, every man he'd killed: the Jihadist posing as a soldier in Afghanistan, the bomber in Pakistan, the enemy that had gone after him in Paris, all flashed before his eyes. When he was working for the Russians, he'd seen enough bloodshed to make the average person want to quit, but he had learned long ago that he was anything but that.

"Do you enjoy death?" someone had asked him years ago.

"Not any more than the average person." had been his response to the shock of many.

Had he enjoyed killing those people? Of course, he'd be lying to himself if he denied that. But there was a part of him that didn't want to admit that he'd had.

He could feel René's eyes on his back, waiting, he thought, for an answer to her question. "No." he finally whispered, his head bowed.

She had removed her hands from her face and was now looking at him evenly. "Aren't you afraid they'll come after you?" she asked.

"Who?" he questioned.

"The FBI. The police. The six other members who are still going to be out there." Her voice had a frightening edge to it.

He shook his head. "We're all after the same monsters, but it's just a matter of who gets there first. And besides, I've been given specific orders by someone who used to work for the government," he said matter-of-factly.

He looked up at the clock: it was half-past eleven, and there had not been any sound from the room in a while.

He wondered what they were doing. Many rounds would be fired between them, but from years of experience, he knew that it only took one, sometimes two, to kill them. The question was, however, when were they going to get the job done? He had been dormant too long. He was itching to give his trigger finger a workout, and he silently asked himself what the next steps to take were.

At half-past noon, the door finally opened and everyone who had gone in came out. As they filed out, he did a mental headcount: twenty people had come out of the inner door, and he assumed that the rest had been told to stay in the outer office and listen during the meeting's progression. He only looked up when he felt someone tap his shoulder.

"Pascal wants to see you." someone said.

"Why?" he asked.

"Hell, if I know, just come on." the person answered, nudging him again.

He followed the person into the small, cluttered office that he and René had been in one day earlier, but he didn't pay any attention until he heard a throat being cleared.

"Thank you for bringing him." a deep voice said, addressing whoever had brought him.

The person he'd followed grunted in response before leaving the room and closing the door.

"Sit." Pascal boomed.

Maxwell sat in the chair opposite him and listened as he clicked a few computer keys. "What do you want?" he asked at last.

It took a moment before Pascal answered. "I've been looking through your file, and I must say that you have an impressive resume." he began smoothly.

"I try my best," Maxwell muttered.

"However, in saying that, I now know your true intentions." he continued in that buttery voice.

"And what might those be?" Maxwell asked innocently.

"Don't be an ass." Pascal snapped, pouring something into a paper cup. "I won't keep you long," he promised, but Maxwell paid no attention to his words, only his eyes.

"I heard you received a rather unsettling message a few weeks back. You're probably wondering who told me about it." He smiled as he looked into the man's blue eyes that must have shone with his thoughts. "Well, I'm afraid that," Pascal said, flipping an unseen switch, "is highly classified information."

Sunlight now filtered through the windows, but the atmosphere in the tiny room was cold as the two men shot daggers at each other.

"I don't give a damn who told you about the message. I want the whole story of why you killed my boss." Maxwell said.

"You shouldn't be so eager for the truth." Pascal cautioned, reaching for a lighter and a pack of Marlboro cigarettes. "Do you smoke?"

Maxwell shook his head.

"I did not ask you in here to discuss the dead." Pascal barked callously, lighting up and blowing smoke rings at the window.

He was about to ask just why he'd been summoned when Pascal put a finger to his lips.

"I asked you in here to congratulate you," he stated, still puffing on his cigarette.

"On what?" Maxwell asked.

"You've finally caught us after all these years." the Frenchman answered casually.

"Maybe if the FBI had had better resources, they would have figured it out sooner." Maxwell retorted.

Pascal gave one quick laugh and reached for a metal ashtray. "Doesn't one of your friends work for the FBI?" he asked, pouring Brandy into another paper cup.

Maxwell said nothing.

"I know that the FBI and the CIA have been getting a bad rap lately, but you seemed to have handled yourself well." Pascal continued.

"I've had my fair share of scrutiny." Maxwell finally mumbled after a moment's pause.

Pascal discarded the first cigarette, then lit up again and stared pensively out the window for a long time before speaking. "Do you drink, Mr. Maxwell?" he asked.

"On occasion."

Pascal pushed the other cup, filled to the brim with liquor, across the table.

Maxwell sipped from it gratefully. "It's strong," he commented, making Pascal chuckle again.

"Would you like to know how we've managed to avoid trouble with the government for all these years?" he asked, chewing on the end of his second cigarette.

"You went into hiding," Maxwell answered tonelessly, now staring out the opposite window.

The oldest member of the GK smiled grimly to himself.

"Don't be an ass," he repeated under his breath before blowing smoke rings at the window again.

"It's funny," Pascal mused aloud, "there's the FBI, the CIA, and then... there's you."

Maxwell tore his eyes from the window and watched the man's face as he took another sip from the paper cup in front of him.

"The FBI and the CIA like to play games, but you and your organization are different," he said, standing up to open the blinds, allowing the bright sunlight into the otherwise darkened room.

"How so?" Maxwell asked.

"Well, they hired you, and from what I hear, you are one of the toughest out there, and you are also quite perceptive."

"That's why they hired me," Maxwell replied sarcastically.

"That message was meant to be a warning, but imagine my surprise and disappointment when I learned that it had not deterred you at all."

Pascal had finished half of what was in his cup and had lit up for the third time.

"Did you hire that man to find me?" Maxwell asked.

Pascal stayed frozen, focusing only on his cigarette and the blue sky above.

Maxwell stared out the other window and waited for the assassin to thaw out. He thought about asking the man again, but he was sure he already knew the answer. After a few minutes, Pascal slowly pulled the cigarette from between his lips, tapped the end of it into the ashtray, and put the butt into the basket under his desk.

"Ah, so eager. Now I'm beginning to see why they keep you around," he observed, avoiding the question entirely.

Maxwell sighed in frustration, tired of playing games. Pascal was only a few feet from him, and he scolded himself for not having a gun or other weapon at the ready.

The Frenchman was now chewing a piece of Spear Mint gum and staring down at his nicotine-stained fingernails. "The man that came to your hotel and left the message on your mirror was hired by us, but the first was hired by X," he admitted unwillingly, bringing his attention back to the situation.

"How did you know I'd be there?" Maxwell asked, fearful that they were stalking him.

Pascal reached across the table and squeezed his guest's fingers.

"Just because we don't like the government doesn't mean we don't keep tabs on them, Mr. Maxwell."

Pascal quickly let go of his hand and watched as Maxwell got up to leave.

"Thank you for the drink and the chat!" he called over his shoulder as he walked to the door, left, then closed it behind him.

Once he had gone, Pascal sighed and reached for a button on the wall.

"Oui?" a bored voice came over a speaker.

"Round up the others and tell them to get ready. It's time." Pascal answered the voice.

"Oui, patron," the voice replied, and the speaker clicked off.

13

Prep Time

The car sped down the highway, swerving at times to avoid pedestrians crossing the street. The passenger in the back seat began to squirm underneath their restraints, prompting the man next to them to bark out a command.

"Stop moving, or you die. Remember, we're being generous."

The restrained passenger had been told ahead of time to keep their eyes shut and to keep their hands behind their back, no questions asked. They had been on the road for more than an hour and the passenger was beginning to wonder how much longer they would be trapped. The window on the driver's side had been opened, and a cool breeze blew in through it, filling the car with the scent of freshly cut grass. The passenger squirmed again and whimpered. The man sitting beside them gave a loud hiss before hitting them on the side of the head with the butt of their gun.

René woke up then, gasping and shivering in her bed before screwing up the courage to look over at the clock on the bedside table. It was now three o'clock in the afternoon.

She had set her alarm to go off in one hour, but her thoughts were racing too quickly to calm her. The scene in the dream began to fade as her heartbeats slowed and her breathing returned to normal.

Had she been the one in handcuffs? She got out of bed, stretched, and went to splash cold water on her face as she pondered the question. She was on the verge of remembering when a knock sounded at her door.

"Just a minute!" she called and hurried to get it, pausing to look at herself in the mirror. After breakfast, she had changed into a blue shirt dress, which she was now looking for wrinkles in, but there were none.

The youngest of the eight members stood outside and a shiver ran down her spine at the sight of his wrinkled face screwed up into his grotesque version of a smile. He was dressed in purple pajama bottoms and a dress shirt. "Sorry to disturb you, Miss," he apologized, hitching up his shorts, his French accent weaker than the others and his breath smelling of fresh cigarette smoke, "but you are needed in the dining room."

She gave a mumbled thanks and resumed calming herself. At four o'clock, she made her way to the dining room, still pondering the dream and the unanswered question in her mind.

"Nice of you to join us," Pascal called out to her when she entered, giving her an equally hideous version of a smile, all his nicotine-stained teeth on full display.

She smiled back weakly and walked to the empty chair beside Maxwell. They exchanged a glance before facing forward again.

He had told her about his unproductive meeting with Pascal, and she had listened while he ranted. "These dumbasses like to play games." he'd raged after all the breakfast things had been put away, and everyone had been sent to get ready for this impromptu meeting. Finally, he'd said that Pascal had avoided the question entirely, using cigarettes and liquor as a way to stall the conversation and to get on his good side.

Her attention snapped back when she heard the sound of clapping and Pascal's raised voice saying something. "The New York Times had no right to publish that article on its website, and Andrea and Jessica had no right to go after the story!" he shouted, almost stumbling over his words in his fury.

"We have asked you here because from this point on will be known as prep time," he announced, surveying the room for a reaction that pleased him.

Some had their eyebrows raised in confusion, and others stared at him in awe, waiting for an explanation.

"For those of you who have been following us, and I'm assuming from your confused expressions that it's not many of you, this is the time for you to practice your shooting with your dominant arm," he stated, a bit calmer now.

Half the people in the room, including René and Maxwell, had their attention glued to him, as they had found that they were unable to turn away. They were afraid that if they did for even a second, they would miss something.

Someone in the back of the room raised their hand, and Pascal turned to face the person vying for his attention. "When do we begin shooting?" the person asked eagerly.

"Tonight," he answered.

"What are our targets?" the person asked again.

"We haven't decided yet," Pascal said, turning to glare at Maxwell.

He gritted his teeth in frustration and gripped the pen he held in his right hand so tightly that René feared the blood vessels in his hand would break. She hadn't done research on the one she now called a partner before they'd met, but from the little that Welsh had told her, she'd learned that this arm was his best bet for shooting dead as many people as he could in under a minute. She leaned toward him and looked at him a second later: his jaw had relaxed, and so had his grip on the pen.

He was taking notes, she realized when she saw the notebook on the table in front of him. Half the page was now stained with blood-red ink, and the longer her eyes lingered on the words, the more she wondered how much he had written. He had his notebook positioned so that no one, not even her, was able to get a clear look at what he had written.

The sound of clapping once again broke through her concentration, and she looked up to see people smiling and rising from their seats. She looked over at Maxwell, the only other person still sitting, and silently asked what was happening.

"It's over; we don't have to be back until six-thirty." he mouthed back as he closed the notebook, put the cap back on his pen, and put the book in his pocket.

Preparations were being made for the kill. That was what he'd wanted to hear, but the joke was going to be on Pascal and his buddies. They were finally going to be brought to justice, but to his dismay, he'd have to play this part for only a little while longer.

What about René's involvement? Did he feel bad for her? Part of him did, but the part that didn't tell him that it was her fault if she died. He'd told her to leave before things got too dangerous, but she had made it clear that she was in it for the long haul, even if it meant her dying.

Back in his room, he wondered what his legacy would be. What would the news reports say after this was all over?

"Andrew Maxwell, Ernest Dumont's last client, has just killed the Greenridge Killers and is now in the hospital with life-threatening injuries." he imagined one reporter saying.

"Andrew Maxwell, the one who is responsible for the GK'S death, has just been murdered," he imagined another saying.

Would anyone blame him for René's death if things went that way? At five-fifteen, René entered, made her way to the bedside table, and sat on the floor next to its right side. "Did you know that was going to happen?" she asked softly.

"I was just as surprised as you were," he replied, keeping his tone light but inside, he hoped that she wouldn't ask what he was really thinking.

"Are you lying?" she asked.

He shook his head with a bemused expression. She looked around the room and saw that her computer and its case sat on another table in the far opposite corner. "Where's the flash drive?" she asked.

"In the case," he said, pointing to the leather container sitting on top of the small machine.

When he next looked up at the clock, it was five forty-five, telling him that they had spent half an hour not doing much of anything.

"What were you writing in your book?" she asked in a quiet voice.

"What he said, the start time and the end time," Maxwell said wearily.

"What time is that?" she asked quietly. He passed the notebook to her, and she looked it over.

They were supposedly going to be done by ten o'clock, eleven at the latest.

"Why so late?" she wondered.

He told her that he didn't know and didn't care, but in spite of his lack of interest, he wondered what kind of targets they had in mind for their first test session. Maxwell hung his head and sighed.

She was about to ask what was wrong, but she kept silent.

He took a deep breath. She was about to get her wish for danger and bloodshed, and once she got it, he hoped that she would leave. At half-past six, they made their way back to the table they had left. Everyone had already gotten there, and Pascal was at the forefront, putting the loaded weapons into plastic bags while the others talked amongst themselves.

Pascal turned to the assembled members at the table and cleared his throat. He was dressed in sweats, a Polo shirt, tennis shoes, and a backpack was sitting on the table in front of him.

"Synchronize your watches," he instructed before turning back to what he was doing.

Everyone who had brought watches with them did so, then waited for further orders.

Maxwell did another mental headcount as he'd had their first night here. Nothing had changed. No names had been added to the list, and he had not seen any new faces in the past few days. He glanced at the familiar faces around him and took in their expressions.

None of them seemed nervous about being assassins-in-training and this fact, for some reason, frightened him.

If their leaders died, they would have to find new ones to follow, and who would they be? He wondered, when the plan had run its course, how many would be dead and if any of these people would be going down with them.

"We will be out for quite a while, so I've packed some bottles of water in here," Pascal said, patting the top part of the bag.

He had finished his task and had turned his attention to the many faces that were waiting for something to happen.

By seven o'clock, they had exited the main room and were walking down the hall and past Ennette's medium-sized room of an office. Her door was closed, and it was dark inside, but Maxwell looked through the window, trying to see if someone sat behind the desk.

"Where are we going?" someone whispered, but no one said a word in response.

Maxwell looked for the seven other members, but they were nowhere to be found. Without him knowing, they had reached another door with bars on the windows and a sign that read:

Members and Personnel Only. If You Do Not Have A Badge, You
Will Be Denied Entry.

It had been written in all caps, and from the look of it, Maxwell guessed that it had been written in the late 1980s, about the same time this place had been built.

Pascal felt around in his pants pocket and pulled out a white card on a red lanyard. He held it against the door's sensor, and a small beep was heard, indicating that it was now all right to enter. He opened the door and everyone filed in after him.

They had entered a heated room that looked like a prison cell, but René did a double-take when she saw who their "prisoners" were. Dummies that resembled various news reporters from various news stations lined the walls, including one that looked similar to Andrea and one that looked similar to Jessica.

All of them were dressed in white, with the exception of Andrea's lookalike. They had dressed it in a black evening gown that reached to its feet, what hair it had been fixed into a messy bun, and its face had been made-up to look like a Barbie doll. René stared in shock and horror at the plastic figures in front of her while Maxwell took a mental picture, hoping to remember it until he left for home.

"They are filled with red dye," Pascal announced proudly.

Both René and Maxwell could see everyones' mouths watering as they watched their "victims" with undisguised anger and pleasure.

"Who gets the first shot?" someone asked.

"I do," Pascal said, removing the backpack and setting it down on the tiled floor.

He unzipped the backpack and put the bottles of water in a mini-refrigerator by the far wall.

"Watch me," he instructed and unclipped his loaded gun from his belt.

He made sure the safety was off, then turned toward his target: a dummy that looked like an editor from the New York Times and fired two rounds into its chest. Red dye poured out in streaks at its feet as it toppled over. One of the other members came in and flipped the dummy onto its back before covering it with a sheet and dragging it away as if it were an actual corpse. The faces in the room had grown white, and everyone had grown still.

"It's your turn," he said, "everybody come up here."

Everyone came up and Pascal handed them loaded guns from his belt. "The first couple of times, I will count you off, but by the fourth or fifth time, you will be responsible for counting yourselves off," he explained to the assembled mass.

Though he had not asked if anyone understood, some nodded with the sound of safeties being turned off soon following.

"Turn toward your targets," he instructed.

Most of them turned toward the dummy they wanted, but Pascal didn't count them off. "Miss, pick a target," he ordered sternly, looking straight at René.

Reluctantly, she turned to face a dummy that looked like a reporter from the BBC and Pascal began where he'd left off.

The carpet was soon stained with blood-red dye as most of their targets fell to the floor with a soft thud. The seven others came in and quietly dragged them away, determined not to be seen and not to interrupt.

The procedure was repeated two more times before Pascal took his part out of the equation. The second part of the day and part of the night was spent in the heated room, with people periodically taking breaks to drink from the bottles of water.

At eleven o'clock, Pascal followed his trainees back to the second floor. Maxwell smiled and flexed his arms, satisfied to have gotten a workout after all this time. "

Great work," Pascal said once they had gotten back to the place they were now calling home.

The other members, he said, were staying behind to clean the carpets. "Get ready for bed," he commanded, "we'll go again tomorrow."

Back in his room, Maxwell wrote another paragraph on the page that was already covered in ink.

We got out at eleven, just as they'd promised.

My hands are stained with red dye, as well as the carpet in one of the rooms, but perhaps the most shocking part of this was our targets for the night: dummies that resembled reporters from various news organizations. My partner was quite horrified, I'm sure. I got twelve and she got nine. We will go again tomorrow.

He laid his pen down on the page and looked over his work. It was not well-written, but it would have to do for tonight. He left the book open to that page and left the pen inside. He stayed up for an extra half hour, alternating between staring at his reddened hands and thinking.

By ten-thirty, the room had looked like a fight had broken out. Dye had stained the floor and some of it had gotten on the walls and their clothes. Most of the dummies had been dragged away, but the few that had been left standing still had to be set up for the next day's target practice.

When he had finally grown tired, he closed the notebook, got up, and tucked it into the desk drawer where he kept his government-issued revolver.

"Any progress?" Welsh asked on the phone the next morning.

"It's prep work," Maxwell said passively.

"You're shooting people now?" Welsh asked quietly but a little surprised.

"No," answered Maxwell, trying to hold back a laugh, "props filled with red dye."

Neither of them spoke for a long moment before Maxwell broke the silence. "Had a hell of a meeting yesterday," he growled.

"Oh?" the voice on the line said, mildly amused.

"Yeah, Pascal is a piece of shit, but I'll give him this much: he knows how to get what he wants."

"Were you able to get any answers out of him?" Welsh asked.

"Yeah, just not the answers I wanted," Maxwell replied.

"Elaborate," Welsh demanded.

Maxwell glanced over at the clock, decided he had enough time before anyone came looking for him, and relayed the details of his meeting to the eager man waiting on the other end.

"Good God," Welsh exclaimed quietly when he was done.

Maxwell heard movement down the line and the closing of a door. "Do you need me to send help?" Simon asked.

Maxwell thanked him but said that he was fine.

"Actually," he said, thinking of something, "send me Pierre's file, will you?"

Simon said that he would and ended the call.

Fifteen minutes after ending the conversation, he grabbed his laptop from the closet, brought it back to his bed, opened it, waited for it to power up, then went online and typed Pierre Dubois's name into the search engine. Many search results popped up, but he chose the first one: an article from

Wikipedia about the Frenchman. He opened it and silently began to read.

Pierre Maurice Dubois had been born in France in 1945 and had just turned seventy-three in June. He'd graduated from the University of Kent at the age of twenty-five with his Bachelor's in literature, planning to become a journalist and a novelist. He'd worked for the French newspaper Charlie Hebdo for four years before quitting to devote all of his attention to his budding writing career.

For twenty years, he'd enjoyed his successes as the author of the best-selling series about a spy-turned-murderer, growing ever more popular as his vast wealth increased.

By 1994, his net worth had been around $700 million, but nameless journalists noted that he seemed tired and upset whenever they asked him about what was next for his main character. In the third paragraph of the second page was an excerpt from an interview that a CNN reporter had conducted with a US journalist only identified as Niki. "I was working for Entertainment Tonight at the time," she recalled, "I had been assigned to work the red carpet at the screening of his last movie. I had interviewed the stars from the movie, the director, the writers, the producers, the makeup artists, and the trainers when Pierre had come up for his turn."

She had gone on to talk about the interview and the incident that had turned reporters off to him. She had complimented him on his looks, though he had gotten wrinkles around his mouth from years of smoking, and he had been in no mood for compliments. "Just ask your bloody questions." he'd snapped at her, according to Niki.

"What happened after that?" the reporter had asked.

She told him that he had answered the first few questions she'd thrown his way, but the last question was what had made him angry.

"What's next for Brooksbury?" she'd answered when asked what the question had been.

"What happened after that?" the reporter had asked.

According to her, he had told her to repeat the question, and when she had done so, he'd reached out, had gotten in her face, and had told her to go to hell before grabbing the mic, throwing it to the floor, and stepping on it until it had become nothing more than parts and wire.

Pierre Dubois had made the news again but for all the wrong reasons. For the next three years, sales of his books dwindled until hardly anyone was reading them at all. By 1997, he'd made a new name for himself as the spokesperson for the anti-establishment party, spouting off conspiracy theories about this and that, gaining a massive following until the government tried to shut him down.

In April of that same year, he'd met up with someone in the GK, and within a month of their meeting, he had become the newest member of the group. However, the group went into hiding in the early 2000s, during which time Pierre met and fell in love with a woman named Denise. They had married three years after meeting, had a child, and divorced six years later.

He'd married again recently but had divorced her two years after meeting. Though the rest of the group remained inactive, he was arrested multiple times for soliciting prostitution and dealing drugs.

He often kept a journal detailing how the cops had banded together to go after him for no reason and talked vaguely about his plans for vengeance.

I vow to get revenge on those bastards, he'd written but had never actually gone into detail about his plans.

In 2016, after fifteen years of not being active, the fourteen members reconvened to plan the murder of Ernest Dumont, a well-known government boss. According to the GK'S official Twitter account, Ernest "had to die" because he'd threatened to tell the media and the police the other thirteen members' whereabouts. One year later, Pierre had gotten a job with Maxwell's organization and has been working at the headquarters of its European branch in London for over a year." the article concluded.

Maxwell walked to the table, opened the drawer, grabbed the notebook, walked back to the bed, opened the book to the page on which he'd left the pen, and began taking notes from the article on the next page, writing down only the facts. It was seven o'clock when he put the pen down and logged out of the article. Then, before turning the computer off, he went back to his e-mail and checked for any new messages.

The screen told him that he had one unread message. He opened it and saw that it had arrived 20 minutes earlier and that Simon had sent it. Though he was now tired of looking at a screen, he opened it and took a quick look.

The e-mail lacked a subject line, but the content in the message made up for it. He had written that although most of the file had been wiped away, they had managed to save the most important bits.

He clicked on the attachment and looked over it. The file was shorter than the article in length, just two pages long, with only the facts as information and an error message for links to the information that had been erased, but most of this he already knew. He turned to his notes and scanned them, filling in the information he had missed.

Pierre had been arrested for soliciting prostitutes 12 times and he had gotten busted for selling cocaine and heroin twice. In addition, he had attempted to murder an undercover police officer that had posed as a rival gang member to the GK and had been sentenced to ten years of prison, but he had only served three years in Fleury-Mérogis. This had all happened during the group's sixteen-year split.

When he decided he'd had enough information, Maxwell closed Simon's e-mail, signed out, and shut the computer down. He looked over at the clock and saw that it was almost eight-thirty.

Breakfast would begin in an hour. He needed to get some sleep, not because he was exhausted, but because he wanted to be well-rested for their little adventure later tonight. Simon had helped him a lot by sending him that e-mail, and he told himself to reply to him later.

He leaned back on his elbows, closed his eyes and sighed, satisfied with his morning's work but dreading the repeat of the previous night's events that would be happening in just a few short hours.

"How did you manage to get Pierre's file?" René asked an hour later as they ate breakfast at the large kitchen table.

"Simon sent it in an e-mail," he said, stirring milk and cream into his second mug of coffee.

"Why are you starting with him?" she asked, taking a sip of orange juice through a straw.

Maxwell shrugged and sipped from the mug.

"Was it useful?" René said, stabbing a few potatoes with her fork.

He shook a sugar packet into his drink and busied himself with the task of stirring.

"Somewhat," he responded, then went back to his drink.

When he was done, he glanced at his notebook that sat on the empty chair beside him, the pen back inside it on the newly-inked page.

René wanted to ask Maxwell what he'd written, but Pascal had tapped his spoon on his water glass, commanding attention from everyone. Conversations instantly ceased, and the room became quiet, except for the sound of metal utensils on glass plates as people continued eating.

"Tonight is the second night of the prep time period," Pascal announced.

Cheers erupted from the table then died down quickly. "Continue eating," he went on, "firstly, I just wanted to congratulate you on a job well done last night.

But we are not out of the woods yet."

Several people nodded to show they understood.

"Our time here is fleeting, so we will have to make the most of it." the Frenchman said, sipping from the mug of orange juice in front of him before continuing. "As I've already said, from now until the time of execution is known as prep time with the guns and props, but we will also have to meet every day to discuss our plan to make sure that it goes perfectly. So now, I would like to propose a toast," he concluded, "to murder."

He said the last two words in a menacing whisper that sent chills down René's spine.

Glasses clinked together and most of the room cheered again. After the cheers had died down, Pascal set his glass on the table and sat back in his chair. "Continue with what you were doing before," he said, getting up from the table and walking to the door that led to the patio, "we will begin in exactly one hour." He then turned on his heel and headed for the patio to take his first smoke break of the day.

"He seemed sure of himself," René commented once Pascal was out of earshot and the rest of the room had resumed their conversations.

Maxwell shrugged his shoulders again and nodded, already digging into his fried eggs, bacon, toast, and potatoes.

"Did you tell Simon about your meeting with Pascal yesterday?" René asked.

"Told him this morning," said Maxwell.

"This morning?" she asked, half-surprised, half-expectant.

"Yeah, he called around five-thirty," Maxwell answered, taking another sip of coffee.

"What was his reaction?" she asked.

"What you'd expect," said Maxwell, "he said, 'Good God.'

"So he was surprised, then?" asked René.

"I wouldn't say that," Maxwell replied.

Neither of them spoke for a long while as they sat side-by-side and ate.

He could see a familiar-looking woman in a black dress and a handsome man conversing quietly at a nearby table in his peripheral vision. He pursed his lips in concentration, trying hard to make out what she was saying and where he had seen her face before. After a few minutes of hard listening, though, her far-away voice finally reached his ears, but only bits and pieces of their conversation broke through all the noise.

"The man with the notebook," the woman was saying, pointing to Maxwell, "do you know him?"

The man followed the woman's finger and studied Andrew Maxwell's features. He shook his head but continued to stare at Maxwell long after the woman had returned her attention to the food in front of her. Then, after a long moment, the man, whose name escaped Maxwell, faced forward again, and they continued their quiet conversation.

"He knows something." the woman whispered, still talking about Maxwell, though she was no longer staring at the man dressed in the workout gear and sneakers.

"Leave him alone," the man hissed from beside her, "even if he does, it's none of your business what it is."

Maxwell waited patiently for the conversation to change to another topic, but he remained the subject for another five minutes. He retraced his steps, beginning with the first night and ending with the previous one, but he couldn't remember ever doing anything to provoke suspicion.

"What are you looking at?" René asked, bringing him back to the present.

He pointed to the table and stared at them once more.

"Why are you staring at them?" she asked.

He turned back to his plate and stabbed at his potatoes with his fork. "They're suspicious of me," he said this a mouthful of egg and potato.

René pondered this for a moment, then leaned toward him. "You haven't done anything to draw attention to yourself," she said matter-of-factly.

After swallowing, Maxwell turned back to the table where the chatty couple sat and listened carefully for either of them to speak again, but both had gone silent and were now focused on their food.

"The good news is, they haven't figured out why we're here," he said, staring at his partner.

Even though he did not say it out loud, he wondered if Pascal had told anyone the details of their meeting. He glanced over at the table one last time, but the couple had already left the room.

14

Round Three

Maxwell stared at the empty table for another few minutes before silently getting up from his own.

"Where are you going?" René whispered.

He turned his back on her, grabbed his notebook and pen, and pocketed them.

"Where the hell are you going?" she asked, louder this time.

He shushed her and made his way out of the room. He waited until he saw the couple begin to move, then trailed behind them. He followed them to their room and watched as the man opened the door for the woman, who was still talking incessantly.

"I know what I saw." she was saying, but the man had his back to her.

Maxwell kept his distance and listened to the woman as she chattered on to no one. "He had a notebook in front of him, but he wasn't writing in it." was the last thing he heard before the man closed the door angrily on her. He waited for another five minutes before making his move. He knocked twice, then opened the door and entered.

Both the man and the woman were sitting on the couch, but neither of them spoke.

"Excuse me?" Maxwell said politely.

Both people looked up at the sound of his voice and stared at the figure standing in the doorway. "I'm sorry to bother you, but may I sit down?" he continued, that disregarding their surprised expressions.

The man pointed to a table in the middle of the room and he gave his host a polite smile.

"Would you like a drink?" the man asked.

Maxwell shook his head and patted his pocket, signaling he wouldn't be here long. "You are most kind," he remarked, glancing around the room before resting his eyes again on his hosts.

"Why are you here?" the man asked, neither irritated nor glad to see him.

"I have to ask the both of you something," Maxwell stated in a flat voice, reaching into his pocket for the pen and notebook.

"Where's your friend?" the man asked.

Maxwell pointed to the door and said harshly, "Back in the kitchen, I hope."

The woman stared blankly as he produced the pen and the notebook and laid them on the table. "Firstly, what are your names?" he began.

They gave them and he wrote them down. "What is your relation to him?" he questioned, turning toward the woman.

"He's my husband," she answered, trying to meet Maxwell's gaze, but he turned away.

"Is this true?" He directed this question toward the man, who nodded.

"What attracted you to this group?" he asked.

They both answered that a Twitter post had alerted them to this group and their plan, but from what they told him, the post had been vague.

"What did it say?" Maxwell asked, hoping that someone would volunteer their phone to him.

The woman got up and grabbed her phone, which was charging on the table opposite him. Soon, she had her Twitter app open and searched through it until she found the tweet she had been looking for. She held the phone out to him and he read it.

The post was dated March 24th and it had only given the building's address and a vague description of their plan.

Bring anyone you think is ready for revenge! We have been betrayed and now we want payback.

He copied the post word-for-word in his notebook, then dismissed her with a wave of his hand.

"How did you know what they wanted?" he said after confirming that the post had been vague.

Both of them answered at the same time. The news had helped them find out what they had wanted.

Maxwell gave a smile as he wrote the information down. "May I have a glass of water?" he asked, and the man got up to get it from the kitchen.

He thanked the woman's husband when he had returned and downed it in one gulp.

"The tweet was vague, yes. But once we got here, we were pleased to hear that there were people that thought as we did." the woman explained. Her voice was high-pitched, like a little girl's, but it also had an air of seriousness about it.

He thought about asking where they were from, but he decided that it was irrelevant to the situation.

"Did you feel any apprehension about coming here?" he asked instead.

They both shook their heads.

His intense round of questioning lasted for half an hour longer than he anticipated before he excused himself, grabbed his notebook and pen, thanked his hosts and left. "Do you believe me now?" he heard her ask as he closed the door.

He reviewed the notes he had taken back in his room, frowning at some parts and smiling at others. The woman had voluntarily given up everything she knew. Thanks to her, he now understood that she and her husband had dropped everything and moved to New York from their home in Boston with another friend. "Were you all going the same way?" he had asked.

She had nodded as the man had looked on.

"What happened next?" he had asked.

The three had taxied their way to JFK airport and from there, they had gone to the Hilton hotel to stay the night. They had left early the next morning and had ended up at the house at about three o'clock in the afternoon.

Thanks to the multiple reports they had been listening to earlier, they were briefed on the situation. They had agreed wholeheartedly that the Greenridge Killers had been wronged. When he next looked up at the clock, it was four-thirty. Where had the day gone, he wondered? He got up stiffly, walked to the door, opened it and looked out.

René had not come to see him in hours, and he thought she was still in the kitchen. He walked back to the bed and dialed her number. After some minutes, he heard someone knocking. He rose again and walked back to the door. René was standing outside, staring at him through narrowed eyes.

"Where the hell have you been?" she asked, not angrily, just out of worry.

He told her and she gradually relaxed.

"Did you find out anything?" she asked. Then, without a word, he got the notebook and allowed her to read the information in it.

"We'll talk later," she said quickly and turned toward the door.

"What's going on?" he asked.

"Pascal wants everyone in the kitchen," she informed him and waited as he got ready.

When they entered, Pascal and the seven others had not arrived, though everyone else had. The television was on again, but no one seemed to be watching it.

The news was on and they were talking about something having to do with politics. Pascal and the others got there within ten minutes of their arrival. They took seats closest to the TV and watched the reporters closely as they talked.

They were gearing up for the next presidential election. There were many candidates to choose from, but none of them seemed remotely interesting to neither Maxwell or the others in the room. The news finally went to a commercial, and Pascal got up to get himself a snack but came back in time to hear the reporter speak their first words. He ate quickly and got up to throw his trash into the wastebasket. The reporter was now talking about the current president, but no one was listening. Some of the group stared out the windows while others stared at the wall.

All was quiet until someone's watch beeped, signaling the five o'clock hour. The last commercial break before the five o'clock reporter took over ended. Then the words Breaking News flashed across the screen as the reporter began.

15

Anonymous Source

Pascal stared at the television screen and again read the words, Breaking News that had been written at the bottom of it.

"The NYPD is on the lookout for eight people, believed to be part of the French group the Greenridge Killers, who have taken refuge somewhere in the states." the reporter was saying.

"How did they know we were here?" Pascal asked in a confused tone.

"It's all over the news," another member spoke up cheerfully, "it's been running all week, but lucky for us, the NYPD doesn't have a lead yet."

"The NYPD was given a tip by New York Times reporter Jessica Morales, though where they are is not yet known." the faraway voice of the female reporter continued.

René and Maxwell sat on, staring at the television screen. The female reporter was dressed in a brown suit, had her hair trimmed and she spoke with seriousness as if this were an emergency. She was staring at the camera, but her eyes were hidden behind dark glasses. She sat straight, with her shoulders back and her spine stiff, and her hair was a mop on top of her head. "If you know where they are, contact the tip line," she said before giving out the number and pointing to a gorgeous redhead who took over for her with the weather.

At that moment, Pascal got up and snapped the television off before throwing the remote down on its stand. "That damn newspaper. Our being here was supposed to be kept secret from the public, but because of her," he spat, slamming his fist into the TV'S stand, "someone will be calling that tip line in just a matter of days!" He was trying hard to keep calm, but his eyes shone with anger.

The other members hung back, waiting for their turn to speak, glaring at the darkened television screen.

"No one even knows where we are. This place is abandoned and old." someone spoke up, sounding both reassured and unsure of themselves.

"What about him?" the woman from earlier asked, jabbing her index finger in Maxwell's direction and turning to glare at him.

Pascal followed her finger and turned to stare at the man sitting only a few feet away from him. "What about him?" he repeated coolly.

René's heart thumped loudly in her chest, and Maxwell turned hard eyes on the woman who had spoken. The woman thought for a moment then spoke again, choosing her words carefully.

"He knows we're here. He might say something to the public." She glared at Maxwell.

Pascal smiled uneasily and turned to meet the woman's gaze. It was silent for a long moment as both Maxwell and the woman seethed inwardly. Then, without moving his head, Pascal riveted his gaze on Maxwell's cold face. "We can trust you, can't we?" he asked, putting on a forced smile.

Maxwell met Pascal's gaze and nodded stiffly. The Frenchman clapped his hands twice and cleared his throat. Then, he turned back toward the television, grabbed the remote, and stared at the screen, his expression still harboring traces of anger. "Who was that reporter?" he asked.

One of the other members stepped up to take the remote from his companion and set it back on the television's stand before shaking his head to indicate that he was unsure.

"What now?" someone else asked.

Without answering, Pascal walked over to a nearby computer desk, tapped its top with his fingertips, and then turned around to face the person who had asked. "We look up their name and where they work." a sharper, more annoying voice answered the man. All eyes were on him as he switched the computer on and waited as it took its time powering up.

Half an hour later, Maxwell and a few others had their pens poised on notepads, their eyes glued to the assassin's face. Unfortunately, they had been unable to find the woman's name but had found out that she worked at both the New York Post and as a correspondent for Fox news.

Minutes felt like hours as Pascal searched the internet, but he finally found an audio cut from the unnamed reporter from a few weeks back. She had been invited to guest-host a radio program based in Washington. "This is not a regular thing, and I am not your regular host," she was saying, "but let's get this party started, anyway."

She thanked the regular host, someone named Richard, for recommending her to be the fill-in for the day in the next breath. There was a brief pause before she spoke again, choosing her words carefully. "For the past few days, I've been watching and listening to the other side practically destroy their party," she began in a calm tone, but Maxwell imagined the smirk on the host's face as she delivered her opening statement, "last night, as I was getting ready to do the show, I happened to turn toward my television screen and heard the audio that I am about to play for you. It's from a rally in California and it describes them perfectly."

For a second or two, there was nothing but wild applause before a commanding voice spoke up. "The other side does not care what happens to you!" the disembodied voice said before wild applause sounded again. "They lie to you and they steal from you.

They just can't face the fact that WE ARE WINNING!"

Just as the applause was starting up again, the audio ended. The guest host gave a short laugh and began to speak again. Still, Pascal turned the video off, logged out, and stabbed the power button with the index finger of his right hand, his face contorted in anger. "For God's sake!" he roared and wheeled around to face the others. He marched across the room to the television. He turned it on, his face a mask of fury as he watched the reporter from earlier speak to the camera, hoping to appeal to anyone that might have had information on these criminals and their whereabouts.

"If you have any information on where these criminals might be, please call the tip line," she said before giving the number out again.

"They are considered armed and dangerous." she finished before the main reporter called for a commercial break.

Pascal turned the TV off once more and scowled into the dimly lit room. "She was on our side," he muttered before walking toward the room's exit and stopping by the wall.

"If anyone calls that tip line, we're screwed," he whispered, pointing a finger at the people still sitting in the kitchen, "and that is bad for all of you. So you think about that."

That bitch was supposed to be on our side, Pascal thought later that night for the umpteenth time while in his cluttered office. He had spent the better part of the night staring out the floor-to-ceiling windows, smoking, and drinking. He was now on his tenth cigarette and his second cup of Brandy. He had tried to clear his mind, but the news had made him anxious.

Pascal reached into his pocket and pulled out his phone. He turned from the windows, sat down at his desk, put his feet up, and looked down at the screen. A text message from an unknown number appeared and Pascal frowned. "What is it now?" he muttered, reaching for his cup.

He downed the rest of his Brandy in one gulp, then threw the cup into the trash can under his desk. Then, still frowning, he opened the message and smiled at the two words on the screen.

Call me.

He replied: I'm busy.

Please. It's important, came the response a few seconds later.

He groaned quietly and relented. The person who had sent the message picked up on the third ring.

"I'm glad you got my message." the voice said down the line.

It belonged to the woman who had broken the story of their reappearance.

"Don't pretend like we're old friends," he answered coldly.

"I was just doing my job, Mr. Larsen." the reporter responded, sounding more serious now.

Pascal gave a pleased smile at this change of tone. "You're lying through your teeth, you dirty cunt." he barked.

The reporter said nothing for a while, but Pascal knew that he had her.

"What?" she finally asked.

Pascal let out a hard, brittle laugh and gripped the phone more securely in his right hand. "Your only job," he sneered, "was to keep the fact that we had come back a secret."

"No. My only job is to report the news, and that's what I did," she corrected emphatically.

"You're friends with Jessica Morales," he said. It was a statement, almost an accusation.

"How did you know that?" she asked in a clipped tone.

"I'm only assuming that you are," Pascal replied.

Though his tone had lost some of its iciness, it still retained its seriousness.

"You shouldn't just assume things, Mr. Larsen." the reporter said softly but firmly.

Pascal chewed on his lower lip for a moment, his expression unreadable. "I'm sorry." he relented.

The woman muttered a reply too low for him to hear.

"Are we done?" Pascal asked his patience with this girl all but gone.

The reporter said nothing for a long time before she cleared her throat. "Unless you have something else to say." she spat, her voice gone cold and hard again.

Pascal smiled into the darkness. "That will be all," he said, mild warmth now in his own voice.

The reporter hung up hastily before Pascal could say anything else. Minutes passed before he took the phone from his ear and pressed the "end" call" button. He looked down at his watch and saw that it was now eight-thirty. The conversation had lasted for less than an hour and he had been in his darkened office for almost two.

He set his phone down on his desk, got up, and walked toward one of the windows. He pressed his forehead against the glass and closed his eyes. His chat with the reporter had given him a slight headache and he was now irritable. He had no idea how long he'd been standing there when someone knocked twice on his door. "What?" he said sharply.

The youngest member of the eight entered the room quickly and stood by a nearby window.

"Where is everyone else?" Pascal asked before the younger man could speak.

Garrett looked toward the door before answering. "Some of them are talking in the kitchen, some of them have gone down to the first floor to get some coffee, and the rest of them are eating in the dining room."

A momentary silence passed between them before the younger man spoke again. "What have you been doing in here?" he asked.

Pascal told him what had happened and the Garrett listened patiently until he had finished.

"It was not her job to betray us," he said with an air of disgust, "it was her job to keep our whereabouts a secret."

"But she says that it was not her responsibility, that her only responsibility was to report the news." Pascal lamented, folding his arms across his chest and throwing Garrett a somber look.

"The news?" he asked, almost laughing.

Pascal nodded once without smiling or speaking. "What about the Englishman and his girl?" he asked at last.

Garrett walked a few feet forward, found an empty chair, and sat down before a fireplace, but no fire was burning. He chewed on his lower lip and thought for a moment.

"It isn't a hard question, Garrett. Just tell me where the man and his companion are," said Pascal impatiently, cutting his eyes at him.

After five more minutes, he finally told him where Maxwell and René had gone and Pascal instantly relaxed. The older man got up, passed Garrett, and walked to the office's door. He opened it and allowed the fresh air from the hall to enter the cluttered building.

"Have you eaten dinner?" Garrett asked.

Pascal had stuck his head out the door and was now letting the air cool his aching, sweaty head, but he looked back when he heard his companion speak. He shook his head and looked down at his watch again. It was nearly nine o'clock.

"Aren't you hungry?" Garrett pressed.

Pascal nodded once and turned back to his companion.

"I will come back and when I do, I want you gone," he said with an edge to his voice.

An hour later, Pascal returned to his office, tired but satisfied. To his relief, Garrett had left and the room had cooled considerably. Night had fallen, and besides the noises of partying from down below, all was quiet. Perfect, he thought. He quickly scrolled through his contacts and smiled once he found the name he wanted.

"What?" the heavily-accented voice answered.

"Get off your ass, Alexander," Pascal said, his voice gone flat and deadly, "I've got something for you to do."

Alexander Ritzkov listened patiently as Pascal explained what he needed him to do. "My victim lives with you?" he asked when Pascal had finished.

"Yes, you have met her before, if my memory serves me correctly," Pascal responded.

"What is her name?" Alexander asked.

The assassin told him and he gave a quiet laugh.

"Will you come out of retirement just once?" Pascal asked, almost pleading.

Alexander hesitated long enough for Pascal to make his case. "You're the only one who can do it without getting caught, and I know that you will show her no mercy," he said.

Alexander thought for another brief moment, then said, "All right."

"Good." Pascal sighed before hanging up his phone and sitting back in his chair. He hoped that Alexander would come through. He glanced up at the clock one more time before reluctantly getting up from his chair and making his way to the office door.

Tomorrow, he thought as he climbed into his bed, Mr. Maxwell's friend will get what she deserves.

16

The Poisoner's Return

The next night after dinner came the call that Pascal had been waiting for all day: Alexander Ritzkov and another man had arrived at the house to collect their victim.

"What have you told her?" Pascal asked.

"That she was taking a little trip." the hooded man that had come with the former assassin replied.

The Frenchman half-smiled and proceeded to call René into his office. Once the girl had entered, orders were given her way.

"Stay calm." the hooded man instructed, grabbing her left wrist in a vice-like grip.

She squirmed under her captor's grip, but the hooded figure only tightened his hold. Maxwell's partner stayed silent as she was led down to the first floor, then out to a waiting car.

She only looked back once to see Pascal coming up with her luggage, but before she could see anything else, she was seized roughly and shoved into the back of the car.

Alexander got in beside her and waited for the hooded driver as he put her bags in the trunk. "Put your seat belt on," he commanded, and she obeyed silently.

"Close your eyes and put your hands behind your back," he said, and she did so.

Five minutes later, the hooded figure climbed into the front seat and started the engine. "Where to?" he asked.

"Just drive."

The hooded figure nodded and pulled away from the house. René stayed silent for the first part of the trip as Alexander and his hooded companion conversed back and forth in Russian.

"What's going on?" she finally asked.

The hooded figure turned around to face René, who turned to stare at Alexander.

"Keep your eyes on the road, comrade!" he almost shouted before managing to calm himself.

With a sharp nod, he turned his eyes back to the road and tried not to eavesdrop. "I've already told you what's happening." Alexander lied smoothly.

René tried to move her wrists from behind her back, but they did not budge. "Why can't I move my arms?" she asked.

"They've been tied behind your back and keep your eyes closed," he ordered.

She obeyed with a frown. Her wrists were beginning to hurt and she was also tired. "Where's Andrew?" she whispered.

"Back at the house," Alexander replied impatiently.

"When the hell are you going to tell me what's going on?" she asked a few minutes later.

He ignored her and turned toward the rear window. René clenched her hands into fists behind her back and bit her lip against the question she wanted to ask.

"Have you got a destination in mind?" the hooded figure asked.

Alexander shook his head and stared menacingly at the girl. "Can you not keep your eyes closed?" he asked coldly.

She shook her head. Alexander reached into his pocket and pulled out a blindfold. "Open your eyes but do not look at me."

She did as he instructed and he slipped the garment over her head. René slept for a while and it was a relief to escape, but the car speeding down the road soon made her jump. She tried to look around but panicked when she couldn't see anything.

It was midnight when they pulled up to another abandoned building, but this one looked older and more rundown than the last one, and shrubs surrounded it.

"Stop here," Alexander ordered of the hooded figure.

The ignition was switched off, and René could hear nothing but the ringing of her ears in the silence. Then, hurriedly, Alexander opened his door and marched away.

"Get the girl," he told the hooded figure, who simply nodded and got out.

In half a minute, René was being dragged out of the car and down a long drive. Alexander had moved ahead of them to open the door and inform someone that they would be having another house guest for the evening.

"How long will they be staying?" the voice asked. It was deep and soft but somehow still menacing.

By now, René and the hooded figure had reached the door and the girl was swaying on her feet from fatigue. Alexander eyed the person standing beside him and gave a grim smile when he saw them. "Only for a day or two," he replied, beckoning them forward.

René, still being dragged by the hooded figure and still wearing the blindfold, walked forward and cringed as the man or woman looked her over.

"What is on her eyes?" the person asked.

Alexander was the one who answered.

"What is your name?" the person asked, now staring at their new guest.

"René Anderson." the girl answered, now more tired than ever.

"Your age?" the person prompted.

René told them that as well. Twenty minutes of questioning followed before the hooded figure was instructed to drag her upstairs and to the room on the end. Only when she entered the room did the hooded figure untie her hands and take off her blindfold, allowing her to look around the room as he kept his back to her. "I will be back tomorrow," he stated in a flat voice and left.

Once he'd closed the door, she took advantage of the opportunity to look around her room. It was small and cluttered, with one bed, dresser, and mirror on the wall. She leaned back on the bed, which was surprisingly comfortable and closed her eyes again. She wondered if her partner missed her or if he'd even been notified about her absence. She wanted to know who had brought her here and why.

What would Simon say when she didn't answer? Would he be worried? The next time she opened her eyes, it was morning, but something was wrong.

The gown she had been wearing was now over her head, her hands and feet were tied to the foot of the bed, and though her eyes were still under the blindfold, she sensed someone near her. "What time is it?" she asked groggily.

"It's morning." a gruff voice responded. The speaker had a thick Russian accent and their breath smelled of mint. "Did you sleep well?" the person asked, a bit sweeter.

"Yes," she answered, still half-awake.

"Great, because I'm going to need you fully awake now." the voice said again, taking a pill from his pocket and grabbing a cup of water from the bedside table. "Open your mouth." the voice ordered.

She did, and he fed her the pill and the water. She suddenly felt wide-awake, but before she could say anything, he injected her with truth serum in her right arm.

"What are you...", but she didn't get a chance to finish because the person shushed her.

"You work with Andrew Maxwell." the person said flatly. It was not a question.

"I do," she answered. Her speech had become slurred and her eyelids had become heavy, and she couldn't make her mind work.

"You live with Pascal and the others in the abandoned office building." the person stated in that same, cold voice.

"Yes," she answered.

The person smiled, then carried her to a chair by the window and sat her down. The person grabbed a pair of handcuffs from a nearby drawer and cuffed her to the wall before pushing the chair back until her head barely grazed the wood.

"I'll be right back," they promised and walked out of the room.

Once they had gone, René closed her eyes under the blindfold and stretched her legs in front of her. She was concerned about how long she would be in this chair, what this person wanted and if they'd let her go when they got it.

The person came back two minutes later with an object in their hand, their face frozen in that icy smile. "This is a cattle prod," the heavily-accented voice said, "do you know what a cattle prod does?"

"Shocks the cattle to make them move when you poke them with it," she answered, her voice now growing heavy.

The person smiled at her words. "That's right, and I don't want to have to use this on you, so please, participate," they whispered, loud enough for her to hear without straining her ears.

She mumbled a reply and closed her eyes.

"Where were we? Oh, yes. How long have you been living with them?" the person continued.

She answered immediately and they smiled at her with mild warmth this time.

"Good girl," they whispered patronizingly.

"How did you hear about Andrew Maxwell's work?" they asked.

"From his employer," she muttered.

"And who is that?" her interrogator asked.

She told them and they seemed pleased by how quickly this was going, but they understood that all "victims" of theirs participated in the beginning. The day is not over, they told themselves.

They continued this routine for several more hours until her interrogator grew tired.

"We will continue this later. You will sleep here," they explained in a tone that told her that his decision was final.

She frowned slightly but nodded at her interrogator as they left the room and closed the door behind themselves.

Her hands, still handcuffed, had become numb from lack of circulation, and she knew that her wrists had marks on them from the metal. Alexander came back at nine o'clock the next morning and they began again, but they were suddenly interrupted by the room's door flying open and a flustered person entering.

"I've just gotten a call from Pascal." the person said. The voice belonged to Alexander's assistant. Only now that René couldn't see him, he was no longer wearing his hooded sweatshirt.

"You have interrupted us for this," Alexander said sharply, turning to the figure that was now dressed in jeans and a t-shirt, "for God's sake! What is it?"

"It's Andrew Maxwell." the man answered, still out of breath.

"What about him?" Alexander snapped.

"He knows that something is wrong." the other man returned, still panicked.

"How the hell does he know this?" Alexander asked angrily.

"The girl's been gone for over seven hours, but they won't tell him anything, just as you have asked."

The former assassin swore loudly again and turned hostile eyes on the man in front of him. "What kinds of questions has he been asking?" Alexander shouted.

The man, sans hood, looked around the room until his gaze settled on René. "He's only been asking one," he finally answered, "where is she?"

"Get the girl," Alexander said, heading for the door.

The driver reached down, picked her up and held her at arm's length. "Where are we going?" the man asked.

"We're leaving," Alexander answered stiffly, "let her walk."

17

Round Four

"What do you mean you haven't gotten the job done?" Pascal asked. He was again in his office, pacing back and forth and smoking. He was staring over his shoulder at his phone that was charging on his desk with a furious expression.

"My partner interrupted us before we could go any further." the voice down the line answered bitingly.

The phone was on "speaker."

"How was the girl? Did she cooperate?"

"Easily enough, though she tried to fight Gordon as he was trying to carry her on the way to the car," Ritzkov answered, almost laughing.

"Who are you talking to?" another, more slurred voice asked.

It sounded distant and heavy with sleep or like the person had been drugged.

"Shhhhh." Alexander snapped, then to Pascal, "What of the man?"

"He still knows nothing," Pascal assured him.

"I've heard that he's been asking about her." the former assassin retorted in a hard voice.

"A bit, yes." the Frenchman answered.

"What has he been asking?" Ritzkov asked after a long pause.

Pascal told him, confirming what his partner had said before their hasty departure.

"Where are you taking her now?" Pascal asked.

Alexander told him that as of now, there was no destination in sight.

"Has she eaten?" Pascal asked, almost sounding as if he cared.

"Of course she has," Alexander answered over the roar of a car's engine.

Half an hour later, he had emerged from his office and went into the sitting room with the seven other members, conversing quietly in French and watching the news.

"Time is running out." the second oldest member murmured.

"If we are going to enact this plan, we'd better do it quickly," Garrett said.

"Where's the girl?" someone asked in a hard voice.

"She's being taken care of by a dear friend," Pascal answered.

"So The Poisoner has come out of retirement, then?" Garrett asked.

Pascal threw the younger man a hard look, then said, "That's correct."

"Where are they headed now?" another member asked.

He repeated Alexander's explanation to his small audience.

"How long have they been on the road?" the youngest of the eight members asked.

"I didn't ask him that."

"Did you at least ask how long he'd be gone?" the same member asked.

"The conversation was fairly quick," Pascal explained.

The eight members glanced at one another before turning to face the TV. Pascal grabbed the remote from the table in front of them and pressed the "up" button until the room filled with the sounds of laughter and chatter.

When they next looked up, it was ten o'clock and it had grown dark outside. The party left the room as one and exchanged another fleeting glance at the kitchen door.

"The Poisoner has made a comeback," Garrett stated again before he and Pascal proceeded into the kitchen for a drink, leaving the others behind.

"Cheers to new beginnings and old returns," Garrett said after champagne had been poured into both glasses.

"here, here," Pascal said quickly and they clinked their glasses together.

They talked little as they drank, only exchanging pleasantries and neither brought up the subject of Alexander's return again. Some hours later, Pascal was awakened by the high-pitched ringing of his cell phone that still sat on the desk along with the charger. He considered letting it go to voicemail but eventually got up and fumbled in the darkness until he found it. As soon as he answered, Pascal was greeted with the sound of a car horn.

"Sorry to call so late, Larsen," the familiar, gruff voice said on the other end, "but we have made progress."

Pascal said nothing and the person on the other end waited for some sign of interest in their words. The person held on for a few more seconds before commenting, "I thought you'd be interested to know that René is safe." His voice had a mocking edge of concern to it.

Pascal gave a smile of mild pleasure at this news but managed a reply.

"Where is she?" he asked lamely.

"In my office, sleeping. She's had a long day," said Alexander.

"Did she tell you everything?" Pascal asked, making a little effort to put some life into his voice.

His friend nodded.

"What will you do with her now?" Pascal asked.

Alexander thought for a long moment but finally answered that he didn't exactly have a clear plan for her.

"What about Mr. Maxwell?" Alexander asked.

It was Pascal's turn to think, but like Alexander, he came up empty. "Does anybody else know that I have come out of retirement for you?"

Pascal nodded and informed Alexander about who else he had told.

"I am only doing this for you. Normally, I would not get involved in such matters." Alexander reiterated.

"I understand, Alex. Thank you." Pascal answered quietly.

The two men talked for a bit longer before Alexander said he had to go and hung up.

Pascal set his phone down on the desk and walked toward a liquor cabinet, then looked up at the clock. He had left Garrett only a few hours earlier, but his mouth had become dry, and he had again become thirsty. He had just set the empty glass down on the counter when two quick wraps sounded on his office's door.

"Come in," he said wearily, not taking his eyes off the glass.

A few seconds passed before the door opened and a figure dressed in sweatpants and a nightshirt wandered quietly into the darkened room.

"Who's there?" Pascal asked.

The figure fumbled for the light switch and smiled.

"Sorry to disturb you, Pascal, but may I have a word?" a familiar voice asked.

Pascal half-smiled at the person in the doorway and narrowed his eyes in suspicion, guessing at the reason for his arrival.

"Oh, of course, Mr. Maxwell. Please, join me for a drink."

He turned back toward the cabinet, grabbed another empty glass and set it down next to his own. Maxwell silently nodded and seated himself in an armchair by the unlit fireplace. He watched as Pascal poured ice cubes and Brandy into his glass and smiled grimly as the Frenchman approached him.

"Set it down on the table," Maxwell instructed and watched again as the assassin set it in front of him before going back to his empty glass. "You're wondering why I'm here." Maxwell intoned flatly.

"What? No thank you?" Pascal asked, smirking slightly.

Maxwell gave a smile of mock appreciation. "Thank you," he said, and Pascal gave one cold laugh.

"I already know why you're here," he said flatly, now filling his glass with Scotch.

Maxwell reached for his glass and grabbed it with both hands without looking across the room at the killer he would soon have to take down.

"Your partner is still missing." Pascal continued, not waiting for a reply from the man sitting a few feet away.

"She's not my partner." he fired back.

"Whatever," Pascal said, a bit annoyed.

"Just get on with it." his guest mumbled, trying to hold on to what was left of his temper.

Pascal downed his Scotch in two gulps, then reached to refill it. "What a shame." he sympathized, a note of sarcasm in his voice.

"You know where she is, don't you?" Maxwell snapped.

Pascal shook his head quickly, grabbed his glass and walked over to sit beside Maxwell's seat on the floor.

"No, of course not." the assassin replied, reaching out to put a hand on Maxwell's shoulder, which he shook off.

"You're full of shit," Maxwell said, showing anger for the first time.

"I don't know anything," Pascal said, determined to keep up his charming facade.

"I don't believe you," Maxwell said, speaking through clenched teeth.

"Have it your way, Mr. Maxwell," Pascal replied, taking a tiny sip from his second glass of Scotch, "but I'm telling you the truth."

Maxwell saw that the time was half past midnight, but he was determined not to leave until he'd gotten some answers. The two men sat next to each other, drinking silently for a while until Pascal spoke. "If you're done interrogating me, I would like to ask you something now." he declared, glancing over his shoulder at the other man's half-filled glass before turning back to his own.

Maxwell grabbed his glass from the table and shook it so that the ice cubes clinked together and frowned. "What is it?" he sighed, putting the glass up to his lips and taking a long swig of liquor.

"Who told the reporter that we had come back?" Pascal demanded. He watched Maxwell drink and waited until he had set the glass down before continuing. "Well, you must have some insight into this situation."

"Just ask me what you want to know. You're wondering if I'm the one who told her, is that right?" Maxwell asked in a hard voice.

"So observant." Pascal gave that irritatingly charming smile again, and Maxwell's expression became hard and cold.

"Observant isn't the word for it," he finally managed, jabbing a finger at Pascal, "you're just so... transparent."

The assassin laughed once at what was meant to be an insult. "Do you happen to know the girl's name?" he asked.

Maxwell gave this question some thought as he looked from Pascal's thoughtful expression to the windows and back. He had spoken with many reporters over the years but could not remember ever talking to anyone from Fox News, and the only reporter he'd ever talked to from The NY Times was Jessica. "Got no idea," Maxwell answered in an off-hand manner.

Pascal's expression dropped in mock sadness. "Too bad," he muttered into his glass, managing to get a few drops of Scotch into his mouth.

He glanced up at the clock again and sighed. "Oh, dear," he mused after he had swallowed, sounding quite sorrowful, "it's almost one o'clock, and we haven't gotten anywhere."

Maxwell gave an icy smile and tapped his bare left wrist twice. He glared at the fully-stocked liquor cabinet before turning back to the smug face of Pascal Larsen.

"Will you be needing anything else?" his host asked, getting up and heading for the office door.

Maxwell shook his head and tried to get his thoughts in order.

"In that case, my nerves are bad. If you will excuse me, I need a smoke." Pascal said, grabbing a lighter and his pack of Marlboro cigarettes from a nearby table.

"Wait, before you go, there is one more thing I want to know," Maxwell called over his shoulder, making Pascal stop in his tracks.

"Yes?" he asked, turning his head to look at Maxwell's stoic expression.

"Will you be needing your phone?"

This question caught the other man off-guard, but he quickly regained his composure.

"Does your organization need you to hack into it or something?" he asked sarcastically.

Maxwell let out a hard, brittle laugh before explaining, "I could care less about what you do with your spare time, Mr. Larsen. Just let me do my job."

Pascal chuckled. "So uptight," he remarked.

"Your phone, please," Maxwell repeated.

Pascal frowned but tossed the phone to him. It landed with a thud on the floor next to his chair, still with the cord attached. Then, without looking at Maxwell, he left the room, slamming the door behind him.

After a second, Maxwell grabbed his glass, took a small sip of Brandy, set the glass back on the table and grabbed the phone from the floor. Before going any further, he got up from the chair, sat the phone down on the empty seat and grabbed his notebook and pen from the little table by the door. Once he was back at his seat, he put the pen in his mouth and opened the book to a blank page.

It took him a while, but he eventually cracked the code to Pascal's phone and was soon searching it for any evidence. He had thirty-four contacts, which he jotted down in his notebook.

Next up was his phone call log. Maxwell took a deep breath and quickly scrolled through it. All of the numbers that he had called over the past couple of weeks seemed unfamiliar to him, but none of them stood out.

He was about to give up when he noticed a text on the screen. It was only two little words, but it was enough to get his attention. "Call me," he whispered.

The message had been sent the day before, and it looked to him like the beginnings of a conversation.

He opened the messages and began to read, taking notes as he went. When the page had been sufficiently filled, he put the pen inside the book and closed it. He looked up at the clock and grinned with satisfaction at all that he had just done before frowning at the phone's screen a moment later. The clock read that it was now half-past one o'clock.

He guessed that the reporter would be sleeping by now and not in any mood to answer questions, but his job didn't operate on a 24-hour schedule.

Ernest had told him during one training session that the government doesn't rest just because it's midnight.

A moment later, he had the phone up to his ear and was listening for the sound that he was looking for.

"What is it now, Mr. Larsen?" a voice asked.

"Got the wrong person," Maxwell said before she could continue.

"Who am I speaking with, then?" she asked, a bit softer now.

A momentary pause. "I work for the government," he answered, "and I have some questions for you."

It was on the woman's mind to ask who he worked for and why he wanted her, but she thought better of it.

"I already know everything, and I can tell when you're lying, so will you participate?" Maxwell asked.

Down the line, the woman closed her eyes and frowned before eventually agreeing to talk. "Why don't you begin by telling me your name?"

"It's Ashley," she answered.

He had begun writing in his notebook again. "How long were you at Fox News, Ashley?"

She didn't say anything for a long moment.

"Answer the question, please."

"Five years." she finally said.

"Do you still work there currently?" he pressed.

She said that she'd left the network soon after the GK'S reappearance in the States.

"When was this?" Maxwell asked, reaching over for his glass of Brandy and taking another sip.

She had left in 2017 and soon after had begun working for the NY Times.

"Do you keep in contact with anyone that you used to work with?" he asked.

She hesitated for a long moment before speaking in a hushed tone down the line. "I can't talk anymore," she whispered, "can we meet at my office later today?"

This surprised him. He was not used to being asked to meet somewhere by someone halfway through their questioning.

"Will that work for you?" she asked.

He cleared his throat and hurriedly approved her suggestion. He listened as she told him a time that he jotted down in the notebook before bidding her goodbye and hanging up. He glanced up at the clock for the final time: it was now one forty-five. He grabbed his glass off the table and finished it off in two gulps before replacing it on the table and grabbing the notebook from where he had left it.

He thought about staying to thank Pascal for the drink and the fruitless chat, but he soon grew tired of waiting and made his way toward the exit. On the way to his room, he stopped outside of René's door, opened it a crack and stuck his head in. The room was empty of all her belongings, and a corner of her blanket was still draped over one of the four bedposts. He stayed there for only a few minutes more before softly closing the door and continuing on his way.

18

Revelations

"Where to?" the cabbie asked at eleven o'clock the next morning.

"620 Eight Avenue," Maxwell replied, settling himself in the back seat of the car.

He patted his pocket with the notebook in it and sighed, glad to have a moment to himself. The news on the radio was only background noise, but at times, fragments of the report still reached his ears.

"Missing for only a day now, but police have already been called..." he gathered that they were talking about René, but he did not want to listen to any more.

The cab driver waved his hand at Maxwell 20 minutes later and smiled.

"This is your stop," he called and Maxwell reached into his pocket for a $20 bill.

"Thank you," he said after getting out and handing him the money.

The driver watched as his passenger walked away and headed west down the traffic-filled streets of Manhattan toward his destination. To Maxwell's delight, the building was only a few minutes from the drop-off spot. Fifteen minutes later, he was knocking on the door of the NY Times building. He waited for someone to let him in, prepared to call Ashley if it came to that, but he soon heard the sound of someone's heels clicking on linoleum.

"I've got it, Susan." a voice said before continuing to the door.

He was soon greeted by a woman wearing a businesslike expression. "Got an appointment?" she asked, flinging her red hair out of her face.

"I'm here to see Ashley," Maxwell told the woman.

"Come with me," she said and he followed her to a long counter.

"Your ID please," she asked.

He produced the card from his pocket and slid it across to her.

She looked it over for a few seconds before handing it back to him and watched as he pocketed it. "She doesn't get here for another hour, but you're welcome to wait," she said, extending her hand and grabbing his elbow.

Looking at her up close, he could see that she was pregnant and already beginning to show. She was dressed in black and wore minimal makeup, but in contrast to her businesslike expression, she seemed friendly. "Are you hungry?" she asked, leading him to the elevator.

Maxwell shook his head and continued to follow the pregnant woman. According to the woman, they had reached the elevator less than a minute later and were riding up to the 3rd floor where Ashley's office was, who still had not told him her name.

"Are you Susan?" he asked on the way up.

She shook her head, trying not to laugh. "No, I'm Heather. Susan works with me," she answered and smiled warmly at Maxwell.

Once on the 3rd floor, he was led to a door on the far right and told to wait outside, as the door was locked. "You are welcome to sit on the couch directly behind you or on the floor," she said before asking one more time if he was fine and heading back to the elevator.

Maxwell watched her leave. The couch that he had chosen to sit and wait on was small but comfortable. The hall that Maxwell had been placed in was quiet and gave him a good view of the cubicles opposite him. Every cubicle but one had a person working at it, and he guessed that the empty one belonged to Ashley. He read what he could see of the name tag on the empty cubicle's table and saw that it belonged to an Ashley Cooper.

He gave a slight smile and turned back toward the wall beside the closed door. Framed pictures of a little girl with her parents lined the walls on either side. On the door, itself hung a sign with the words said: Patience is a virtue in red ink alongside a picture of a cartoon owl with its wings folded. When he grew tired, he leaned back, crossed his arms over his chest and closed his eyes. He was woken up five minutes later, or so it seemed, by someone unlocking the door in front of him and muttering under their breath.

He sat up and rubbed his eyes with the backs of his hands and yawned.

"Are you the guy from the phone?" a feminine voice asked.

He nodded and slowly opened his eyes to look at the woman in front of him. She was also dressed in black but unlike Heather, she wore jeans, a t-shirt and some high tops.

She wore no makeup and her sandy brown hair was in a bun at the back of her head.

"You're Ashley Cooper," he said, holding back another yawn.

The woman nodded, keeping her back to him as she continued to fumble with the lock. When she had finally opened the door to her office, Maxwell silently followed her in and to a long table.

"Are you hungry?" she asked, putting a bag down on the table, and Maxwell wondered if that had been the reason for her tardiness. The scent of burgers and fries emanated from the bag and as tempting as the food was, Maxwell shook his head. After getting a Sprite from the fridge, she made her way back to the table, sat down on the wooden bench beside him, unwrapped her burger and began to eat.

"Is that little girl in the pictures on your wall you?" he asked in a conversational tone.

"Yeah," she said after swallowing a mouthful of burger.

"Are those your parents?" he asked.

She nodded and wiped her hands and face with a paper towel.

"Thank you for agreeing to meet me," she said, gathering up her trash. She had finished the burger in two bites and the fries, he assumed, had been finished in the car.

"Not something I'm used to, but..." His voice trailed off and he produced the notebook and pen from his pocket. "How does this work?" Ashley asked, coming back to sit beside him.

Maxwell fixed Ashley with a confused gaze.

"Do I get to ask you any questions or are you the only one that gets to?" she clarified.

"By all means, ask me whatever you want," Maxwell said coolly, setting the notebook on the table and opening it to the page from the night before.

"Now, I believe the last question I asked you was if you kept in contact with anyone you worked with at Fox," said Maxwell, his pen poised to begin.

"Just the ones that left after me." he scrib4 as she spoke.

"How many left after you?" Maxwell asked, reading the next question from his list.

There was a beat of silence as Ashley thought. "Seven." she finally answered.

"What are their names?" he asked and listened as Ashley listed them. "What was your reason for leaving?" he asked.

It only took half a second to answer this one, and he was pleased with the rate this was going. He questioned her for fifteen more minutes before he finally got up from the bench.

"Do you have a ride?" she asked as he got up to leave.

"I'll hail a cab," he said, closing the book and grabbing it from the table. "One more thing," he said as he headed for the door, "who told you about Pascal's return to the States?"

Ashley had half-risen off the bench, but she now lowered herself back onto it. The room fell silent, but Maxwell didn't need words to know the answer to his question.

"Why did you keep it a secret?" he asked, turning his penetrating gaze on her reddened face. "I... I..." she stammered, flushed with embarrassment and shame.

"Who told you about their reappearance?" he repeated in a hard voice.

"He did." she finally whispered.

He came close beside her and sat down on the floor next to her side of the bench.

"Who?" Maxwell asked, narrowing his eyes in suspicion.

"Mr. Larsen," she mumbled, keeping her gaze on the floor.

Maxwell kept his expression blank as he continued. "How much did he pay you to keep quiet?" he asked. He had opened his book again and was now scribbling in it.

"He paid me nothing. It was just supposed to be a favor for an old friend," she said, panicking inwardly.

"Where did you two meet?" Maxwell asked, getting on his knees and setting the book and pen down on the floor.

"In Paris," she answered, her voice barely above a whisper.

Maxwell leaned toward her and rested his chin on the bench. "Why were you in Paris?" he asked.

Ashley turned away from Maxwell's penetrating gaze, but their eyes met wherever her eyes moved.

"To do a story," she answered reluctantly.

"How long ago was this?" he asked.

She rose from the bench and walked toward the wall beside her desk, ignoring the warning look that Maxwell gave her as she went. Maxwell continued to stare as the woman ignored the wall in front of her and went instead to the Landline phone that was surrounded by papers on her desk.

She picked it up from its cradle with one hand and carefully dialed a number with the other, avoiding the livid expression that was clearly meant for her. "How may I help you?" a raspy voice asked in her ear.

"Yes, I need security sent up to the 3rd floor, please." he heard her say and threw her another hard look.

"What room?" the disembodied voice, sounding weary now, asked.

"Room..."

She felt someone grab her ruthlessly by the hair and pull her until both the phone and its cradle fell to the floor before she could finish.

"Hello?" the person on the other end called. The phone was on "speaker" now. "Ma'am? Are you there?" the voice asked urgently.

"She'll have to call you back," Maxwell said, letting go of her and going for the phone.

"What the hell are you doing?" Ashley demanded after Maxwell had hung up and set the phone back on the table.

He didn't answer but simply pointed to where she'd been standing only a moment ago. They glowered at each other for a long moment, neither of them speaking. "You agreed to tell me everything." he finally said.

"Why? So you can report me and I can lose my job?" she shot back.

"You certainly weren't worried about that when it came to keeping a secret for your dear friend, were you?" he asked, reaching into his other pocket and wrapping his hand around the revolver. He hoped he wouldn't have to use it on her, but he knew people sometimes became combative when questioned.

"Look, I don't know who you are, but..."

"My name isn't important," he said, cutting her off.

"But please, leave my office and this building before I call security again." she went on.

They were standing only a few feet apart, both of them glaring at the other.

"Not until I've had every question answered," he said defiantly, taking two steps toward the lady in black.

"I've answered enough of your questions." she snapped just as defiantly, walking back toward the phone and picking it up again, but a metal object digging into the back of her head made her jump and slammed the receiver back down into its cradle. She spun on her heel and confronted Maxwell, now holding the revolver in his right hand. "You lunatic." she choked, looking away from the menacing expression on her guest's face.

Maxwell's mouth twitched slightly, but he said nothing. She took two steps back but was immediately met with the butt of Maxwell's revolver again. Do whatever it takes to keep them talking had been Ernest's other motto, and now was one of the few times that he was glad that he had taken that advice to heart.

"I don't want to shoot you," he said, lowering the gun from her forehead and backing up a few paces.

Ashley shook her head in disbelief.

"But I will if I have to." Maxwell continued.

"How do I know that you're even from the government? How the hell did you even get in here?" she asked, fury now in her voice.

"I was asked, by you, to come here to continue my questioning," he said, trying to stay calm.

"Yes, but that was before I knew what you were bringing to the table."

"If you didn't want me to ask about it, then why did you keep it a secret from the public? Why didn't you just report that they had come back here?" He was fuming now.

"Because he said that if I did, I'd be out of a job," she admitted with a sigh.

"How long ago was this?" Maxwell repeated, rubbing his temple.

"Last year," said Ashley, looking at the phone again.

She hoped that he wouldn't go for the gun again, but she knew that if he made up his mind to do so, she was prepared to call for backup to deal with him.

"So am I correct to assume that you had only been away from Fox for two years by this time?" He had begun writing in the notebook again.

She nodded, still exasperated.

"That will be all," he concluded, gathering the notebook, pen and gun.

Ashley smiled with relief and walked him to the door. "Thanks to you, I've wasted half a day's work."

After pocketing the pen, book, and gun, he reached out to shake her hand. She returned the handshake, then let it go to hurriedly open the door to let him out.

When his taxi pulled away from the curb nearly half an hour later, he welcomed the cool air that radiated from the car's air conditioner. Though he hadn't realized it, the front of his shirt had become soaked with sweat. Due to traffic, the ride back to the house was long, but it gave him time to regroup.

His head aked and his palms were slick with sweat from the revolver. He had had no intention of threatening Ashley with it, but it had been his last resort and it had worked.

She had calmed down enough to give him the answers he had needed, making his job, and maybe even hers, much easier.

"Your stop." the cab driver called in a low voice 20 minutes later as he pulled into the dilapidated garage.

Just like before, after Maxwell paid, the cab driver watched as his passenger left before driving away.

Ennette met him at her office's door as he passed by it. "So sorry to hear about your friend," she murmured, taking both his hands into her own.

Maxwell closed his eyes and sighed.

"Thank you," he said after a momentary silence.

They stood there for a time before Maxwell gently pulled his hands free of hers.

"Did you have a nice meetin'?" she asked in her thick Irish accent.

He nodded and turned to leave but suddenly turned back to face her with curious eyes.

"Ennette?" he called, staring after her as she began to walk away.

"Aye?" she said, taking the few steps she had taken back to him.

"How do you know that I was going to be having a meeting today?" he asked.

"I heard you talking to the cab driver," she answered innocently.

"You were listening?" he asked in a hard voice. He saw her eyes dart to the right and left with nervousness.

"No," she said with a chuckle, "I heard you as you passed by my office door."

She pointed to the door of her office and gave a tiny smile.

"Where are the others?" he asked.

"In the room," she said, pointing behind her to another door.

He thanked her and turned around to join them.

Maxwell was not surprised to find that there was little movement in the big room when he entered. Everyone was seated around the dining room table, watching TV and taking notes, their lips moving rapidly. He wanted to ask someone how long they had been at this but thought better of it and sat down. "Pens down." someone instructed when the program they had been watching switched to a commercial break and the TV had been turned off.

"I have something to tell you." the voice added when all movement had ceased. "In a few weeks, our plan will have to be enacted." The speaker stopped to quickly survey the surprised faces around him. "Phase one has already been completed, but it will be your turn to help soon."

The speaker sighed and Maxwell clenched his hands into fists at his sides.

He was beginning to realize that René's disappearance was phase one, and this fact only made him worry about her safety even more.

"What do you want us to do?" someone, a woman he presumed, asked.

"Kill the enemy." the main speaker answered.

"How will we prepare?" the same woman asked a second later.

The speaker and his companions laughed, but the sound abruptly stopped.

"We sit and watch them make fools of themselves," he said, "but do not worry, my children, we will soon come out of the woodwork and exact our revenge."

The TV was again switched on and everyone, Maxwell included this time, began taking notes. His irritation with the lying murderers in front of him aside, he wanted to know how many phases there were to this plan and what their endgame was going to be. Many scenarios ran through his mind, but the one that made the most sense to him was the one that seemed the most pleasing to them: the one in which he and René were dead.

"We have to stop these people." the male reporter's voice cut into his morbid reverie. His eyes snapped to the television screen.

The reporter and a woman were sitting across from each other, deep in a conversation. "I do not disagree with you. I'm just saying that the only way to take these people down is to let them do it themselves." the woman said in an even tone.

The reporter gave his guest a %slight smile. "One last question," the man said over the music that signaled a commercial break, "do you think they're doing a good job of it already?"

With a smile, the woman nodded. The man let out a laugh, thanked the woman for coming, and teased the next segment.

Maxwell turned his stony expression toward the window and looked out at the streets that were, as usual, busy. Some smoked as they walked, while others held cell phones to their ears.

"Do you know what's happened to her?" Welsh asked later that evening on the phone.

Maxwell leaned back on his bed and rested on his elbows on the pillow. "They've been very tight-lipped about her situation," he said.

He had been on the verge of sleep when he got the call from his boss.

"What exactly have they told you about her disappearance?" asked Welsh.

"Nothing," said Maxwell.

"Well, I have some news that you might be interested in."

Maxwell heard the sound of Simon's fingers tapping on computer keys. "What's that?" he asked wearily.

"It seems that Alexander has come out of retirement."

"Why is that news to me?" Maxwell asked.

"We don't have all the facts yet, but an eyewitness told the police that a girl was seen tied up in the back of a speeding car," Welsh answered.

"So?" Maxwell asked.

"Put the facts together, mate," Welsh said.

Maxwell's boss stayed on the line as his client and friend mentally put the pieces together.

"Did the eyewitness see his face?" Maxwell asked after a short time.

The sound of tapping was heard again. "The report doesn't say." Welsh sighed.

"Have you figured it out yet?" he asked anxiously.

"Did they see a driver?" Maxwell asked.

Simon clicked a few more keys and read. "The witness did not recall that, either, but they may have gotten a glimpse of a brown hood," he concluded.

Maxwell considered this for a moment, then gasped. "You don't think..." he finally said but broke off mid-sentence.

"My colleagues at the CIA have checked and double-checked this information, and it seems accurate," Welsh answered softly.

"When was this report published?"

Simon scrolled to the top of the screen. "Nearly 20 hours ago," he answered at last.

Maxwell ground his teeth and clenched the phone in his right hand. He suddenly wanted to wring Pascal's neck. "Does the report give any information about her current whereabouts?"

Simon acknowledged his question with a low grunt but otherwise stayed silent.

"How is everything going? Making any progress?" Simon asked a moment later.

Maxwell sighed and quickly told his boss the unfortunate news.

Simon clicked his tongue twice down the line and exhaled deeply.

"Call me if there's more news, will you?" Maxwell asked ten minutes later. Simon said that he would and hung up. Half a minute passed before Maxwell's phone buzzed.

Be careful, the message said.

He smiled at the screen and quickly typed a reply before tucking the phone under his pillow and settling in for the night.

Pascal stared at the arsenal of weapons he kept on the wall by the dresser in his room, then turned back to the mirror. "Just a few more weeks and we shall be reunited," he whispered.

He smiled at the reflection that stared back at him in the mirror. In just a few short weeks, he and his friends would be back in the news, and this time, they would emerge victorious.

19

Bombshell

"Remove her gag," Alexander instructed.

The other man nodded and removed the piece of cloth from the girl's mouth. René's screams had ceased long ago. "Where am I?" she croaked, her voice now gone hoarse.

Alexander turned toward his captive and glared down at the body lying on the couch. "I've brought you to my office, I told you," he answered coldly.

"Where's Andrew?" she asked.

Alexander stared at the pale face that stared weakly back at him. "Your partner is... away," he replied.

"I... I have to tell him where I am," she said, reaching forward with her left hand, but her torturer seized it and roughly pulled it back.

"Your phone is gone," Alexander answered.

"Where is it?" René croaked again.

"My partner has taken care of it." The former assassin pointed to the hooded figure standing by his side.

René turned her head to the right and looked at the man that stood in front of her in disbelief. Broken pieces of her phone lay at his feet and a match sat next to them. "Has he burned them?" she asked softly.

"No. He was gracious enough to wait until you became more... coherent to do the job."

René stared up at the stern face that hovered above her with as much outrage as she could muster.

"When did he break my phone?" she asked, moving her eyes back to the broken object on the ground.

"After the gag was put into your mouth." the other man answered. It was the first time he'd spoken to her since their arrival.

"How long have we been here?" René asked.

It took Alexander a moment to answer, but he seemed reluctant and frustrated when he finally did. They had arrived at the three-story building fourteen hours earlier, but they had only been in the small room of an office for twelve.

"Why did you gag me?" she asked.

Alexander frowned slightly, but the other man maintained a stoic expression. "You wouldn't stop screaming," he said.

"Why was I screaming?" she asked.

Alexander pointed to a small object lying on a table nearby. The cattle prod lay on the edge of the table, and René gasped at the sight of it. "You used that on me," she stated dully.

Her torturer nodded and smiled coldly at the pale face that was now turned away from him.

"Because I wouldn't answer your question about Andrew," she remembered.

"Correct again," Alexander whispered, going for a glass from the cupboard.

Even with her cheek pressed against the cushions of the couch that had been her bed for the last few hours, she still heard the gurgling sound of liquid being poured from a bottle.

"I told you, I don't know anything beyond what I've already said," René explained, her speech muffled by the couch cushion.

"Liar." Ritzkov spat.

René sighed.

"Why was Mr. Maxwell picked to go after my former group?"

René didn't answer.

Alexander sighed and a moment later, the little room was filled with the sounds of René's cries. "Will you answer my questions now?" Ritzkov asked menacingly, leaning toward his victim.

The girl nodded weakly and her torturer smiled, mollified now.

"Good girl," he said softly, "forgive me. You must be thirsty."

René nodded and listened as liquid and ice cubes were poured into another glass. Alexander handed the glass to the other man and the girl watched as he approached her. "Sit up." the sharp voice commanded. She did what she was told.

"Careful not to choke her. We need to keep her talking."

The man nodded and held the glass out to her. "Drink," he instructed, inching toward her until the tip of a straw touched her lips.

She had taken several pulls from the straw when the cup was suddenly yanked away and she was left gulping at air.

"You have had enough," Alexander said sharply.

She gave a muttered thanks and watched as the two men went their separate ways.

Moments later, Alexander was back at the cupboard and the other man was kneeling beside the broken pieces of her phone. The man on the floor lit the match and smiled coldly up at René's pale face. He showed no interest in the task at hand, but he knew that it was a crucial part of his boss's plan.

His smile faded as he lowered the flame to the broken pieces of plastic, wires, and glass. René watched helplessly as it burned. She hoped that she would be able to explain the reasons for not returning Maxwell's text messages and phone calls when and if he ever saved her.

"Now," Alexander said, bringing her back, "what is your friend's reason for going after the others?"

"They killed his boss two years earlier," she said, feeling as though she had just betrayed a best friend.

"That bitch betrayed me." she heard his voice say in her ears.

"I think I remember hearing something about that." Alexander smiled.

"You did?" René couldn't hide her surprise.

"Yeah, he was knifed," Alexander answered casually as if they were having a conversation.

Spare me the details, René thought.

"Can't say I'm sorry." Alexander continued.

She wanted to ask how he could be so cold-hearted, but she realized that you had to keep your emotions in check to be a stone-cold killer. "You knew him?" she asked instead.

He nodded once stiffly. "He and his friends in London conspired to have my Olga killed," he explained, taking a swig from his glass.

"Your Olga?" she asked, confused.

"She was my dear friend as well as my partner in crime," he revealed.

"Isn't he your partner now?" she asked, jerking her chin at the man who was still on the floor.

"Nyet, Gordon is only my assistant."

The man on the floor looked up and nodded in agreement.

"You have a grudge against Andrew," she stated.

Alexander nodded.

"He used to work for Ernest," he said sourly.

"He also used to work for Olga." René offered.

"Correct, but we have a right to be angry at your precious partner for what he did." Ritzkov took another drink.

She was not about to argue with the likes of him, but she thought it stupid to hold a grudge against someone who didn't work with you anymore.

The room lapsed into silence for a beat before the sound of a phone ringing filled the quiet.

"If you will excuse me." Ritzkov apologized, walking to a table and picking up the phone. "Hello?" he said into the receiver.

"Where the hell have you been?" René heard faintly from the other end.

"Here. Why?"

"Because I've been trying to call you for two hours, that's why! We have a problem." Pascal snapped.

"What is it, comrade?" Alexander asked.

"Have you checked the news lately?" came the answering question.

"No," Alexander replied, "what's the top story?"

"The top story is that a girl has gone missing." he hissed.

Alexander glanced over at René and narrowed his eyes. "Have the police been called?" he whispered.

"Yes, an eyewitness called them late last night," Pascal answered through clenched teeth.

"How do they know it's René?" he asked.

"Because her name's been printed, you idiot!" Pascal was shouting now.

"Does Mr. Maxwell know about any of this?" Alexander said.

René's ears perked up, and she prayed that he did.

"I would imagine so." He had calmed down a bit, but he still sounded angry from where René sat.

"Has he asked anything?" Alexander asked, still whispering, forgetting that both René and Gordon were in earshot.

Pascal muttered something down the line, making Alexander frown and groan quietly.

"Have you heard of a woman named Ashley Cooper?" Pascal asked.

Alexander thought for a moment, then shook his head and answered that he hadn't.

"She's a reporter for some news network, and she was alerted to the news of our reappearance in the States." Ritzkov's eyebrows shot up at this announcement.

"Who told her?" he asked in a hard voice.

"I did, but that's beside the point," the disembodied voice replied hastily, "we trusted her with a secret and she betrayed us by revealing it to the world."

"What did she say when you questioned her about it?" Alexander asked.

He listened as his former partner briefly described their phone conversation. Alexander took the phone from his ear and glared at the other two people in the room. "Oh, no," he whispered before putting the phone back to his ear.

"Thank you for the information," he said and hung up.

"What's wrong?" Gordon asked, noticing the expression on his boss's face. Alexander pointed at René, then at the phone that was still in his hand.

"They know, don't they?" Gordon guessed.

Alexander nodded and buried his face in his hands.

"How long do we have?" Gordon asked.

Alexander stayed silent for a few more seconds, then turned to face René, who now had her back to both men.

"I will not apologize for burning your electronic device. However, I will say that there was no need for it," he told her.

"Why?" she said, stunned.

"Your partner already knows that you have gone missing," Alexander explained tonelessly.

She smiled, but it quickly faded. "Does he..." she started, but he silenced her with a glower.

"He does not know where you are or who took you. All he knows is what's in the news," he said, still glowering at the girl lying on the couch.

"What's in the news?" she heard herself ask, though she didn't care.

"An eyewitness told police that they saw a car speeding down the road with a girl tied up in the back seat." he sighed and walked back to the cupboard.

"How long are we staying here?" Gordon whispered when his boss had come back to his side.

The older man shook his head and sighed again. "Watch her. I'm going to get some sleep," he finally said and left the room.

"Did you know about this?" René asked once Alexander had turned the corner.

Gordon ignored her question and turned toward the windows. "Get up, girl," he said sharply. But before she could manage to do it, he grabbed her wrists and marched her toward his boss's office.

"I'm very sorry, Sir, but I think we should go now."

"Put her in the car." alexander agreed without looking her way.

Gordon nodded and grabbed her left wrist.

"Wait," Alexander said, getting up and going for a syringe.

In half a minute, René felt herself being lifted off the ground.

"Stay still, girl." a voice said as the needle went into her arm.

When she next awoke, it was to the sound of somebody yelling and a car speeding.

"How many cars are following us?" Alexander was saying.

Gordon looked out the driver-side window and frowned. "There's only one car." he finally answered.

Alexander muttered something under his breath and turned to stare out the passenger window. Damn, he thought and turned back to the man that was once again wearing the hooded sweatshirt.

René was drowsy but not unaware. Her hands were again behind her back, but unlike before, she had limited range of her arms.

"Where am I?" she asked, her speech slurred and her throat heavy.

Both men swore softly this time, but it was Gordon who answered. "We're on the road again," he said in a hard voice.

"Why? What's going on?" she asked.

"We can't risk the cops seeing us," he answered.

The tires spun on the road and Gordon honked the horn as the car sped toward them before going forward. "Dammit," he whispered under his breath but otherwise kept going.

"Are they coming after us?" René asked, concerned now.

"I didn't see any flashing lights," Gordon said, keeping his eyes on the road.

"Pascal just texted." Ritzkov piped up suddenly.

"What did he say?" Gordon asked.

Alexander didn't answer. The car lapsed into silence, with only the motor and the heater humming. René wanted to know how long they'd been on the road and how long she'd been out.

Alexander's phone buzzed again half an hour later and he looked down at the message that had come through. He quickly typed a reply and smiled. "Speed up," he announced gravely.

"Who's following us?" Alexander asked an hour later.

"I don't know, but it's an unmarked car," Gordon said, his eyes still on the road ahead of them.

"It's probably a detective." René offered.

Alexander threw her a look as the car sped forward, but it took less than a minute for the car to catch up to them.

"Oh, hell," Gordon muttered, picking up speed.

The unmarked car had slowed down a bit and was now a few cars behind them.

"Can we stop for a bite to eat?" René asked softly.

Alexander looked from her to the man in the front seat and for a moment, she feared that she had asked the wrong question.

"All right." Gordon agreed and pulled into a nearby Burger King parking lot.

"We can go in since the news hasn't broken the story of runaway fugitives yet." Alexander chuckled as all three undid their seat belts.

"What time is it?" Alexander asked a few minutes later as all three sat at a table in the half-empty eatery.

"Five minutes to midnight," Gordon said, looking around at the few tables that were occupied.

No one looked like a detective or an off-duty cop, and no one appeared to be listening to their conversation. "How long do you think it will take for the news to get wind of this?" Gordon asked as their food arrived.

"I hope it takes a long time," Alexander replied, digging into his burger.

As René ate, she wondered where Andrew was and if he was worried about her. She resented the man sitting across from her for burning her phone, but she suddenly understood their paranoia.

As the three of them prepared to leave fifteen minutes later, Ritzkov felt his cell phone vibrate in his pocket. He pushed his chair back, muttered an apology and answered the call immediately. "What's wrong?" he asked urgently. He listened as the voice on the other end answered and let out a gasp. "Dammit," he said loudly, forgetting the other diners in earshot, "what time did he leave?"

20

Hot Pursuit

The cab driver threw his passenger an exasperated look and sighed. "It's almost midnight, I'm tired and some idiot wants me to drive him somewhere. Are you him?" the short, stocky man asked in an irritated voice.

Maxwell nodded and made his way to the back of the car.

"Where to?" the driver asked after he had gotten in, clearly not in the mood for introductions.

Maxwell didn't answer, only buckled his seat belt and pulled his phone from his pocket. "Where to?" the driver repeated.

"Hold on for a second, will you?" Maxwell asked with a hint of impatience.

The cab driver tapped his thick fingers on the steering wheel as Maxwell pressed his phone to his ear, visibly distressed as he waited for whoever he was calling to answer. "Dammit." he groaned a minute later when the call had gone to voicemail. He eyed the driver slowing at him in his rear-view mirror but pretended not to notice as he dialed another number.

"Yeah?" the voice answered on the third ring, filling Maxwell with relief.

"Thank God you've picked up, Simon. Listen, have you seen René? I've just tried to..." The retired government agent cut him off mid-sentence with a groan. "What's wrong?" Maxwell asked.

"I was hoping to have more details for you before the next time we spoke, but she and the others have disappeared," he said apologetically.

"Who's with her?"

Simon told him and he pressed his lips together in a thin line. The driver glared at Maxwell again and he pretended not to notice as he continued his conversation with Simon.

"Where are you now?" he asked after a minute.

"In a taxi," Maxwell answered, finally meeting the driver's stony gaze.

Simon told him to hold on and switched to the other line. He was back in two minutes and now spoke with urgency. "I've just talked to a colleague of mine from the

CIA, and he's reminded me of a tracker that had been put on Alexander's car sometime earlier," Welsh said.

Maxwell looked up in surprise.

"What happened to it?" Maxwell asked.

"It was deactivated some years ago," Welsh answered.

"Why?"

The answer Welsh gave put a small smile on Maxwell's lips, which was quickly replaced with a look of seriousness. "Activate it again," he ordered.

"Already done," Welsh answered.

"Thank you, Simon," Maxwell spoke softly now, "can I keep you on the line?"

Welsh agreed and the cab driver looked relieved at now having someplace to take him, even if he had no idea of their final destination.

Maxwell had put Welsh on "speaker" and had turned the volume down to keep the driver from hearing too much. "Look out your window," Welsh instructed.

"Why?"

"The car should be in front of you," Welsh said.

It took a moment for Maxwell's eyes to adjust to the darkness, but Maxwell eventually saw the headlights of a small, unfamiliar car speeding down the highway. "Go faster," Maxwell said, and after a moment, the unfamiliar car was only 20 feet in front of them.

"You can't stop for anything," Welsh said.

Maxwell nodded and continued to stare out the window.

"Where's the car now?" Welsh asked.

Maxwell assured him that he had not lost sight of the car and told the driver to go faster, as they were now falling behind. He sped up, and they were once again 20 feet apart.

"Keep your eyes on the car. Watch when it changes directions and lanes."

Maxwell gave one quick nod and turned toward the driver. "Get closer to it," he instructed and watched as the driver eventually caught up to the speeding vehicle.

Someone had turned their headlights off, but he could now see well enough in the dark to make out the shadow of Alexander's car.

"Can you see who's in there?" Welsh asked.

He craned his neck to take a look out the back window.

"Just let it down." the driver instructed without looking in Maxwell's direction. He pushed the button and within a few seconds, the car filled with the cool night air.

The car was still in front of them, but Maxwell could now see that the road was filled with other drivers, some of whom were throwing the speeding Russian dirty looks.

"Dammit!" Maxwell almost shouted.

"What?" welsh asked, now in high alert.

"She's in the car with him and another man," he replied, again craning his neck to see the vehicle and its occupants.

"Can you catch up to them?" Maxwell asked.

The driver looked at his watch and frowned. "It's almost one in the morning," he said and pursed his lips.

The traffic had picked up and they were now several cars behind their target.

"Where are the others?" Welsh asked.

"They're probably trying to find me," Maxwell answered, not taking his eyes off the road.

"We've lost them, Simon," Maxwell announced over the roar of the engine.

"Can you see them at all?" Welsh asked and waited while Maxwell stared out the open window at the two lanes of heavy traffic. They were now moving at a slow pace, and Maxwell tried once more to search for the Russian's car, but all he could see were tire tracks. "I think they've left us behind," he muttered in frustration.

"Are you moving at all?" Welsh asked.

"Barely. There's too much traffic." Maxwell tried hard to keep his voice calm, but he was running out of patience.

"They've sped up and went east on Broadway." Welsh was talking animatedly now.

The cabbie followed Welsh's directions and then soon found themselves on Alexander's tail again. Though there was still heavy traffic around them, the driver sped up, avoiding more dirty looks and honking horns from angry drivers. Alexander and his two companions were only a few feet in front of them, but it was clear from the speed he went that the chase was on. The driver looked at his speedometer and frowned again. "I have to get this car back before my boss throws a fit," he said, speeding up again and narrowly avoiding a head-on collision.

"Tell your boss that you had something more important to do," Maxwell growled, still looking out the window.

The flow of traffic had let up but only a bit. He could now see that the car had turned left and had veered into the first lane of traffic.

Despite everything, Maxwell asked himself if the people in the car in front of them could see him as clearly as he saw them. The driver sped down the road, filling the car with more cold air, raising goosebumps onto Maxwell's skin. Over the roar of the engine, he faintly heard the "call waiting" signal. He sighed and with shaking fingers, answered the other line.

The person had called from an unknown number, but Maxwell's stomach muscles tightened when he heard a car engine in the background. He was about to ask who had called when the sound of muffled voices filled his ears. Several more minutes passed before a clear, unfamiliar voice finally broke through. "So sorry to hear about your friend, Mr. Maxwell."

The voice oozed sympathy and he would have believed it had it not been for the slight Russian accent.

"Who is this?" Maxwell asked.

"I'm... a friend." the voice said.

"What do you want?" Maxwell asked.

"First off, I've called to offer my sympathies," the voice said, "but my second reason for calling is ..." His voice trailed off, but Maxwell filled in the gaps.

"Where are you?" Maxwell asked, ice in both his voice and veins.

"Doesn't matter. All you need to know is that I'm with someone very close to you."

"Right now?" Maxwell asked stupidly.

The person gave a derisive chuckle down the line and Maxwell inwardly cursed himself for asking this question. "Where are you?" he repeated.

The person didn't answer immediately and Maxwell feared that the call had ended, but when the person did finally respond, their voice was harsh. "You're an idiot."

"Excuse me?" Maxwell asked, slightly offended.

"An idiot, a moron, a simpleton, do I have to explain it to you?" The person had become enraged.

Both cars were still speeding down the road in the same direction, but it was just a question of where they would end up and who would get there first. "I know what you meant," Maxwell shot back frustratedly, "but did you just call to insult me?"

"You're making this too easy for me, Mr. Maxwell." the voice muttered.

"Who have you got with you?" Maxwell asked, as though he had not heard him. The line went silent again, but instead of hearing muffled voices, Maxwell heard the squealing of tires on pavement and someone shouting in the background.

"Oh, piss off!" someone said. This voice, Maxwell noted, also had a slight Russian accent, but unlike the person who had called him, this one was deeper and more menacing.

"Why am I an idiot?" Maxwell asked after the shooting had stopped.

"Look out your window." the voice commanded.

Maxwell obeyed and was mildly surprised to see that the car had, inch by inch, gotten closer to the cab and was now only a few feet in front of them. "I see the car. So what?" Maxwell said.

The person gave another derisive laugh and hung up.

Maxwell sighed and switched back to Simon's call, but before he could get any words out of his mouth, the car was sprayed with a shower of gunfire. The driver cursed under his breath and watched helplessly as the driver's-side window dissolved into nothing but shards of broken glass. It was over in a matter of seconds.

There were no casualties and the party responsible sped down the road, tires squealing. The driver, who had put his head in his hands to protect his eyes, now lifted it and carefully assessed the damage.

Broken glass from the driver's-side window littered the pavement, both front tires had holes in them and were going flat, and the windshield wipers were now on their way to falling off. The driver made a frustrated noise, and Maxwell looked up from his phone for the first time since switching calls.

"Can you fix it?" he asked, staring at the driver's pale face over his shoulder.

"I got two spare tires in the trunk, but on everything else, I'm screwed.

Who was that anyway?" He directed the question to no one.

The driver looked at his watch again and clucked his tongue three times. "It's after one o'clock in the morning and I have to deal with this shit," the driver muttered before opening the door, undoing his seat belt and stepping out of the car. He slammed the door in anger and walked around to the trunk, careful not to step on the glass that now littered the street.

"Bloody cowards," Maxwell muttered when the driver had left.

"Where have they gone?" Welsh asked.

Simon pushed a button on his computer's screen and frowned. "I can't find them anymore." he lamented after a moment of silence.

Maxwell pursed his lips and turned his head toward the back window. The driver had managed to get the tires out of the trunk, and it appeared that he was also on the phone with someone.

"Are you hurt?" Welsh asked, looking once again at the tracker on his computer's screen, but to his disappointment and frustration, it still showed him nothing.

"Everyone is fine. It's just the car that needs mending."

"How bad is it?" Welsh asked.

"Not that bad," Maxwell replied and went on to describe all that had been done to the car in the shooting.

"Where's the driver?"

"Putting tires on the car," Maxwell said and stared out the window again. Where has the other car gone, and where are we headed? he wondered.

Despite everything, he also asked himself if René was all right and why she wasn't bothering to pick up her phone. He did not, however, disclose any of these worries to his friend.

Maybe she's busy, he thought and looked again out the window at the driver that was now striding back to the car.

"Ready to go?" he asked after the doors had been closed and his seat belt had been fastened.

Even though there was once again no destination in sight, Maxwell nodded and watched with a blank expression as the cabbie put the car in gear and began to drive.

"Where's that other car?" Welsh asked.

"We're not exactly sure," Maxwell said slowly.

The driver showed no emotion at this news as he stared out the broken window. He jammed his foot on the brake in anger. "I just talked to my boss and he wants to know who smashed up the window and nearly shot off the windshield wipers."

He glared at his watch and saw that it was now after one o'clock.

"Was your boss angry?" Maxwell asked.

"Yeah, and you would be too if somebody called you to say that the car given to you had just been shot up," the driver snapped and clenched his fists on the steering wheel.

"I've finally got something," Welsh announced, "tell the driver to go right and to hurry."

Maxwell repeated Welsh's command to the driver, who gladly sped off in that direction. "For how long?" Maxwell asked.

"Two miles," Welsh said and it took no time at all for the two cars to catch up to each other again.

Although the cab was fast, the other car was faster and they eventually collided. Shots rang out again, and when it was all over, the back windows and the front passenger windows had been blown out; the tires were flattened, and the windshield wipers were now fully on the ground.

"Pull him out," Alexander ordered, staring straight into the eyes of Andrew

Maxwell.

"What about him?" Gordon asked, pulling the agent through the broken window.

Alexander stared at the driver, took out his gun and held it to his head. "You saw nothing, understand?" he said.

The driver nodded and waited for more instructions.

"Step out of the car," Alexander said and watched as he carefully made his way over the broken glass.

"Tie their hands behind their backs," he said.

Maxwell watched as the hooded man went over to the driver and whispered something in his ear. The man lowered his head and put his hands behind his back.

"Wait for me." Gordon sneered and kept his eyes on his soon-to-be captive as he strode back to his car. "The driver's hands have been tied," he announced seconds later, turning the driver in circles by his new rope leash.

Alexander clucked his tongue twice in approval before opening the back door of his car. "Shove him in." he threw Gordon's way, turning his stony gaze on Maxwell's pale face. "Your turn," he said, seizing his right hand roughly and shoving it behind his back.

Maxwell closed his eyes and waited as Alexander did the same with his left. "Shove him in," he said, dragging him over to Gordon, who ruthlessly shoved him in between the cabbie and the girl.

"What will you do with his cell phone?" Gordon asked.

It was then that Alexander looked down and noticed the cracked object lying on the ground at his feet. He picked it up and threw it across the open space. "If someone finds it, it will be theirs," he whispered before slamming both doors and locking them.

They were on the road less than ten minutes later, but aside from the GPS, little speaking was being done. René lay on her back with her feet up in the air. Her expression was panicked and a little frustrated, but she did not turn to see who had been laid out beside her.

The drive to their destination was short and when they emerged from the car 20 minutes later, it was dark and quiet. It reminded René of a cemetery, but she did not say this out loud for fear that she might end up buried alive or dead.

Both prisoners were dragged by their ropes to a dimly lit building. Maxwell never saw what happened to the girl. He suddenly found himself alone in a cozy-looking room, but he did not remember hearing the doors open and close, nor did he feel the temperature as it changed from cool to mildly warm. A fire burned in the hearth in the center of the room and he smelled candles, but he dreaded what was coming next.

"Take a seat, Mr. Maxwell," a voice said, "it's time we had a little chat."

21

Bruised and Bothered

The Poisoner walked over to an end table and grabbed a lighter and a pack of Karelia cigarettes. "Do you smoke?" he asked and lit up without waiting for an answer.

Alexander walked over to a chair near Maxwell, sat down and crossed his legs at the ankles. "Have you figured out the identity of the person who contacted you earlier?" he asked.

Maxwell didn't respond.

"You see, everything that's been happening to you is no coincidence."

Maxwell clenched his hands into fists behind his back and closed his eyes.

"You're probably wondering why your hands are tied up." Alexander went on, still speaking softly and still smoking. Maxwell nodded and Alexander smiled.

"Well, I shall tell you," he whispered, getting up and going for something else, "it's the end of the road for you, Mr. Maxwell. You think you have won but you haven't."

"What the hell kind of game are you playing?" Maxwell asked.

"Funny, I should ask you the same question. Do you like hide-and-seek?" His torturer spun around and revealed what was in his right hand: a long piece of rope that almost reached the floor.

Maxwell twisted his face into a grotesque smile at the sight of it.

"You lived in that house with your girlfriend. Were you happy?" Alexander asked, a mocking edge of concern to his voice. He was now kneeling on the floor in front of Maxwell. He held one leg tightly in both hands and gently squeezed it.

"Ah, very muscular." Alexander complimented.

"What have you done with René?" Maxwell asked, trying to struggle out of Alexander's grip, but he had already tied his right leg to the chair.

"She and your cab driver friend are with Gordon in another room and as long as you cooperate, nothing will happen to any of you." The Poisoner was now working on the other leg. "I didn't realize that you cared so much for her." he sneered and stepped back to admire his handiwork.

He left again to throw his cigarette butt into the trash can under his desk before coming back to his side.

"We can't have you escaping before your big finale," Alexander muttered to himself as he bent down to untie Maxwell's shoes.

"What do you think you're doing?" Maxwell demanded angrily.

"The real fun begins now," Alexander said, untying first Maxwell's right leg, then his left.

"Take off your shoes and socks," he said before chuckling, "oh, that's right, you can't. I'll have to do it for you."

Maxwell clenched his teeth and fought back a wince as his captor untied and wrenched his right leg, then his left away from the chair and yanked off both his shoes and socks before tying them back to the chair's legs.

"I realize you are uncomfortable right now, but you must understand something." He paused and reached up to begin unbuttoning Maxwell's suit jacket. "After what you've subjected my friends to, you owe me something. Don't you agree?"

Alexander had managed to remove Maxwell's jacket and was now working on his shirt. He got it off on the second try and threw it on the floor, where his shoes, socks and jacket now lay. "Lean back on your elbows," Alexander instructed.

Maxwell silently obeyed.

Alexander smiled and walked over to a shelf.

He got on his tiptoes, reached up with both hands for a wooden board and brought it down. "You look rather vulnerable lying there like that," he commented, holding the board by the top, careful to avoid the nails sticking out from the bottom.

He silently envied the man with the long, sculpted legs and shining blue eyes in front of him.

"Now, let me think," he mused, "what can you give me in return for the hell you've put my friends through?"

He had come back to his spot, but instead of sitting, he laid the board down on the seat. It hung off the end of his chair but neither noticed. "Have you got any ideas?" he asked, gazing intently at his guest. "Oh, I know," he finally decided, "killing you seems perfect."

He laid his hand on the board and stroked its wooden surface with his fingertips. "Somebody once suggested to me that I should just call the police and have you locked up, which was a good idea at the time, but then I decided that that would be too easy."

He licked his lips and picked up the board. Maxwell flinched as he came closer but otherwise stayed still. "My friends deserve vengeance against you, Mr. Maxwell." he went on.

He banged the board, nail side down, onto the empty spot closest to the chair Maxwell occupied. "You see, my job is to inflict pain on my victims, and since you're here and refuse to talk..." he said no more but lunged at the unsuspecting man with the board.

The nails dug into the skin on his right shoulder and part of his back. Alexander removed the board after half a minute, and Maxwell fought back a shriek of pain by clenching his teeth.

"I admire your stamina. Most men in your situation would have given up after the first hit." He struck Maxwell again, this time aiming for his torso. The nails again dug into his flesh, and blood dripped from the cuts onto his white suit pants.

They had left long gashes on his skin, and the area around him was a sea of red.

Alexander turned the board over and stared at the blood that was now drying on the points of the nails and the bottom of the board. He dropped the board to the floor with a bang and once again untied Maxwell's legs. In one swift motion, he had removed his pants and had thrown them to the floor with the rest of his clothes. "I have to take you to the back," he explained, "I realize that you're in pain right now, but you're strong. Your young body can take a beating."

He somehow managed to carry both Maxwell and the board to a room that was only used for this one purpose and laid them both on a long paper-covered table.

Maxwell shivered as the cool air came in contact with his freshly made wounds, but he would not let Alexander know that he was getting to him. The snapping of rubber gloves brought him back from his reverie. He looked up to see his torturer now holding a bottle and he automatically tensed up.

"You know, maybe I won't kill you after all."

"Why not?" he choked.

"You're the government's best worker and if you went missing, I'd get blamed for your disappearance," Alexander said, setting the bottle down on the end of the long table.

"Who else knows I'm here?" Maxwell asked.

"Only Gordon," he answered and ran to the door.

"Gotta take a piss. Don't go nowhere," he said and rushed out of the room.

Maxwell looked around at his makeshift prison.

Only one light shone in the room, and it was from the lamp that sat near him. The table that he had been placed on was the kind that was usually reserved for hospitals.

Now only in his underwear and with bruises already beginning to appear, he felt exposed and helpless. He took a deep breath and looked around the room for the second time, noticing now that the bottle that had been brought in was gone.

The Poisoner had forgotten to close the door, but fortunately for them, not many people were in the building.

"Wake up, asshole." a sharp, familiar voice said, and Maxwell looked up to see The Poisoner standing in front of him. "Miss me?" he asked sarcastically and jabbed a finger at Maxwell's bruised torso. He replaced the bottle where it had been earlier, then turned his back on his victim and exited the room once more.

He reentered the room moments later, now carrying a tray with two plastic cups, a pot of coffee, and little packets of cream and sugar upon it. "Do you remember a woman named Jessica Morales?" he asked, setting the tray down on another table and pouring himself a cup of coffee.

"Yeah, why?" Maxwell asked.

"She died this morning."

"How?" Maxwell asked, picking himself up and balancing himself on his elbows.

"Would you believe me if I said that it was of natural causes?" The Poisoner asked, suppressing a laugh. He had removed his rubber gloves and had disposed of them.

"No," said Maxwell.

"Well, then you're smarter than I gave you credit for," Alexander answered, sipping from his coffee, "she was... what's the right word? Murdered."

"Who killed her?" Maxwell asked.

Alexander smiled as he stirred cream and sugar into his cup. "I didn't know the guy, but according to a colleague of mine, she'd had a hit put out on her." He took another sip of coffee and glanced around the room until his gaze rested on the man lying on the hospital-like table. "I quite like seeing you that way," he commented, "tied up and bruised. I'm just sad that the others couldn't join us."

"You know where they are?" Maxwell asked and watched Alexander wipe his mouth clean of brown liquid before crossing the room in two long strides.

"I do, but telling you would be a breach of trust." He smiled at Maxwell's knowing expression.

"They still want me dead," he stated flatly.

Alexander nodded in agreement. "After Olga's death, things were never the same," he began, going back and pouring himself another cup of coffee, "she held the whole operation together. Her death was felt around the world. Anyway, after her burial, her mother made a statement. In this brief speech, she came out with some startling information."

"Oh?" Maxwell said, suddenly interested.

"Would you like to hear what she had to say?" Ritzkov asked, turning away from the tray.

"Yeah," said Maxwell.

"She admitted that someone had conspired against her daughter to have her killed." The former assassin tentatively watched Maxwell's face for any flicker of emotion, but his expression stayed stoic. It was clear the apology that he was hoping for would never come. "It was your boss," he said, going for the board again.

"Pierre did this?" Maxwell asked, not at all surprised by this information.

"It was not Pierre, it was Ernest," he admitted. The room fell silent for an instant as The Poisoner scrutinized Maxwell's incredulous expression before continuing. "She was very detailed in her descriptions," he said, "it was as though she had known what he was thinking firsthand."

Maxwell put his head back on the table and closed his eyes. He had known that Ernest, like everyone else, had had his flaws, but he found what The Poisoner was saying now hard to believe.

"Yes, I too found it difficult to believe," Alexander said, unexpectedly reading Maxwell's mind.

Though he didn't look up, he sensed it when Alexander neared him.

"That's fascinating." he offered.

"Yes, but do you know what's even more fascinating? It appears that he had a co-conspirator." The Poisoner said quietly.

"Who was that?" Maxwell asked before he could stop himself from doing so.

"Funny you should ask," Alexander answered, picking up the board and bringing it close to Maxwell's face.

He flinched at the contact.

"Why?" he asked, trying to keep his expression even.

"Because," Alexander replied, brandishing the makeshift weapon at the man lying on the table, "it was you."

Maxwell opened his mouth to object but was greeted with the pain of being hit repeatedly with a board and the sharp stabbing of nails. When it was finally over, he again clenched his teeth and looked up to find The Poisoner staring down at him with a calm smile. "Did you enjoy that?" Alexander asked, holding the board that was sticky with wet blood.

Maxwell's skin began to hurt, and as he looked down at himself, he realized why he had been stripped. The board and the nails had made contact with the front half of his body, and more bruises were beginning to appear. The skin on the lower half of his body stung and burned, and he could feel the muscles in his arms and legs beginning to spasm. He feared losing ability in all four limbs. He had been the one to call when there had been a long-distance emergency and most of the other agents had not been in any condition to work.

He had always jumped at the chance to fly to faraway places for his kill, but he now wondered if he had finally met his match.

"What happened once you found out Olga had died? Did you rejoice? Did you and Ernest go for a celebratory drink?" Alexander spoke with a mocking edge of excitement to his voice.

"I didn't conspire with anyone to do anything." Maxwell choked, still shuddering from the pain.

"Why would a grieving mother lie about something like this?" Alexander asked, picking up the bottle and shaking it. He set the board down on the other side of the table and sneered at his captive, still holding the bottle in his hand.

"You've had your chance to apologize," he whispered, moving closer to the unsuspecting man's already bruised body, "you have wasted my time, and I have nothing more to say to you. I'm sorry, I wish there was another way, but you have left me no choice."

Maxwell opened his mouth but snapped it shut when Alexander put his finger to his lips. "Your precious government will miss you, I'm sure, but hopefully, someone will notify your boss, er, bosses, that you've been... laid up for a while." Alexander snickered.

"Would you like a drink?" he asked, still sneering at Maxwell.

Without saying anything, he nodded and reached for the bottle.

Alexander closed his eyes, leaned over him and poured the clear liquid out onto the bruised man's body.

Within seconds, the room was filled with Maxwell's agonized screams. He watched as the agent writhed in pain and glared at the former assassin's smooth expression. "You son of a bitch." he said, shuddering from the pain of his burns.

"Enjoy your payback, Mr. Maxwell. Maybe now that you know the reason for your boss's murder, you can stop going after my friends," he whispered, grabbing the board and jamming the nails into the flesh on his belly.

Alexander turned his back on Maxwell for the last time and made his way to the door. The last thing he heard before shutting and locking the door behind himself was the agonized screams of a well-known agent.

Maxwell gritted his teeth against the sharp pain that escaped his lungs whenever he breathed. The realization that he was helpless suddenly hit him.

The GK would kill again, and he wondered who would be their next victim. He immediately thought of René Anderson and his now-boss, Pierre Dubois, sighed for them, then winced at the effort. One of them was innocent and the other already worked for the enemy. He raised his head, looked down at his naked body and shuddered inwardly at the sight of it.

He was covered in bruises and dried blood from the nails and would undoubtedly be in worse shape once he got cleaned up. He closed his eyes as he considered his situation.

Were both their lives worth saving? Would he be happy if only the girl lived to tell her side of the story, or would he be happier if they both took their secrets with them to an early grave?

He wondered how long he'd been lying on this wettable and how much longer it would be before anyone realized he had gone missing. The circulation had gone out of all four limbs and he feared losing everything. He clenched his fists in anger at this thought and didn't let go until his hands began to ake from his nails digging into his palms. "You ruined my life," he shouted, opening his eyes and glaring up at the ceiling, "I trusted you to help me, and because I did, I'm now lying on a table in my Goddamned underwear and you're laughing your ass off! I swear, when I get out of here, I will kill you and every other son of a bitch that works with you!"

He hoped that Alexander heard him from wherever he was, but a small part of him doubted it and wished that he had done something sooner. He turned his head to the side and stared at the clock. It was now half-past three. He asked himself who, if anyone, missed him at this moment and if anyone had tried to contact him. The last thing he felt before he laid his head back, closed his eyes, and drifted off to sleep was the sharp pain of the nails piercing his flesh as he inhaled for the last time.

22

Deadweight

"Who did this to him?" a voice asked.

It was muffled and the words sounded distant, as though the speaker stood far from the person they were addressing. Another person spoke, but this voice sounded more muffled and faraway than the first.

"Do we know where his clothes are?" the first person spoke again.

The second person shook their head and frowned.

"There was somebody else with him. Where is she?"

The second person responded, then gave a tiny smile.

"What about the other guy?" The second person asked.

The first person gave a terse reply and walked away.

Maxwell squeezed his eyes shut and pursed his lips. Had René been saved? Had both their lives been spared? He struggled to make his brain work, but he felt stupid and trapped.

He tried to remember where he was and how he had gotten here, but all he had were gaps where information failed him. He slowly opened his eyes and looked around. He was now lying in a bed with the curtains drawn, and as he looked down at himself, he realized that he had been put into a purple hospital gown. Maxwell stared up at the ceiling and a tiny smile came to his lips as he finally realized where he was.

"Look who's awake." a cheery voice greeted him, making him jump and turn his head toward the voice. It sounded familiar, and he soon figured out why.

"How long have I been here?" he croaked.

"A week and a half. I'm glad you're awake," the lady smiled a tiny bit at the last part.

Maxwell opened his mouth, then snapped it shut.

"You were messed up when they found you," she said, going to stand beside him.

"Who found me?" he asked.

"I didn't get their names, and I didn't see their faces. Come to think of it, they didn't speak at all."

"What's wrong with me?" he asked.

Without answering, the nurse turned toward a laptop sitting on her desk and switched it on. He listened as she described to him what had happened.

"Did somebody else come here with me?" he asked when she'd finished.

The woman nodded and proceeded to tell him the good news. René had not been harmed but had refused to talk when questioned by the nurse or her assistant.

"When we asked her why she explained that she would only talk to you," she said with a laugh.

He acknowledged her remark with a small smile, then raised his head and once again looked down at his body. The place where the board had been was now stitched up and the front of his gown was streaked with dry blood. "How many stitches?"

"Ten. That cut looked pretty nasty. You'll have an ugly scar on your torso.

Try not to get it wet for a few days." The nurse gave him a stern look.

"What happened to the board?"

The nurse looked confused for a second, then her expression morphed into one of understanding.

"It's been disposed of, that thing had so much of your blood on it. It was disgusting." She gave a dry laugh and turned toward the door. "I should go. I have more patients to see, but call me if you need anything."

He promised that he would and watched her leave. Once she had left, he thought about all that she had told him. She had said that he would be sore for a little while but that she was confident that he would be better by his next visit. The spot on his shoulder where the nails had first come in contact was now bandaged, and that too had required a few stitches.

He wondered if Simon would give him time off once he understood what had happened and where he had been, but he also knew that just because you were down and out, evil never took a break. Two quick raps on the door disturbed his train of thought, and he did his best to put a smile on his face as he permitted his visitor into the room.

"I thought you'd look worse from the nurse's description," René said cheerfully.

She was dressed in jeans and a white t-shirt. Her hair looked like it had just been done.

She smiled at the pale face that greeted her and stepped closer to his bedside. "You still look like hell," she admitted, smiling.

He gave a short laugh, then winced. "Thank you." He smiled back at her.

She sat on the edge of his bed and glanced around the room before her gaze rested on him. "Alexander and his companion left about two days ago," she told him.

"Shit, Simon's going to murder me. Where'd they go?" he asked.

"Back to their office, I think. He was fairly satisfied when he saw your unconscious body lying on that table."

She frowned, but Maxwell smiled humorously at her words.

"I'm not surprised. That's been their ultimate goal since the beginning." He looked down at the dried blood on the front of his gown again and winced.

"What did the nurse say?"

He described to her what the nurse had told him and when he had finished, he watched her face, which stayed empty.

"When are you getting out?" she asked after a moment's pause.

"Don't know," he said forlornly, staring at the grey wall.

She felt sorry for him and herself. He had almost sacrificed his life for her, but it had been at the mercy of a psychopath, and she felt sorry for herself because the same fate had befallen her.

"He ruined my life," he muttered and shut his eyes again.

"Where do you suppose they are now?" she asked.

He didn't answer; he just stared at the door as though he were waiting for someone to burst through it. As far as he knew, The Poisoner and Gordon were probably on the other side of the world by now. He was going to have to live with the fact that millions of lives would be lost because of it. "Probably halfway around the world by now." he lamented. The pressure of this mission was beginning to get to him. He had two enemies on his back: the main group and the man that had parted ways with them.

She stayed for another hour and tried to comfort him, but she soon had to leave and promised to visit him tomorrow.

Once the door had closed, he resumed his train of thought. Pierre had betrayed him for the last time and he no longer considered him his superior. He would ask Simon for time off the first chance he got, but he knew that the government couldn't stand to lose him, no matter how temporary the loss was. It seemed he had only been asleep for a few minutes when a commotion woke him up. He pressed the "call" button repeatedly until someone came.

It was the nurse that had come to see him when he'd first opened his eyes, but she was now wearing a panicked expression. He heard the screams as soon as she opened the door and saw the red lights of the fire alarm when he opened his eyes. "What the hell is going on?" he demanded.

"Someone's broken into the building, says he's looking for a particular patient here."

"Who is he"" began Maxwell, but he was interrupted by a loud bang. He recognized right away that it was a gunshot, but he couldn't place where it had come from. "Nurse, nurse, are you all right?" he asked, but his face fell when he saw what had happened.

The nurse had been shot in the back and now lay dead on the floor in a pool of blood. He struggled to get to his feet and successfully made it on the third attempt.

He was dizzy and weak from his imprisonment, but he willed his legs to move quickly as he made his way down the hall in the direction of the screams. He was greeted with shouts and curses as people ran and hid, accompanied by the ringing of the alarm and a voice over the intercom that kept repeating the same message.

"Attention, attention, active shooter, please get to a safe place. This is not a drill."

He scanned the chaotic scene for the shooter but the hospital was now a mass of people, all running for their lives. He stood frozen and listened until the popping sounds reached his ears again. He watched, horrified, as one by one bodies went down, but he wasn't sure which ones were dead and who was only pretending to escape the wrath of the shooter. The chaos only began to calm down when the shooter put his gun in its holster and seemed to give up, but Maxwell was startled when someone came up behind him and said in a menacing whisper, "Missed me, asshole?"

Maxwell spun on his heel and surveyed his surroundings. Many bodies lined the walkway and pools of blood were everywhere. "What the hell is wrong with you?" he hissed.

The gunman slipped the holstered weapon into his pocket and smiled through his face mask. "I knew you'd be here, and I knew that someone would save you," he said in Maxwell's ear.

"I thought you'd be back at your office or somewhere out of the country by now," Maxwell replied.

"I couldn't leave without paying my friend one last visit, could I?" Alexander smiled against Maxwell's neck.

The screaming had died down and the alarm had finally been shut off, but people were still scattered everywhere.

"What did you do with my clothes?" Maxwell demanded, taking two steps forward, with The Poisoner behind him.

"I burned them," he answered calmly.

Maxwell silently counted the bodies that were on the floor, then gasped. He counted ten bodies in front of him and ten behind him, but more people were going to die as a result of what Alexander had just done.

"Just be happy that I didn't harm you or your friend. You didn't try to escape and neither did she, but as for your cab driver..."

He licked his lips and touched his pocket with the gun inside. "He had to get back to his job, he told me. I assured him that no one was going to care if he missed a few days, but he wouldn't hear of it, so..." He pointed his finger at Maxwell's torso.

He glared over his shoulder at the man that had come to see him. "You killed him?" he asked in disbelief.

"No, but I watched Gordon do it." Alexander touched his pocket again and smiled as a look of confusion crossedMaxwell's face. "Allow me to explain. Gordon is my assistant, as well as my driver. He'll do anything I ask him to and because the cab driver disobeyed me, he's now dead."

"Where's the cab?" Maxwell asked after a brief pause.

"Where we left it." The Poisoner said, frowning slightly.

Maxwell winced again. His midsection was beginning to hurt and he felt like his legs were going to give out at any second. "Have you finished?" he asked, turning in the direction of his room.

"There's one more thing I came to tell you. The others and I have been in constant communication, and I am pleased to tell you that you will be seeing all of us sometime soon, and they say they have a surprise for you."

Maxwell frowned again and walked away, careful to avoid the mess on the floor. The hospital now looked like a war zone: windows had been shattered, nurses' stations were in disarray, and dead bodies were everywhere, including the nurse that had been at his bedside. Aside from a few workers that had managed to find hiding places under tables, it was mostly void of life.

He paused outside the door to his room and glanced down the hall. He smiled when The Poisoner finally disappeared out of the building, but the excitement was soon replaced with worry when René managed to slip into his thoughts. He now regretted telling Simon that he would watch out for her. She had been warned to leave before she'd gotten in too deep, and now it was too late. They had both been put in danger, and as much as he hated to admit it, he feared for their safety.

He tapped his chin twice, looked into the tidied room, then looked back at the body of the nurse. The white dress she'd been wearing was now stained with blood, her right shoe had fallen off at some point, and her glasses were now broken, probably from the impact of her fall.

Her brown hair had come loose from its ponytail and was lying in the pool of blood that had dried up. He took two steps toward her body and carefully touched her arm.

It was cold, rubbery and hard. He stared at her blood-stained dress for another minute before turning to the open door and retreating into the shadows of his room.

Though he was exhausted, he had no desire to sleep. He closed the door, wandered over to the table by his bed and opened one of the drawers. He looked through it until he found a pen and pad, then closed it and sat on the end of his bed. He opened it to the first page, then stopped with the tip of his pen only a few inches from its destination. Maxwell scratched the small mustache that had grown on his upper lip in thought, but nothing came.

The pain in his torso had dulled and was now tolerable, and he felt some of the strength return to his legs. The hand that held the pen didn't shake, but the relief of this didn't ease his mind, nor did it help him think. Alexander's promise had seemed genuine, and the threat of being killed suddenly filled him with anticipation.

He was not excited to die, but the prospect of finally getting the answer he needed, even if knowing them got him killed.

After a moment of fruitless thinking, he shoved the pen and pad aside, got out of bed and walked to a computer desk that was only a few feet away. As he waited for the computer to boot up, he quickly glanced around the room once more, trying to get a mental picture of it before he was due to fill his gaze with words on a small screen. It took him less than one minute to get logged in and onto the website he had in mind. He typed only one letter into the search engine when it finally came up: X.

The search results he'd been waiting for were disappointing when they finally appeared on the screen, but he would just have to make do with what he had. The first one was some information on X the band, the next was about the Model X from Tesla and the third was x.org. He scanned over the top three he had chosen, then softly banged his left fist on the table in frustration.

He sighed and closed out of the website.

He reopened it a moment later and without looking at the screen brought it back to the search engine, then typed in the question he most needed the answer to: "Who is X?"

He silently read through the first page of results when they finally appeared on the screen, but they disappointed him again. After another half an hour of fruitless searching, he gave up and logged out. He considered sending Simon a brief e-mail but knew it would probably find its way into the trash bin. Thirty seconds passed before he finally made up his mind and opened the "e-mail" tab. He decided that even if his message did ultimately end up there, at least Simon and his companions would have a way to contact him for the time being, if needed.

He typed in his address and pressed the Tab key until he found it, but when he finally got to the subject line, he stopped dead. This and the actual body of the message were the two tricky parts, and he thought about skipping it, but he eventually chose the two first words that came to his brain. The message was quick, only one paragraph long, but it had enough details to fill Simon in on the situation.

Sorry for not calling you back. Alexander broke my phone and tied me up. I am now in the hospital and so is René. But don't worry, she isn't hurt.

He read it over twice before pressing the "send" button, then logged out and walked back to the edge of the bed, and sat down. He grabbed the pad, closed it, and held it on his lap. He wondered if Simon would ever get back to him and if he would understand what had happened. He imagined his phone lying in pieces somewhere and his hands clenched into fists around the pad.

He relaxed his grip after a few seconds, but his face stayed set in a grim line. Ten minutes passed before he dropped the pad back on the mattress and walked back to the computer desk. He tapped his fingers on the wood, then leaned over, turned it on, opened up his e-mail, and was pleased to find a message waiting for him.

Re: Useless Hunter was the subject line.

No need to apologize. I guessed that something had happened when I didn't hear from you for a few days. I can give you time off if you need it, just let me know.

He scrolled down, typed a quick thanks, and sent it. Before going back to his bed, he looked out the window and saw the flashing headlights of a car in the distance. He raced across to the door, opened it a crack, stuck his head out, and waited for something to happen. Muffled voices reached his ears again, but they were louder this time.

The sound of an argument made its way to him and from what he could hear, it was between two people: a male and a female.

"This was your fault! You weren't paying attention to who was coming in and going out!" The man's voice was deep and hoarse as if he had a cold, but he still managed to shout at his companion.

"What do you want me to do about it now? It's done, they're dead, the killer's gone, and besides, I didn't get a good look at their face, they were wearing a face mask, and people were running around..."

"Did you think to call the police?" the man interrupted sharply.

The shouting stopped for a moment and Maxwell imagined the hurt look on the girl's face.

"Look, you screwed up, Stephanie." The man had gained control and now spoke softly. It was silent for a long time before anyone spoke again.

"I'm sorry, Mr. Valasquez," Stephanie mumbled.

Ned Valasquez whispered something to Stephanie, who then let out a loud sigh, turned away from the man and walked off. "I need an aspirin." he heard Ned mutter and carefully walked closer to the door when the man-made his way to an entrance down the hall. Ned was short and balding. He was dressed in a Knicks jersey and he wore Coach tennis shoes on his feet.

Maxwell ducked back inside his room when he heard footsteps approaching and closed the door. He sighed at the thought that someone had survived his assassination attempt. He looked at the clock and saw that it was now almost midnight. Avoiding the computer entirely, he went straight to his bed, replaced the pad and pen in the drawer of the desk he'd gotten them from and climbed in. As he began to wind down, he asked himself when he would see Alexander and the others again and what his surprise would be, but he knew how it would end.

He thought about where he would go once he was released. The cabbie was dead and he didn't want to be separated from René again. The image of the nurse's dead body filled his mind and he shuddered. She, along with others, was now a blood-soaked corpse in blood-stained rags. He had been lucky that time, but he knew that his mortality was on the line.

For the next few weeks, he rested, e-mailed Simon about his progress, and talked with René when she came to see him. She was pleased that he was getting better and so was Simon, but he was itching to get back to work. He would have his revenge one day, but it wouldn't be for him. More people were going to die, but the bad guys would be the victims this time.

He had not seen Alexander for three weeks by the time this popped into his head, and his promise of a surprise was almost non-existent but not forgotten. Though Maxwell tried to hide it, he was constantly on edge.

"Where are you going to go once you've been released?" René asked a few days before Maxwell was finally due to leave.

His new nurse had been delighted to share the good news with him: he had healed nicely, and it was now safe for him to go home. "I'll probably check myself into the Hilton in New Jersey," he said.

They were having breakfast in the hospital's spacious cafeteria. He was still wearing the gown they'd given him, but he was now wearing purple sneakers to match.

The place had somewhat gone back to normal. Most of the staff had come back and patients were now coming in droves.

"How's your new nurse?" she asked, tearing open a sugar packet and putting it into her coffee. She now wore her hair in curls on top of her head and she was wearing blue jeans and a tank top with pink sandals.

"All right," he answered, picking up his fork and digging into his ham and eggs.

He had hidden his matted hair under a baseball cap that his nurse had given him. "He's on duty right now," he said after swallowing a mouthful of scrambled egg.

The female nurse had been buried in the cemetery across the street from the hospital. As he'd expected, the shooting had made the news rounds. Alexander had killed 20 people, including the nurse, and had injured dozens more but as of now, nobody except Maxwell and his companions knew the identity of the killer. The police chief had held a press conference a few days before his new nurse had been due to arrive, and he had told reporters that in addition to trying to find out the identity of the killer, they were now trying to find a motive, but both he and René knew that it had been a botched attempt on his life.

"Do you think he'll try something like this again?" she asked, sipping from her coffee cup and looking around the room. It was half-empty and the tables that were occupied weren't in earshot of them.

"I wouldn't doubt it," he answered.

"When do you think they'll catch him?" she asked.

Maxwell shrugged his shoulders.

"Would you be willing to come out and tell them what he wanted?" asked René.

"Yeah, if I have to," said Maxwell, remembering Alexander's promise of a surprise. He doubted that that's when the surprise would come: while he was camped out at the hotel.

"Does it still hurt?" she asked.

"A little," he said.

Maxwell stared at the occupants of the nearest table to them. Two parents sat on either side of their daughter. The family was all dressed in black like they had just come from a funeral.

"Did he hurt you?" Maxwell asked, turning back to face the girl that sat across from him.

René shook her head, keeping her eyes down on the mug of coffee she now held in her hands. "We just got questioned a lot. Did he tell you about the cab driver?" she asked.

He nodded and knitted his eyebrows together. "Were you there when he was murdered?" he asked.

She took a long sip of coffee, then swallowed and shook her head. "We were kept in different rooms, but even with both doors closed, I still heard it when it happened," she said, shuddering at the memory.

"What did they do with his body?" Maxwell asked.

She didn't answer his question, just sipped her coffee again, then looked up at the clock and sighed. Neither of them spoke again for a long moment. They were now in their worlds, each thinking about something different.

The Poisoner plagued Maxwell's thoughts now, but he kept reminding himself that there were more important things to worry about. He still had to find Pascal and the rest of them, and besides the millions of other people, there was someone in front of him that he needed to protect. He glanced over at René and tried to smile, but the worry showed on his face.

"How much time do we have left?" she asked, and he could tell from her tone that she meant until their partnership ended and he headed back to London.

The question hung in the air for a long time, but he would not give her the answer she wanted. She was just a name to him, an extra burden, but he would never tell her that. "I don't know," he said.

They finished the rest of their meal in silence, neither one of them looking at the other.

Maxwell spent the rest of the day packing and trying to forget about the past few weeks. Once his room had been emptied of all his belongings, except for the clothes he would need for the next day and his toiletries, he sat on the edge of his bed and glanced down at the blood-stained gown for the last time. He scooted toward the pillows and sighed and gently patted his midsection. He winced as he laid on his back and rolled onto his right side, then closed his eyes and frowned into the darkness.

23

Winners and Losers

"Two, please," Maxwell said, stepping onto the elevator.

The dark-haired man that had come on before him gave him a slight nod and without saying a word, pressed the "up" button.

Maxwell had ditched the hospital gown in his room before leaving the hospital and was now dressed in all black.

"Where're ya comin' from?" the man slurred.

Maxwell looked the man over for a moment before answering. He was dressed in blue jeans and a baggy sweatshirt. He wore no shoes on his feet and a Yankees cap on his head. Thick-framed glasses covered his eyes and he held a half-empty can of Bud Light by his side. It was clear from his appearance that he'd been drinking.

"The hospital," Maxwell answered.

The dark-haired man studied the man in black for half a minute, then looked away. "Lookin fine to me. A little thirsty, though. How long ya in town for?"

"For a while," Maxwell answered.

The dark-haired man held the bottle out to him, but Maxwell politely declined. "You from around here?" the man asked, turning to face his riding companion.

"No, from London. I'm just here visiting friends." Maxwell said.

The intoxicated man and Maxwell exchanged a sideways look. The elevator doors opened a moment later and the two men went their separate ways.

"I'll be seeing you." the unidentified man called as he walked the other way.

Maxwell nodded and walked down the other end of the hall to the room he'd booked for the next few weeks. He turned the corner and glanced down the hall. He sighed when he didn't see the man from the elevator. The man had looked familiar, but as he walked now, he could not remember how and where they'd met before.

Later in bed, Maxwell tried to sleep off his day's travels, but the memory of the man's face from the elevator came back to him whenever he closed his eyes. He got up, stretched and went to his bag. He had bought a laptop earlier that day and intended to use it now. After it had booted up, he typed in his former boss's name and scrolled down until he found the list of people who had worked with and for him.

He spent the next forty-five minutes scrolling through the images on the screen, but a shiver ran down his spine when he realized that none of the people matched the man from the elevator's appearance. He played the conversation from earlier over and over in his head, focusing intently on the look in the man's eyes before he departed. He had seen that cold, sideways look before, but trying to figure it out now exhausted him.

He got up from the computer, walked to the door, opened it a crack, and listened. He stood there for several minutes but when he heard nothing, he closed the door and locked it.

The man's face stayed in his mind, but aside from the interaction on the elevator, they barely saw or spoke to one another.

He spent the next few weeks recovering and getting stronger. He stayed in contact with both René and Simon, who'd made their concern for him clear. He had told Simon about the drunken man, and the retired agent had confirmed his suspicions that he had never worked for Ernest or their organization.

"I don't remember him ever working for the government." he'd said when Maxwell had called him from his hotel room.

He frowned when he realized what Simon's words meant. The man wasn't one of the good guys. He regularly searched the internet for information about him: where he worked, who he worked for, and with whom he worked, but there were very little details on him.

He was born in Michigan and grew up in a working-class family. His father worked on an oil rig and his mother was a stay-at-home mom. He had gone to MIT to study Aerospace engineering but had dropped out after the death of his father. He'd gotten in trouble with the law a few times, but the site never went into specifics.

According to the site, the man had applied for a government job but had not gotten it.

Maxwell jotted his findings down in the notebook he'd brought with him from the hospital. He had found out everything about this man but two things: his name and the reason for the government turning him down.

He turned the computer off and closed the notebook. He breathed a sigh of relief as he turned out the light and climbed into bed. He felt strong enough to go back to work, and he was determined to resume it eventually.

He would have to prove that he was strong enough to use a gun, which scared him a bit. He had always been a perfect shot, but due to his aching torso and shoulder, he wondered if he would be able to hold it long enough to complete the job. He rolled over on his side and welcomed the sleep that soon came to him but was woken up what seemed like minutes later by a bright light in the room.

He pulled back the covers and pursed his lips. "Oh, hell," he muttered groggily, sitting up and reaching for the lamp.

There was a note lying on the table beside it.

Carefully, he grabbed the sheet of paper and put it beside him in bed. He rubbed his eyes and picked up the note.

Three words had been written in big black letters:

See you tomorrow.

He turned the note over and over in his hands. He got up from the bed and made his way to the lamp. He squatted beside the table and carefully studied the note, but the author had only signed with the initial A at the bottom right corner. The ink was beginning to run, leaving black splotches on the tiny sheet.

After a while, it began to resemble a woman's mascara-stained face after crying. He stared at the note for another five minutes before replacing it on the end table beside the lamp. He looked up at the clock and sighed. It was only ten after midnight.

He scooted toward the end table and felt around until he found another piece of paper. He held it up to the light and saw that this one had also been written in black ink. This piece of paper had more on it, which he soon realized were a message and a time. Maxwell studied it closely. The entire note read:

Meet me at the hotel's entrance at ten o'clock A.m. sharp. We have a long drive ahead of us.

He searched for the other note and smiled to himself when he found it. Whoever had written both of these, noted Maxwell, had very messy handwriting. He then opened the top drawer of the end table and shoved both notes into it.

The telephone woke him up at a quarter to nine the next morning.

"Mr. Maxwell, sorry to bother you, but you have a guest in the lobby. He says you have an appointment this morning." the concierge said when Maxwell, still half-asleep, had answered the phone.

"Oh, shit. Tell him to give me fifteen minutes." Without waiting for an answer, he hung up the phone and hastily got up. He arrived in the lobby fifteen minutes later to find the man from the elevator, now in a pressed black suit and tie, sitting on a couch with his back to him.

"You clean up fast." the man snickered, peering at Maxwell out of the corner of his left eye.

Maxwell gave a half-smile, walked toward the couch, and sat down on the opposite end.

"Well," the man said, checking his watch, "we have a little time before we have to leave. How about some breakfast?"

Maxwell didn't answer.

"Come on, let's go get something to eat. You're going to need your strength." the man tried again, his tone darkening.

Reluctantly, Maxwell got to his feet and walked in the direction of the cafeteria with the man following after him. Each had eggs and bacon and black coffee, but neither of them spoke for a long time.

"Where are we going?" Maxwell finally asked after they had finished and the dishes had been cleared.

Now it was the man's turn not to answer. He reached into his pocket, grabbed his phone, then glanced around the room. Some diners that sat near them stared back at the well-dressed man, while others kept their gazes on their food. He set his phone down on the table and turned to face his breakfast companion. "An old friend wants to see you," he said to Maxwell and turned his back to him.

Maxwell shifted his eyes away from his neighbor and watched the other patrons as some of them got up to leave. At nine-thirty, the two men exited the cafeteria and made their way back to the lobby.

At nine-forty-five, Maxwell's companion fished his car keys from his pocket and turned them over in his hands. "Come on, it's time to go." the man said and turned to leave.

Maxwell followed him to a black sports car and watched as he opened both doors with the touch of a button. Half a minute later, the black sports car sped down the road with Maxwell sitting in the passenger seat.

"I said at ten o'clock." the man stated with a tight smile.

"Your friend won't mind if we're a bit early," Maxwell replied.

The driver scowled out the window at the skyscrapers they passed. "I think my friend will be excited to see you." the driver said suddenly.

"She doesn't even know me," Maxwell objected.

The driver put his hand over his mouth as if he'd already revealed too much, then he turned on the radio and flipped through the stations until he settled for rock.

The radio stayed on for the duration of the ride, but Maxwell barely paid attention to the lyrics. They arrived at a dimly lit house at 11:00, but instead of getting out, the driver ordered Maxwell to stay in the car with him for a moment.

"I would like to ask you something before we go inside." the man explained, his expression serious.

Maxwell unbuckled his seat belt, turned toward the familiar-looking man and waited for him to speak.

"You don't know who I am, do you?" he asked and crossed his arms.

Maxwell gazed at his companion's face for a long moment, then dropped his eyes and gasped.

"You're the man from the elevator," he exclaimed quietly.

The dark-haired man smiled at his response. Maxwell opened his mouth but immediately snapped it shut.

"Yes," the dark-haired man said after a few seconds, "but do you know my name or what I do?"

Again, Maxwell opened his mouth but only stared at him wide-eyed.

"I know you work for the government, and I know you've been keeping tabs on me." the man clarified.

Maxwell gave a half-smile before composing his expression. "We keep tabs on everyone." he finally said.

"Then I suppose you know that I applied for a job at your organization?" he pressed.

Maxwell shook his head.

"Do you know why they turned me down?" the man asked, turning off the ignition.

Maxwell shook his head again.

"They turned me down for being a damned drunk! I was so wasted that when it was time for my interview that the man asking the questions threw me out on my ass." the man said bitterly.

Maxwell gave his driver an apologetic look, but the man waved a dismissive hand at him. "I don't need your sympathy," he said, looking out the window, "my friend was there for me and she was also there for you."

Without elaborating, the man opened the door and walked out, with Maxwell following a few steps behind him.

"Ring the doorbell," he commanded.

Maxwell pushed the button twice and the muffled chimes sounded from inside. Half a second passed before the occupant, a slender man with graying hair, answered and smiled at the men standing in the hallway. He was dressed in a black Polo shirt and pants, and his hair was cut close.

"Hello, the lady of the house has been expecting you."

He led them through the entryway and into a dimly lit parlor, then left.

"Put this on." the man ordered, handing Maxwell a blindfold before turning his back.

Once the blindfold was covering Maxwell's eyes, the man turned and walked up the stairs.

"I'll be back," he called over his shoulder.

Maxwell sat on the couch in silence and waited for what seemed like hours until he heard footsteps coming back down the steps.

It sounded like a woman was following the man and like she was wearing high heels.

"Ready for your surprise?" he asked.

Maxwell nodded and waited as the man whispered something to the woman, then came and put his hands over the blindfold. "Keep your eyes closed until I tell you to open them." he hissed.

Maxwell nodded again.

He pulled the blindfold off and ordered Maxwell to open his eyes. It took a minute for his eyes to adjust, but once they did, he gasped and blinked in shock. "Olga," he whispered in disbelief.

24

Bitter Reminders

"Hello, Andrew," she whispered.

Olga was thin and frail; her face was covered in wrinkles, and her gray hair was in a ponytail on top of her head. She wore a black dress and black high-heeled sandals on her feet.

"I thought you were dead," Maxwell murmured once he'd found his voice.

She smiled and reached for a cigarette from a pack on the coffee table. She put it between her lips and the dark-haired man walked over to light it. She blew smoke rings toward the ceiling and turned to face the man that had brought her former employee. "I had no intention of resurfacing, but my dear friend Alexander reached out to me a few weeks back, saying that one of my former agents couldn't wait to see me."

"Where are they?" Maxwell asked.

Olga pointed the finger at the front door.

"They'll be coming shortly. In the meantime, I thought you and I could have a little chat," Olga snapped her fingers twice.

"Get him some wine," she ordered, addressing the man that had shown them in.

Without saying a word, the man nodded and walked to the kitchen.

"I believe you call him The Poisoner," she said with a slight smile.

"Don't you?" Maxwell retorted.

"No. Alexander, myself, Pascal, we're all a part of the same group. You used to be a part of that group, too, until you changed your mind at the last second."

"And what group is that?" Maxwell asked as the well-dressed man set a glass of red wine in front of him on the table before turning and walking off.

"Power-hungry loyalists," she answered quickly, snapping her fingers again.

"Bring the bottle and another glass," she ordered and watched the man, now flustered, head back to the kitchen.

Maxwell and Olga shared a long look across the table until her former employee dropped his gaze to his glass.

"Who exactly are you loyal to?" Maxwell asked, taking a sip of wine.

"Not who. What." Olga corrected curtly, putting the cigarette out in an ashtray on her side of the table.

"All right. What exactly are you loyal to, then?" Maxwell asked, taking another sip of wine.

"Our countries and our jobs," she replied tersely.

Maxwell opened his mouth and began to speak, but Olga silenced him with a look. "When I hired you, I was given your guarantee that you could be trusted," she explained.

"You accused the Americans of doing something to sabotage your country. You lied."

"We have no way of knowing now because you burned the Goddamned codes!" she said angrily.

She paused as the man set the bottle of red wine and the glass on the table before walking away again.

"I'm not going to apologize for anything," he told her defiantly.

"If that's how you feel," she said, pouring him another glass of wine, "but before we go any further, you should know how badly you fucked up. You're a traitor, and you should be thanking God every day that Nikolai didn't kill you when he had the chance." She put the cork back in the bottle, got up, and headed for the door.

After she had gone, the man who'd brought him took her place and pushed the glass away.

"I knew there was a reason for coming here today." he snickered.

"Piss off." Maxwell barked.

"I think her guests are coming." the man said, looking toward the kitchen.

Maxwell followed the man's gaze and saw that several familiar-looking people were trailing behind Olga.

"You may turn around now," she instructed when they had gotten to the table.

One by one, the men turned around and gave Maxwell a polite wave. To his overwhelming relief and dismay, Pascal, along with three other members of the group, stood in front of him.

"Didn't think I'd ever see you again," he said, addressing everyone at once but only looking at Pascal.

Pascal smiled back at him. "It was a surprise to us, too, but when Olga called us the other day, we couldn't exactly say no to her. Did you enjoy your ordeal?" he asked.

"No one enjoys being almost bludgeoned to death by a board with nails," he answered, throwing his former boss a hard look.

"That wasn't meant for you in the first place."

"I know who it was meant for." Maxwell snapped.

Pascal fingered the strings on his sweatshirt and walked to an empty chair across from Olga's seat.

"I would like my chair back now," Olga announced.

The dark-haired man got up and headed for the kitchen.

"Remain there until we need you," Olga called and waited until he had disappeared from the room.

"Get up, please," Olga said and watched Maxwell rise to his feet.

"Raise your shirt," Olga commanded and Maxwell silently obeyed.

She studied the bandage on his torso for a long minute. "What happened?" she asked, concerned.

Maxwell quickly told her, and she wrinkled her nose in disgust.

"I do not condone violence." Olga snapped, glaring at Pascal.

"I did not tell Alexander to do this to him." Pascal defended.

"Then who was it for?" she asked and listened as he explained it to her, then turned her icy stare on Maxwell.

"It was my understanding that you were to take care of Miss Anderson," she said in an icy whisper and smiled at Maxwell's surprised expression.

"Alexander told me about your girlfriend," she explained, reaching for her empty glass and the bottle of wine.

Maxwell said nothing.

"You put her in danger." his former boss accused.

"I warned her that this was no job for someone of her experience level before she took this on," he said, "but I'm only keeping her on because she seems to have the stomach for it."

"For not getting assassinated?" Olga guessed.

Maxwell gave a slight nod and the others turned to look at him. "When did you talk to him?" he asked in a whisper.

"Doesn't matter.

You sold your country out for another one. Just imagine all the people you've hurt, all the lives you could've saved." Olga said, her voice breaking on the last word.

Maxwell grabbed his glass and took a long sip of wine, then turned to give his former boss another hard look.

"You're still up to your old tricks," he remarked with a grim smile.

She grimaced, then tapped her wrist twice. "Enough of this idle talk. Let's get down to business," she said, opening the bottle and filling her glass to the rim with wine.

"Pascal," she said, turning away from Maxwell's gaze, "is the car ready?"

The Frenchman nodded and pulled a set of keys to a minivan from his pocket.

"Where's the other one?" Garrett asked.

Olga silently pointed in the direction of the kitchen and waved her hand at the figure in the doorway. The dark-haired man acknowledged Olga's wave with a dismissive look but stayed where he was.

"Antonio, stop conversing with the help and get over here," she ordered.

He flashed Olga an irritated look before rejoining the others in the parlor. Maxwell stared at his driver's face, then looked into his eyes and held his steady gaze for a long minute before lowering his eyes in realization. "I knew you'd help her," he whispered.

Antonio smiled cruelly at the agent and chuckled. "Very good," he said, clapping his hands slowly.

"She talked about you nonstop. She loved you. Of course you'd help her," Maxwell continued, still whispering.

"You're damn right."

Maxwell raised his head and opened his eyes to see Antonio standing only a few inches in front of him, now pointing a revolver in his face. "You've been on this manhunt long enough, Andrew. You've been branded as a traitor by your country. It's time you paid for your mistakes." He edged the gun closer to Maxwell, but the agent stayed still and said nothing.

"I was the original person who was sent to kill you but at the last minute, she sent me somewhere else," he explained, jabbing a finger at the woman sitting at the head of the table, "she told me to leave you to the big boys, but they turned out to be useless."

"He was murdered," Maxwell answered.

"That's the only reason you're still alive, but that all changes in a few seconds." Antonio finished, putting his finger on the trigger.

"Tony, not here," Olga snapped, looking out the window and getting to her feet.

"Get up," she said and walked on without looking back.

Antonio and Maxwell were the last to leave, with the hitman gripping the backs of the agent's arms so tightly that he began to squirm. They walked to a waiting taxi and as soon as they were settled in, Olga gave the driver orders in Russian and they sped off.

Maxwell was handcuffed to the cushioned seat between Antonio and Pascal. "I need to make a phone call," he said, stretching his legs in front of him.

Antonio and Pascal exchanged a quick glance, then the hitman glared at the man sitting to the left of him.

"Give me the number," he growled, taking a flip phone from his pocket and gripping it in his right hand.

Maxwell gave Antonio René's number and listened as he dialed.

"You've got two minutes," he whispered, putting the phone to Maxwell's ear.

He took a deep breath and closed his eyes.

"What's wrong, Andrew?" she asked a moment later, sounding distressed.

He took another deep breath and began to explain, only giving her the important details.

"Where are you headed now?" she asked, pacing in a bathroom. René stood in front of the mirror in a robe and slippers, nervously twisting a lock of hair in her left hand. She stared intensely at the towel rack as she listened to his reply. "How many of you are in the cab?" was her next question.

There were four, including him.

"Where are the others?" she asked. She tightened her grip on the phone and frowned as he spoke in her ear. She turned her intense gaze on the bathroom door, then turned back to the towel rack.

"Where are you?" Maxwell asked.

"In the house," René answered.

She had stopped twisting the lock of hair and now stood still.

"I'll call you back in a few minutes," she promised.

"Where are you going?" Maxwell asked as the cab sped down Main Street.

"I'm getting ready to come find you."

Maxwell opened his mouth to object, but René had already gone.

Antonio snapped the phone shut and laid it on the seat next to him. "She's coming to save you." he guessed.

"Who?" asked Maxwell.

"That bitch you hired to do your dirty work for you." Antonio clarified, clenching his hands into fists at his sides.

"She's better off dead," Pascal said callously, looking over his shoulder at Maxwell's wan face.

"You've seen her?" Antonio asked, looking out his window at the minivan driven by Garrett. The two cars were ten feet apart, but Maxwell had a sinking feeling that two vehicles were about to become three.

"I have," he answered.

"Is Alexander coming?" Antonio asked.

Pascal nodded and stared out the car's other window for a few seconds.

Antonio's phone buzzed a minute later, and he briefly glanced down at the screen before frowning at Maxwell's stoic expression.

"Did you tell her to call me back?" he asked crossly.

Maxwell shook his head, too stunned and a little angry to speak. Antonio gripped the phone in his right hand, closed his eyes in concentration and angrily opened it with his left.

"Say hello," he growled, clamping the phone to Maxwell's right ear.

"René, what the..." he began but stopped when he heard a car's engine purring in the background.

"Tell me where to go," she said over the car's engine.

"Where are you headed?" Maxwell demanded.

"To find you. The driver gave me his phone when I told him that somebody I knew was in trouble."

"Who's with you?" he asked and paused to listen to her speak. "Is he driving?" Maxwell asked, ignoring the exasperated looks his riding companions gave him.

He glanced out the window, saw a tail light flashing a few feet behind them and groaned inwardly.

"René, this is too dangerous for you," he said, eyeing Pascal, who now had his phone in his lap and was furiously texting someone.

"Speed up," he heard someone say away from the phone, followed by the honk of a car horn and the roar of an engine as someone stomped on the gas pedal.

"Go faster," Olga said and put her hands on her knees as the car sped forward.

She pursed her lips for a second, then reached for the radio's volume knob, turned it up and listened as an intro to a talk show began.

Antonio took the phone from Maxwell's ear and listened to the sound of movement down the line. He turned his head toward the window and looked out at the traffic-filled streets, ignoring the voice now emanating from it.

"Andrew, answer me." René was saying, her tone tinged with anger.

The minivan, he saw, was now three feet behind them and in no hurry to pass.

"Garrett's behind us," Antonio told Olga, who had become engrossed in what was on the radio.

"How many came today?" she asked without looking up.

"Including Pascal, four," he replied.

"What about the other ten?" asked Olga.

"The other four are at the house, but the members that didn't come decided to stay behind in Europe to monitor the situation."

By this time, the minivan had inched closer and was now two feet from the cab.

"I know you hear me." René spat through clenched teeth. Her voice had become an angry squawk, but Antonio had no intention of answering her.

Let the girl talk herself out, he thought.

"Andrew Maxwell, I swear to..." The hitman snapped the phone shut on René's unfinished threat and resumed staring out the window.

The minivan was now speeding toward their cab, and the car being driven by Alexander was only a few inches behind it.

"I see their vehicle." Antonio sighed, turning to glare at Maxwell. He held the closed phone out to him and smiled.

The cab driver honked his horn twice, then went on, ignoring dirty looks from other drivers. They were now speeding down Fifth Avenue and the three cars had caught up to one another.

"Makes you think, doesn't it?" Antonio whispered, pocketing the phone.

Maxwell looked confused for a second, then his eyebrows pulled together, and he sighed.

"She's just trying to be a good friend. You didn't have to anger her like that." he fired back, wincing slightly at the pain in his arms.

"I know, but it was entertaining to hear her squawk," said Antonio with a short laugh.

Olga fumbled around until she found the radio's volume knob, turned it up, and listened.

"A three-car chase has just ensued down Fifth Avenue. An eyewitness has told police that one of the cars was driving erratically down the road, and they were sure that one of the vehicles contained the girl that had gone missing a few weeks back."

Olga glared out the window and saw the two vehicles speeding in the same direction. "I suppose the police are going to be after us now," she said irritably, turning back to glare at the radio, which had resumed its program.

The host was taking calls on a variety of topics, but Olga did not appear to be listening. She turned to the window and glared out at the light rain that was beginning to fall.

"Turn that damn thing off," Pascal said, looking over the back seat at the male driver.

He nodded and pushed the button, cutting the woman caller's sentence short.

Antonio glanced over at Maxwell, who had fallen asleep.

"Nobody's driving erratically."

He turned his head to find Pascal scowling out the window and talking on the phone.

"How's the girl?" he asked and waited for the person's response.

"We're almost at the house. Just another hour and he'll get what's coming to him," he said, looking at Maxwell's sleeping face.

Antonio smiled at his partner in crime as the car sped forward, then turned right, narrowly avoiding hitting the car in front of them.

"What time is it?" Pascal asked, still scowling out the window.

"Almost three in the afternoon," Antonio answered, still staring at Maxwell's sleeping face. He reached into the pocket of the seat in front of him and grabbed a pistol from it.

"Wake up," he said, hitting Maxwell on the side of the head with the butt of the gun.

Maxwell slowly opened his eyes and winced as he tried to stretch his arms.

"We're almost there," Antonio said, removing the gun from the side of Maxwell's head.

"Almost where?" Maxwell asked drowsily.

"The house. If the girl is going to save you, she'd better get her ass in gear." Antonio growled.

Maxwell started to move, but Antonio slapped him on the side again.

"Ow," he whispered, closing his eyes and breathing deeply.

"I thought you said you didn't like her," Maxwell said and blinked twice.

"I've never even met the girl." Antonio laughed, lowering the gun to his side. He smiled derisively at him and closed his eyes.

"You really should get some sleep, Tony," said Maxwell, eyeing Antonio's exhausted expression with concern.

He opened his eyes and shook his head. "Who will look after you?" he asked, running a hand through his messy brown hair.

Maxwell pondered this for a moment, then looked over at Pascal on his phone.

"I'll look after him. He can't go anywhere." Pascal snickered.

"Fine," Antonio agreed, "but you better wake me up if he moves."

Pascal nodded and Antonio rested his head on the leather seat. Pascal glanced out the window and furrowed his brow. "Where's Alexander's car?" he asked, still staring out the window.

Olga turned her head and gave him a confused look. "Garrett's minivan is right on our heels," he explained, pointing to the window, "but the other car..." His voice trailed off and he lowered his gaze from the window. He grabbed his phone from the seat beside him and began dialing.

"Put him on "speaker," Olga ordered.

The assassin nodded and they all listened to it ring.

"Pascal, to what do I owe this pleasure?" the voice asked casually.

"Why aren't you following us anymore?" Pascal asked.

"Car broke down," Alexander answered, softly banging his fist on the vehicle's window.

As he talked, his assistant came to stand beside him, and he took the phone from his ear. "What's the good word, Gordon?" he asked, looking at a mud puddle a few feet away from him.

"A tow truck will be here in less than an hour," he said.

Olga eyed Pascal's phone and waited for Alexander to get back on the line.

"Where's the girl?" asked Alexander, putting his phone on "speaker.

René walked slowly toward he and Gordon, then stopped.

"We don't need you anymore," he said coldly, putting his finger in her face.

Maxwell opened his mouth to speak, but Olga held up her hand to stop him.

"You're still on with us, Alexander," she said, trying her best to hide a smile.

Alexander stopped talking for a moment, then went on as if he had not heard her. "Will we be there in time for his execution?" he asked, hope coloring his tone.

They didn't hear Gordon's answer.

"How far out are you?" Alexander asked, returning his attention to the phone call.

"30 minutes," Pascal answered.

"You can't discard me like that, you asshole!"

Alexander looked over his shoulder to find a fuming René running toward him, her hands balled into fists. "Don't forget I spared your life, you ungrateful bitch." he said, eyeing her with open contempt.

She seized the phone from him and turned away as he called out to her. She took a deep breath and walked a few feet forward, then hurled the phone into the nearby mud puddle and watched it sink.

"Tell me where they're taking him." she snapped, turning around to face Alexander.

Alexander's expression was livid as he stalked toward her.

"Your boyfriend ruined everything for me!" he roared, raising one hand as if to strike her.

"He didn't make you leave," she shouted, "or make you lie about Olga's death! So what the hell did he ruin for you?"

"He didn't just ruin things for me. He ruined them for my entire country when he did what he did. Nobody from my side has ever forgiven him for that." He looked up when he saw the tow truck round the corner and silently walked toward it.

René looked down at the mud puddle by her feet, then fought back the tears as she turned to Alexander's assistant. "Gordon," she said, "tell me where Mr. Maxwell's cab is going."

25

Endgame

"Try to get him on the phone again," Olga said, anxiously staring out the cab's open window.

"I did, but he's not answering," Pascal said, glancing back and forth between the screen and her anxiety-ridden face.

"We're two minutes out, and one of our key allies can't be reached." she laughed, gripping the phone in her lap with both hands. She turned to the window and glanced up at the now-darkened sky, but the ringing of her cell phone brought her attention back to the matter at hand.

"Garrett." she breathed.

"Nice to hear your voice, too, but I don't have happy news." he began.

"What's wrong?" she asked.

Garrett's answer was brief, but it made her frown, then her expression hardened as the impact of his words hit her.

"Thank you for telling me." she whispered and stabbed the "end call" button with her thumb. "We need to move faster," she said with an air of urgency.

"But Ma'am, we're almost over the speed limit." the driver told her, looking at his speedometer.

"What's happened?" Pascal asked.

Maxwell leaned over the seat, but she ignored his questioning look. "Miss Anderson has tracked us down," she explained, letting the window up.

"Did Garrett tell you where she is now?" he asked, but before Olga could answer, they heard a knock on the car's back window.

"Drive faster," Olga ordered, "and Pascal, grab the gun out of Antonio's hands."

The driver sped forward and Pascal took the gun from the sleeping man.

René crossed the street in her muddy sneakers, keeping pace with the car in front of her.

"I know you have him!" she screeched, all control gone.

"Go!" Olga shouted, but the driver shook his head and looked out his window.

"The light's red," he said, and Olga gave an exasperated sigh.

René crossed the street to the car in front of her and stood next to it.

"Please, hurry up," Olga said more calmly when the light had changed.

The driver sped forward again, unaware of the girl running alongside his car. "Let him go!" she shouted, keeping her eyes forward.

Pascal fired one shot through the window and she fell to the ground, surrounded by broken glass and covered in blood. She got up and dusted herself off, then looked around and saw that the car had gone. Though she ached all over, adrenaline made her run until she had caught up to the car again. The back window had been blown out by the bullet and she was bleeding, but she was determined to save Maxwell's life.

She glanced back at the shards of glass on the pavement, then she turned to stare at Maxwell's cold expression.

"Where's the minivan?" she heard him ask, disregarding the face staring up at him.

She strained to hear the answer but sighed when nothing came.

"Get ready," she heard Pascal say over the roar of traffic, "we're almost there. You should say your final goodbyes now."

The car had slowed a bit and René was now jogging alongside it. Out of the corner of her eye, she saw Maxwell give the assassin an icy stare.

"I won't be the one saying goodbye today," he answered.

René chuckled at the sound of his voice.

A moment later, the car turned into a residential neighborhood, slowed and stopped.

"This is you." the cabbie said and unlocked Olga's door.

After unbuckling her seat belt, she turned to the driver and quietly thanked him before getting out and going around to the back. "Hope you're ready to see your friend die," she said as she passed René, who had backed away a few paces.

Olga silently looked over her bloodied clothes and gave a satisfied smirk as she walked away.

René watched the driver get out and walk to the back. He unlocked the doors and stepped back as Pascal got out, then watched Antonio and Maxwell exit.

"Will you be needing me anymore?" he asked, shutting the doors.

Pascal shook his head and walked after Olga, not bothering to look at their new guest.

"I just got word that your girlfriend is here," Antonio said, grabbing Maxwell by his shoulders.

Maxwell didn't respond.

"Are you nervous?" Tony asked a moment later, his voice fading into the distance.

After the cab had disappeared, René followed after them and found herself standing in front of a run-down building that resembled the house she'd just left.

She climbed up three porch steps and braced herself against a brick wall for several seconds before pushing the front door open and striding into the hall. She looked around until her eyes rested on a container sitting on the end table. She walked over, pushed it near her, and silently examined its contents: two-gallon cans of gasoline and a box of matches were inside.

She picked up one of the cans and weighed it in her right hand, then she set the heavy can back in the container and walked around to the other side. The house keys and a long chain sat near the edge. She shivered and walked in the direction of the main room, where she found Maxwell seated in a chair with his hands folded in his lap.

"Are you alone?" she asked, coming up behind him.

He looked up at the sound of her voice. "I thought I told you to stay out of this," he said coldly.

"You might die today," she answered.

"You're doubting me now?" he asked, rising from the chair and going to her.

"I saw what was on the end table in the hall," she said, ignoring the question.

"And?" he asked.

She pointed in the direction of the table, and he followed her finger.

"I've dealt with worse," he said, unfazed by what he saw.

"I just want you to be careful," she told him and stared after him as he walked to the kitchen.

Olga gave him a cold smile when he entered. "Well, I must admit that your friend has some admirable qualities," she said, looking over her shoulder at René, who had not moved from where Maxwell had left her.

He smiled at this compliment but said nothing.

"She's loyal, I'll give her that.

I don't know anyone who would put their life on the line for someone like us." she added, still looking at René.

"Why are they here?" he finally asked, gesturing over his shoulder at the crowd that was now forming by the door.

"Looks like the other four came after all." she mused, seemingly unaware of his presence.

"One person is needed to pull the trigger, so why are the others here?" he asked.

"It's the drama of the thing. They don't want to miss the murder of the government's most valuable asset." She gave one hard laugh.

He looked away and sighed.

"Let's get this show on the road," she said and marched toward the den.

Maxwell followed her out and waited in the den for the crowd to come. They arrived seconds later, and Maxwell gasped to see that his housemates were among them.

Antonio made his way to the front of the line, grabbing the long chain from the table as he went.

"Is that supposed to be for me?" Maxwell asked, but Antonio didn't hear him over the roar of the crowd.

Antonio laid the chain on a chair and walked back to where Maxwell stood. They stared at one another, both wishing that the other would die.

"Come with me," he ordered, and Maxwell walked with him to his spot.

"How much?" he asked after he had been seated.

"How much what?" Antonio whispered back, standing in front of Maxwell's chair.

"How much did Olga pay you to kill me?" he asked.

"Only his arms," Olga said and Tony walked behind him with the chain.

"$3,000,000" he answered, chaining first his right arm, then his left to the chair.

Maxwell closed his eyes and let his head fall forward. It was only a few months ago that he had received a call from Welsh demanding $3000000 in cash. At the time, he'd claimed it was for himself before explaining that Ernest's killers were the ones who were asking for it. "But that money was for..."

"The GK, I know. Your boss wasn't lying about that, but after it was given to them, one of the members gave Olga the money to give to me." He pointed to a book in the center of the coffee table and sighed. "It's not in the book if that's what you're wondering. What is in there, however, is the key to the briefcase containing the money."

The crowd had gathered around them and had fallen silent.

"I've kept every cent given to me by my clients in there. It dates back to 1999, but you see, it's a rarity for me to be speaking with someone that was supposed to have been killed and refuses to die," he said, turning around to smirk at Maxwell's dumbfounded expression.

All eyes were on Antonio as he reached into the right pocket of his pants and pulled out a rifle. He counted to three and put his finger on the trigger, but the gun suddenly fell to the floor and Antonio followed, falling onto his stomach. Everyone looked up to see René standing over Antonio's motionless body. She looked down at the pool of blood surrounding him with an air of finality. Antonio's index finger was still on the trigger and his legs were stretched out behind him.

She didn't look up from the body until she sensed someone watching her. Maxwell was looking at her with a mix of anger, shock and relief on his face.

"That bitch killed my friend!" Olga shouted, grabbing a pistol from her pocket and lunging at her.

The crowd cheered as Olga repeatedly punched and kicked René in the face and ribs before pointing the pistol at her head.

"He was going to kill Andrew." she panted when Olga had finally gotten to her knees.

"Because he betrayed an entire country!" Olga yelled back.

The two women wrestled for the gun, both of them now covered in Antonio's blood, but neither was willing to give up.

"He was only doing what he thought was right," René answered, wincing from the pain caused by Olga's blows.

After several more minutes, Olga finally relented and shoved away from her opponent, gun in hand.

René tried to sit up but almost cried out from the pain. She flopped back onto the floor and looked down at herself; her clothes were covered in blood, and the area around her ribs was red and swollen.

Olga left and ran down the hall to the bathroom, her expression weary.

"Are you all right?" Maxwell asked, looking at his friend with concern.

"Don't talk to her." someone ordered harshly.

Maxwell looked up to see Alexander standing over him.

"Hello, Alexander," he said evenly.

"The time for pleasantries is over, don't you think?" Alexander asked, meeting Maxwell's even gaze with a fierce one.

"Did you know the dead man lying on the floor?" Maxwell asked.

Alexander shook his head. "My deepest sympathies go out to Olga," he sighed,

"I'd only met him once when he came to Russia in the early 2000s. He seemed nice."

Maxwell's gaze returned to the girl lying on the floor.

"I was not there when she killed Antonio, but I heard the cheering from outside and decided to wander in, though I have to say, I was disappointed that it wasn't you," Alexander said, moving closer to Antonio's body.

"They were not cheering because somebody died," Maxwell explained, "they were cheering because someone was getting hurt."

Alexander walked over to René and knelt beside her. "You've made a mess of yourself," he commented, edging closer to her.

"You're a piece of work, Alexander," she said with what little anger she could muster.

He grabbed a knife out of his back pocket and pushed the button to reveal the freshly-sharpened blade. She eyed it warily, but he backed away from her.

"Luckily, you're not my target today," he said and got up.

He walked over to Maxwell's chair, put the knife down and unchained him. Alexander watched as Maxwell rubbed his wrists before advancing toward him.

"These good people," he said, pointing to the crowd, some of whom had diverted their attention from the situation, "want a show. So let's not keep them waiting any longer."

Alexander pushed the chair from the front and Maxwell fell backward.

He laid sprawled on the floor, but he quickly got up and ran for the end table with the former assassin chasing after him, brandishing the knife. He stopped and stroked the gleaming handle.

"Giving up already?" Maxwell asked.

He held his revolver in his right hand, which was aimed at Alexander's chest.

"No, I'm just getting started," said Alexander, rushing up from behind and ramming the blade into Maxwell's back.

He fell forward but kept the gun clutched in his hand.

Blood oozed from the knife wound and dripped onto his suit jacket. Maxwell got up, turned and fired two rounds in Alexander's direction but missed. He looked and saw Alexander's former friends rushing toward them, nostrils flaring and weapons drawn.

The crowd followed behind with their phones, ready to capture the murder of a government official in real-time.

Maxwell rounded a corner and moved behind the couch. He put his fists on either side of it and rested his head on his left arm. His palm had become sweaty from holding the gun so tightly, but all he prayed for right now was a perfect aim. He closed his eyes and lifted his head at the sound of a nearby gunshot.

"Come out of your hiding place!" someone shouted, moving closer to the couch.

Maxwell didn't move.

The gunman held a pistol in his right hand and looked over at Maxwell. The two stared each other down for a few seconds, then the gunman rushed at him.

Maxwell ran out from behind the couch and headbutted the man. He doubled over in pain, then reached up and wrapped his left hand around Maxwell's throat. He let go after a second and watched the agent catch his breath, then Maxwell pointed his revolver at the gunman's head and pulled the trigger. Blood poured from the man's wound and made a red line that ran down his left cheek and continued to his chin.

Maxwell's eyes flashed open and he peered up at the man he'd just shot. "You just can't stay away from me, can you, Alex?" he asked, looking at the blood that was now trickling down his chin and onto his shirt front.

Alexander chuckled and pointed his weapon at Maxwell's face. He closed the distance between them and leaned into him.

"Don't flatter yourself," he whispered, then backed off.

Maxwell turned and fired his revolver twice and watched with a cold expression as Ritzkov stumbled, then fell onto his back. He stared up at the ceiling with a peaceful expression, then his eyes closed.

Maxwell knelt down, dragged Alexander's dead body back into the main room, and laid him next to Antonio.

René looked up at him through swollen eyes and winced when she breathed.

"He's gone," Maxwell said simply.

"Where's his knife?" she asked.

He pointed to the spot where he'd left both the knife and the gun.

"What about the others?" she asked.

Maxwell thought for a moment, then looked over his shoulder to see Pascal pulling a semiautomatic rifle from the waistband of his jeans. "Get in the bathroom," he said fiercely.

René gave him a lingering look but struggled to get into a crawling position, made her way to the bathroom and closed the door.

"Lock the door!" he shouted.

She locked it and looked around. Olga's motionless body was on the floor by the toilet with a gunshot wound through the head and the pistol beside it. She pressed her ear to the door and listened for a minute, then returned her gaze to Olga. She painfully walked over and sat beside her.

The gray hair that was left was covered in blood, as were her dress and shoes. Pieces of her skull lay scattered in the center of the room and some of her brains, as well as some of her blood-stained one of the walls. Blood poured from her nose and her eyes were haunted; the wrinkles around her mouth seemed more prominent now that she could no longer move.

She had just gotten to her hands when the commotion reached her ears. She heard a distant scream followed by the sound of broken glass and heavy footsteps coming down the hall. She closed her eyes and listened to shots being fired, followed by more screams and more glass shattering. She returned to the door, pressed her ear against it, and listened.

The semiautomatic went off nonstop for five minutes, and then all was silent again. René looked around, then went over to the toilet and collapsed next to Olga's body.

Garrett had grabbed the rifle and was leaning over Pascal, who was covered in blood. "We're still not done." he was saying.

Pascal stared at him wearily but got up and took the gun back. He staggered forward and began limping toward Maxwell, who stood near an open window with his back to him but turned when he heard Pascal approaching.

He shoved him roughly to the side and closed the window. The room had grown cold from the evening air and the crowd had dispersed. "I'm not through with you yet," he growled and limped to Maxwell's side.

Maxwell looked at the bathroom door for an instant, then turned to face Pascal, who was holding the gun by his side.

His jeans and sweatshirt had been ripped, he was covered in sweat and he looked exhausted. "I don't have the energy to chase you anymore," he whispered, leaning against the wall and breathing heavily.

"Did you kill the others?" Maxwell asked.

Pascal shook his head and straightened a little. "They're waiting for you," he whispered.

"Where are they?" asked Maxwell.

Pascal pointed a bloody finger at the kitchen door.

Maxwell turned to leave, but he suddenly turned back to face Pascal. "Alexander's dead," he said gravely.

The Frenchman stared at him incredulously, then raised his eyebrows. "You killed him?" he asked.

Maxwell nodded and looked at the broken glass and blood on the floor. Several windows had been broken during the shooting and two people had been shot, but nobody was seriously injured.

He turned and headed for the kitchen, making sure to avoid the mess on the floor.

The door swung open upon his arrival.

"Keep your weapon with you," Garrett ordered and directed Maxwell to a table a few feet from the entrance.

Maxwell laid his revolver on the table in front of him and pulled out the chair. "The time for this has passed," he said, addressing the small group in the room.

Three members: Garrett and two others, were already sitting, waiting for him. He sat and stared off into space.

Garrett nodded and excused himself. He rejoined the group two minutes later, holding the rifle.

He walked over to Maxwell and jabbed him in the right side with it. "Yes, the time for this has passed, but my friends and I still haven't accomplished what we set out to do," he said, edging closer to him.

Maxwell shoved his chair back and rushed at the younger man, knocking him to the ground before spinning on his heel and running out the kitchen door.

Garrett screamed and raced after him with the other members on his heels. They rounded a corner and found Maxwell standing by the front door with his arms crossed.

The youngest member of the GK pulled the trigger, and Maxwell ducked to avoid getting hit. The glass on the door shattered, then broke.

Maxwell crawled back to the kitchen and grabbed the revolver from the table, then crawled back and met Garrett in the hall.

"You're prepared," Garrett said and pointed the rifle in Maxwell's direction.

"I always am," he answered and kicked the young man in the groin.

He grabbed his groin, sank to the ground and dropped the gun to the floor. More gunshots rang out, and Garrett looked up to see the agent with his finger on the revolver's trigger, but he was not facing him.

Maxwell was twisting Garrett's fellow member's arm behind his back and the other held tightly to the gun. "There were nine of you," he was saying, "your former partner is dead and your leader is half-dead. Where are the other seven?"

The man pointed to seven chairs in the living room, and Maxwell eased the pressure on his arm.

"Do you have a family?" Maxwell asked.

The man shook his head and Maxwell smiled.

"Well, it will make this a lot easier," he whispered and pulled the trigger one last time.

When he was sure the man was dead, he laid the gun by the front door and dragged his body to a spot between Alexander's and Antonios' bodies.

He went to the bathroom door and knocked twice. "René, open up!" he called and waited for an answer. When he didn't get one, he kicked the door down and was shocked by what he saw.

Olga was dead and René was passed out beside her with the pistol resting between them. He went over and shook her gently.

She opened her unfocused eyes and spoke in a whisper. "Andrew, you know what you have to do now."

He shook his head.

"You have to burn it down," she said.

He looked at her in alarm, but she smiled up at him blissfully. "Burn this fucking house down," she said, then was gone.

He stepped over the broken door and walked to where Alexander had left the knife. He picked it up and one by one slit the throats of those who had been left alive before dropping it back to the floor and going to the end table for a can and a match.

Epilogue

Andrew Maxwell climbed the last of the stairs and walked a few feet to Simon's office. The door swung open before he could knock, and Welsh came out to greet him.

"René's parents called," he said when Maxwell had taken his seat across from him, and the door had been closed.

Though it had been one week since her death, he still heard René's last words to him as clear as a bell. "What did they say?" he asked.

"They wanted to thank you for trying to keep their daughter safe," Welsh answered somberly.

Maxwell had escaped from the fire unharmed, but Antonio and the rest had perished along with the house. The firefighters had been able to save the charred bodies of René and Olga before the house had burned down, and autopsies had been performed on them immediately. The coroner had concluded that Maxwell's former boss had died from a self-inflicted gunshot to the head, and René had died due to what had been done to her.

"Did you know that Olga was still alive when you asked for the money?" Maxwell wondered.

Welsh shook his head but remained silent.

"I still don't know what their plan was, and X's identity is still a mystery to me." he sighed, getting up and going for a drink of water.

"How's your back?" Simon called.

The knife wound had required stitches, but not as many as he'd expected. "I get my stitches out next week," Maxwell answered, filling a plastic cup from the sink.

"A letter came for you today, but I was instructed to tell you not to read it until you got home," said Welsh, rising from his chair and taking an envelope to Maxwell.

He mumbled thanks his boss's way and pocketed the letter. "Should I come tomorrow?" Maxwell asked after he had finished what was in his cup.

He would not be needed for the foreseeable future, but Welsh promised to call him if anything changed. Maxwell disposed of his cup and walked to the door. "Simon, I have one more thing to ask," Maxwell said suddenly, turning back to face the other man.

"What's that?" he said.

"Why did Olga do it?" Maxwell asked.

"It was ultimately because of you," Welsh answered.

Maxwell's eyebrows shot up in disbelief; he opened his mouth to speak, but Welsh gave him a stern look before continuing.

"After that fiasco in Russia, there was a part of her that wanted you dead, but when everything blew up in her face, she believed that she had failed. Antonio had been her only confidante and when René killed him and it was clear that you were going to survive, it was all too much for her. She felt that yet another employee had betrayed her."

Both men stayed silent for several minutes before Maxwell spoke.

"Thank you," he said, pausing with his hand on the knob.

"Be careful." Welsh cautioned and watched Maxwell exit his office.

The drive home was short, but he finally had time to process everything that had happened over the past week. The police had been quick to determine that an arsonist had set the fire, but the case had been dismissed due to the fact that everyone who could have been brought in for questioning was dead. Maxwell had left New York two days after the fire to avoid news coverage and journalists who might have wanted him to answer their probing questions.

He stopped the car in front of his apartment complex forty-five minutes later, turned off the ignition, unbuckled his seat belt, and got out. He looked around for a minute, then slowly made his way to the building on the second floor. Once inside, he closed the door, set his car keys down on the nearby table, unbuttoned his suit jacket, and walked to the couch. He took the letter from his pocket, sat down, and ripped the envelope open. He looked inside but only saw a card with a short message on it.

Tune into the news tonight at ten o'clock.

Maxwell crumpled the note and the card in his hand but made no move to throw it away. He got up, turned his TV on, and flipped through the channels until finally settling on a movie.

He barely paid attention to it and was soon asleep when he remembered the note in his hand and woke with a start. Maxwell flipped through the channels again until he found the news and waited. He was still questioning why the person had wanted him to tune into this when he heard the sirens blaring and looked up.

The BBC news building was behind a heavyset male reporter with short hair, and he periodically looked at it as he talked.

"The fire was called in early this morning, and police have begun investigating the motive behind it." he was saying.

"Was anyone in there?" a female anchor asked. She was dressed in an all-black pants suit and wore her hair in a messy bun.

"Yes. Rosemerry had been getting ready in her dressing room."

"Do we know if there have been any casualties?" she said.

"Rosemerry and most of her team have died," he confirmed.

Maxwell clenched his hand into a fist around the note and the envelope as he stared up at the building engulfed in flames. The New York Times and CNN buildings had also been set ablaze, but there was no word on whether anyone had died or if it was connected to this. Maxwell glared at the screen and jumped to his feet, but something told him to stay where he was. He sat back down and watched the broadcast all the way through.

A video was brought up at the very end, and a familiar face popped up on the screen.

"Who is the message for, Mr. Dubois?" the anchor asked.

"This message is for Andrew Maxwell," Pierre said and leaned in.

"Am I on?"

The anchor nodded and Pierre began to speak.

"You've probably guessed that I was the author of the note. I'm glad you're home, but it's time you knew the truth. Firstly, I was informed that eight of my group members were killed and burned in an abandoned house. Who told me is not important. Secondly, I didn't tell you that Olga was alive because I was hoping you'd be dead before anyone had the chance to tell you, or maybe you'd apologize before it came to that. And lastly, you should know who X is, er, was."

Maxwell's eyes were riveted to the screen as Pierre continued.

"X was Olga's code name. She was the one who recommended you to work for Ernest. Why she did, I don't know, but I'm sure that you already know by now that she hired Antonio to kill you. And she hired Nikolai's killer. That's right, she hired the good guys and the bad guys too."

Maxwell put his head in his left hand and continued to listen.

"Well, that's it, but I will make you a promise: I will be back for you, and I won't rest until your head is on a platter."

The video ended then, but neither Maxwell nor the anchor could move. He closed his eyes and opened his mouth to speak, but no words came out.

He lifted his head a moment later and dropped his hand to his side to turn off the TV but otherwise stayed rooted where he was. The new phone he'd gotten only days earlier rang just then, pulling him out of his trance.

He reached behind him and grabbed it from the arm of the couch. "You've made your point," he snapped when he'd answered, "but you can't intimidate me into apologizing."

"It's too late for apologies," Pierre said in a tight voice.

"Was that your plan all along? To kill me?" Maxwell asked quietly.

"Yes, but the recent incidents have been an added bonus," Pierre answered.

Maxwell took a deep breath and waited.

"It was gruesome what you did to them," Pierre told him.

"We can't play nice with people like you," Maxwell said, gripping the pieces of paper tightly in his other fist.

"All I know," said Pierre in a hard voice, "is that you should watch your back."

Pierre hung up immediately, but Maxwell held the phone to his ear for a few more seconds before hanging up. He got up, slammed the phone down on the coffee table, and went to the kitchen. He threw both the note and the envelope into the trash can before turning and heading for the door.

He opened it and glared out at the cars that passed for a long minute before grabbing his keys from the table and stepping out into the cool evening.

"Shit," he whispered seconds later as he closed the door and walked away from the building.

Meagan Collins is available for interviews or personal appearances. For more information contact Meagan via email: info@advbooks.com

To purchase additional copies of this book, visit our bookstore at
www.advbookstore.com

Longwood, Florida, USA
"we bring dreams to life"™
www.advbookstore.com